Praise for **Michael HARVEY**

"Michael Harvey is a magnificent new voice." —John Grisham

"Michael Harvey has finally done for Chicago what Raymond Chandler did for Los Angeles and Dashiell Hammett for San Francisco. . . . Dazzlingly good." —*The Plain Dealer*

"Harvey doesn't waste a word and keeps you glued to your seat reading." —*Boston Herald*

"A major new voice." —Michael Connelly

"[Harvey] composes punchy noir sentences that he stacks into punchy noir paragraphs that have all the rhythm, irony, and wit of the genre's manly classics of the 1920s and '30s."
—*Entertainment Weekly*

"The efficiency of [Harvey's] cinematic style suits the brisk, animated shots of Chicago that give the story both grit and authenticity." —*The New York Times Book Review*

MICHAEL HARVEY

THE Fifth Floor

Michael Harvey is the author of *The Chicago Way*, as well as a journalist and documentary film producer. His work has won numerous national and international awards, including multiple Emmy awards and an Academy Award nomination. Mr. Harvey earned a law degree from Duke University, a master's degree in journalism from Northwestern University, and a bachelor's degree in classical languages from Holy Cross College. He lives in Chicago.

www.michaelharveybooks.com

ALSO BY MICHAEL HARVEY

The Chicago Way

THE
Fifth
Floor

Michael
HARVEY

Vintage Crime/Black Lizard
Vintage Books
A Division of Random House, Inc.
New York

In memory of
Mary Lyons and
Margaret Kelly

This town was built by great men who demanded that drunkards and harlots be arrested, while charging them rent until the cops arrived.

—MIKE ROYKO, CHICAGO COLUMNIST, 1976

THE
Fifth
Floor

CHAPTER 1

I pushed the slim volume of poetry across my desk and into her lap. The woman with auburn hair, perfect posture, and a broken life picked it up.

"I can't read this," she said, and lifted her head.

"That's because it's in Latin," I said. "Why don't you take off the sunglasses?"

"Why don't you translate for me?"

"Take off the glasses."

The woman slid the dark frames up and off her face. Her left eye was green and watering. Her right was black and swollen shut. The cheekbone below it offered a study in shades of purple, blue, and yellow.

"You get the picture?" she said.

"The poem is by Catullus. First line reads *Odi et amo*. Translates as *I hate and I love*."

"And this is my life?"

"People say it's a love poem, but they're wrong. It's about abuse, about not being able to get out, even when the door is wide open and the whole world is yelling that very thing in your ear."

"I can't just leave. It's not that simple."

"It never is. Let me ask you something. How do you think this ends?"

The woman dropped her gaze back into her lap.

"You're a smart woman, Janet. You can figure it out. You wind up hurt real bad. Maybe dead. Or . . ."

She raised her head again. "Or what?"

"Or he winds up dead. Either way, it's not good."

She thinned her lips and set a hard edge at the corners of her mouth. There'd never been anything soft about Janet Woods' face. Beautiful, yes. Even through the bruises. But never soft.

"What do you want?" she said.

"Same thing I wanted three months ago. Get you out of there. Today. Taylor's in school, right?"

She nodded.

"Okay. We pick her up. I take you to a safe place. No one knows but me, you, and your little girl. Then I approach your husband. Explain the situation to him."

"Johnny will never go for it."

"Johnny doesn't decide, Janet. He just listens."

She hesitated, then shook her head. "I can't. Not right now."

I leaned back in my chair and looked toward the front windows. The sun had cracked through my blinds, and dust floated in panels of afternoon light.

"Don't make this personal, Michael."

I swept my gaze back across the room. "Excuse me?"

Janet had brought a cup of Starbucks with her. She took a final sip and dropped the cup into a wastebasket near her feet. Then she crossed her legs and deflated a little with a sigh.

"I said, 'Don't make this personal.'"

"What does that mean?"

She shrugged and stared at the line of her calf, the angle of her shoe.

"I don't know. Just don't."

I breathed lightly through my nose and let the silence between us settle. Old friends make lousy clients. When that friend was once something more, things only get worse. I considered the tangle of history that bound us to each other, but got nowhere with it. Then I sat forward, tented my fingers on the surface of my desk, and smiled. "How about some lunch?"

Janet closed the book I'd given her and dropped the glasses back over her face. "Sounds good."

"Let's go," I said. "There's a new place down the street."

She unfolded slowly from her chair, moving stiffly for a woman in her thirties. I figured Johnny Woods might be doing a little bodywork as well, but didn't comment.

We made our way out of my office and down the corridor. I stopped about halfway down. My client stopped with me. She kept her eyes fastened on her feet as she spoke. "What?"

"Let me at least approach him. Just once. I can run into him by accident."

"What good will that do?"

"Maybe I can get to know him. Talk some sense into him."

Janet put a hand to her temple and rubbed. Her fingers were long and thin. Old, but not with age. Then she dropped her hand back to her side and gave a small shrug.

"He can't know I've hired a private investigator."

"I understand."

She nodded once and we started down the corridor again. It wasn't everything I wanted. In fact, it wasn't even close. But at least it was a start.

CHAPTER 2

I double-parked on Michigan Avenue, popped my blinkers, and cruised the FM dial. I was tapping along to a-ha singing "Take on Me" and wondering whatever happened to my inner Led Zeppelin when Fred Jacobs walked out of the Tribune building.

Fred was six feet two and weighed slightly less than your average house cat. He was chasing sixty, with an Adam's apple that earned every bit of its moniker and a head of black hair the color and consistency of shoe leather. He wore a brown Ban-Lon golf shirt over a pair of green-and-gold-checked polyester pants with inch-and-a-half cuffs. His socks were white and his loafers black. His skin was yellow when it wasn't just grim, and an unfiltered Camel hung from rubber lips. Fred was a lifelong bachelor. Suffice it to say, he didn't get a lot of chicks. What Fred did get was information. The man shambling along Michigan Avenue had won two Pulitzers and was probably the best investigative reporter this side of Bob Woodward. I pulled the car up but Fred just kept walking. I'd seen this before and rolled down the window.

"You getting in, Fred?"

He squinted through a layer of cigarette smoke, motioned with one hand, and talked out of the side of his mouth.

"Keep moving. I'll meet you around the corner."

When it came to paranoia, the NSA had nothing on Fred Jacobs. I pulled around the block and waited. It took a minute or two, but he finally slipped alongside my car and got in.

"Just drive straight."

"It's a one-way street, Fred."

"Even better. Get going, for chrissakes."

I popped the car into drive and found my way around the block.

"A lot of people watching you these days, Fred?"

"Fuck off, Kelly. First of all, you're never anything but trouble. Second, you don't work my beat. You don't do what I do. So you don't know anything about what people see and don't see."

Like I said, great reporter. A little touched in the head, but what the hell.

"Where are we going to eat?" he said.

I'd told Fred I'd buy him lunch. He knew that meant I needed information. Of course, Fred expected something in return. Like a story. Maybe another Pulitzer. Probably not. But for someone who weighed no more than the typical calico, Fred Jacobs also liked to eat. Big time.

"I thought we'd go over to Mitchell's," I said.

"We're going to the Goat. Take a left here."

I swung a left off Michigan Avenue and then another at State Street. Jacobs sucked up the last quarter of his cigarette and pushed the butt out an open window. Smoke curled softly from each nostril as the reporter rolled up the window and chuckled to himself.

"Got to hand it to you, Kelly."

"What's that?"

"You stuck it to that TV bitch but good."

He was talking about Diane Lindsay, former Chicago news anchor, convicted killer, and someone I used to sleep with.

"You think so, Fred?"

"Fuck, yes. Talking heads think they invented the news. No respect for journalism. No respect for the process."

"And putting Diane Lindsay in the slam made that right?"

"Didn't make it right. But damn, it was fun to watch. Pull over here."

I dropped into an empty spot on Hubbard Street and the two of us got out. The Billy Goat Tavern was located on the lower level of Michigan Avenue. Most people walked down a set of stairs in front of the Wrigley Building on upper Michigan. Apparently that was a little too public for Jacobs, so we came in from Hubbard.

"The Billy Goat isn't exactly low profile, Fred."

"Not a problem. I eat here eight days a week. Someone like you sits down at my table, what am I supposed to do? So I let you buy me a burger and listen to your bullshit."

"That's the story?"

"That's the story. Come on."

Jacobs opened the heavy metal door, painted red with a black-and-white goat. We walked down a greasy set of steps and into a Chicago legend.

CHAPTER 3

The Billy Goat was more cave than tavern and everything Royko and Belushi ever made it out to be. Four sets of Greek eyes watched as we walked through the door. Spatulas in hand, they started jabbering about cheeseburgers and chips even before we stepped up to the counter. The menu board was a mildewed version of yellow with black plastic letters, forming words that were mostly misspelled. A cheeseburger cost three bucks. Everyone ordered a double, of course—mostly because it was only a buck extra. Also because that's what the guy behind the counter was making no matter what you ordered. Throw some onions and pickles on your double, then go sit at the elbow of the bar with the white linoleum top. Also known as the Wise Guys' Corner. Watch the regulars drink beer, talk about the mayor, the Bears, the Sox, Chicago. Then, now, forever. Leave the Billy Goat, walk the world for a year or two, and return. They'd still be there. Same guys, or ones just like them. Drinking a Billy Goat draft. Rolling out the history of their city. Pushing at the past, pulling it into the present. Arguing and exaggerating. Preserving what's been and making it come to life again. All for the price of a drink and available seven days a week, in the home of the Goat.

"Double cheeseburger, Mr. Jacobs?"

The counterman knew my reporter friend, which wasn't a surprise. Jacobs ordered two double cheeseburgers, which wasn't much of a surprise either.

"Give me a couple bags of chips too," Jacobs said, and lifted a thumb my way. "He's paying."

The counterman winked and waved a spatula at me.

"Double cheese, sir?"

I nodded. We got our burgers, wrapped in wax paper, dressed them up with onions, pickles, and ketchup, and headed to the VIP section, a grouping of cracked brown tables, dimly lit and pushed together in the very back of the place. A little privacy. Apparently enough for Jacobs, anyway.

"What are you drinking?" he said.

I ordered a can of Bud. Jacobs got himself the house special, something called a Horny Goat, and took a furtive look around. Four tourists took pictures of one another at a table near the door. Other than that the place was empty, save for a drunk at the end of the bar who kept reciting the lineup for the 1984 Cubs to himself. Every time he came to Jody Davis, the guy took a hit on his beer, shook his head sadly, and ordered a shot of Old Grand-Dad. The bartender ignored him and the drunk lapsed back into his play-by-play.

"I think we're okay here, Fred."

"What is it you want, Kelly?"

All I knew about Johnny Woods was what I had learned from Janet. He was a control freak who liked to muscle his wife. Never touched his stepdaughter—not yet, anyway—just liked to have a few drinks, come home, and punch the little woman around. All that plus one more thing. He worked downtown. On the fifth floor. For the mayor, John J. Wilson.

"Johnny Woods," I said. "What do you know about him?"

Jacobs took a bite of his burger and stirred a swizzle stick through his Horny Goat. One exercise of his Adam's apple and the drink was half gone. Jacobs wiped his lips with a napkin, finished off the rest of one burger, and pulled the second in front of him.

"Johnny Woods, huh?"

The reporter dug one paw into a sack of chips, filled his mouth, and began to crunch.

"He works for the mayor. Fifth Floor."

"I know that, Fred. What's he do there?"

"What the fuck do any of them do? Why you so interested?"

"It's a case, Fred. No news value. At least not yet."

I didn't see how this case could ever make it into the news, but keeping Fred Jacobs on a string was probably a good idea. Besides, I was paying for the Billy Goat feast so why not push it.

"And if it becomes a story?" Fred said.

"You're my first phone call. Now, what does Woods do on the fifth?"

Jacobs nodded, bit into his second burger, and talked with his mouth full.

"If you looked him up on the payroll, he'd be some PR flack. Probably pulling a hundred K a year. Wilson's got half a dozen of 'em stashed there."

"And what does Johnny really do?"

The reporter spread a smile across his face. "He's what we call a fixer."

"A fixer?"

"Yeah, a guy who fixes problems for the Fifth Floor. Makes things go away. And greases the machinery. All at the same time."

Jacobs' cell phone chirped. He held up a hand and flipped the phone open. "Yeah." He listened, grunted a few times, and began to scribble furiously on a napkin.

When he finished with one napkin, Jacobs gestured to me. I pushed a pile more over to his side of the table; the reporter continued to write. I finished my burger, then my beer. Jacobs snapped the cell shut and stood up.

"You want to know what Woods does?"

I nodded.

"Let's go."

Jacobs headed to the door. I followed. A primer, apparently, was in the offing. On how problems got fixed in Chicago.

CHAPTER 4

We got in my car, drove back around the block, and stopped short of the Tribune building. Jacobs went inside and came back out with a black duffel bag. Then we drove south on Michigan.

"Head down to the Loop," the reporter said.

I cruised up and over the Michigan Avenue Bridge. Jacobs picked at his teeth with a toothpick and talked.

"That was one of Woods' buddies on the phone."

"Another fixer?"

"This guy actually works for Woods, but it's all the same thing. He dropped me a bit of information only a guy like him would have. Could be good."

We were into the Loop now, heading south on Wells Street. Taxis cruised by on our left and right. An El train clattered overhead, throwing a shower of sparks down onto the street.

"Pull up to the corner of LaSalle and Washington," Jacobs said. "Then we wait."

I pulled the car over and wondered what it was exactly we were waiting for. My passenger filled in the blanks.

"Like I told you, these guys get their orders from the mayor.

Do all his dirty work. Sometimes it's a private thing. Sometimes, however, they use the media."

"The machinery?"

"Exactly. Reporters like me who need a story. Someone like Woods puts out a call. We get our headline, and a problem gets fixed. Very efficient, very convenient. Keep your eyes peeled for a guy in a light blue Crown Vic. He'll be driving on municipal plates."

Jacobs checked the napkins he had brought with him from the Billy Goat.

"Tag number M 3457."

"Who's this guy?" I said.

"The guy in the Vic?"

I nodded. Jacobs' smile conjured up the ghosts of Chicago muckrakers past.

"Name's David Meyers. Vice chairman for the mayor's Department of Aviation."

"Never heard of him."

"That's because he doesn't do a fucking thing. Patronage job: pull down a hundred and a half a year and take lunch at the Union League Club every day, buy a summerhouse down in Grand Beach, and kiss the mayor's ring whenever summoned."

"Nice."

"Yeah. But David's got what we call an issue. Actually two issues."

Jacobs raised two lengths of bone he probably called fingers.

"First goes by the name of booze. Guy likes to drink his breakfast."

"And?"

"Second involves a young lady named Margaret Hurley. Graduated last year from DePaul. Masters' in public service. Not particularly smart. Not particularly charming. She is, however, the mayor's niece."

"I'm not following you."

"Pretty simple. The mayor wants to give her a job, David Meyers' job. Thing is, he can't just fire Meyers. Piss off too many people. To be specific, one of the VPs at Boeing. Got Meyers his gig in the first place. Contributes some heavy cake to the Wilson war machine."

"So?"

"So one of the mayor's fixers steps in. Calls a guy like me. I get a story. They get an excuse to can the guy without pissing off the folks with the checkbooks."

Jacobs pointed as a car exited from an underground garage onto LaSalle. "Here's our boy."

The Crown Vic with city plates pulled out and headed north.

"Stay a couple car lengths back," Jacobs said.

"I know how to do this, Fred. Where's he headed?"

"According to my source, the boozer. 'Course, I've heard that before."

"You tailed this guy before?"

"Three times."

"Nothing?"

"Not yet. He drives around a lot. Likes to follow fire engines. Sits at the fire and watches them work."

"Must have a scanner in his car."

"Yeah, well, I told my guy on the phone. This is it. If Meyers doesn't get drunk today, I'm taking a pass."

"What did your source say?"

"He said today's the day. Damn sure. So I go."

We followed the Crown Vic west on Randolph, south on Halsted, and then onto Taylor Street.

"Looks like it's Little Italy," I said.

Jacobs nodded. We cruised past the University of Illinois at Chicago and into a block full of pasta, spiced with espresso and smoke shops, over-the-counter delis, and stands selling Italian ice. Just past the corner of Taylor and Racine, the Crown Vic pulled into a pay lot, and a middle-aged man in a suit got out. He gave his keys to an attendant and walked down the street to a tavern called Hawkeye's.

"He's going in." Jacobs said it like tumblers rolling, gears shifting, and the fate of one David Meyers falling into its predestined slot. From his duffel, the reporter pulled out a camera and snapped off a couple of quick shots as his man walked into the bar. Then he put the camera down and sat back in his seat.

"Now we wait."

"How long?"

"Long as it takes. You okay with that?"

"Sure," I said. "You going to ruin this guy's life?"

Jacobs lit up another Camel and looked at me across the cut of smoke. "You think this is dirty?"

I shrugged.

"Let me ask you something," Jacobs said. "You pay taxes. You like the fact this guy is going to sit in that bar all afternoon and drink the day away? On the city dime?"

"I hear you."

"Sure you do. Let me tell you something else. Those guys downtown, they play rough. But hell, this is a big town and if you don't know that, then get the fuck back to Iowa or wherever it is you come from. Fact is, David Meyers opened himself up to this."

Jacobs held up his camera, two fingers pinching the cigarette as it burned down.

"If he didn't have his nose in the booze bag all day, the Fifth Floor wouldn't be able to put out the call to guys like me."

"Doesn't mean they wouldn't take him out. Somehow."

"Maybe," Jacobs said. "But they wouldn't be able to use me. Or any other journalist worth his salt. If the guy's clean . . ." Jacobs shrugged. "Like I said, it's a big town. Tough town. And the Fifth Floor plays it that way."

I knew that from hard experience and decided to let the whole thing lie. So we watched the front door of Hawkeye's and waited. Two hours later, Meyers was still inside. Jacobs had gone in to check on things. Now he slid back into the car.

"Nice pub. Flat-screen TVs, good jukebox, great-looking waitress."

I had been sitting in my car for the better part of the afternoon and was getting sick of the coffee, not to mention the company.

"What's he doing?" I said.

"I talked to the bartender on the side." Jacobs rubbed his fingers together in the universal sign of currency changing hands. "He let me get a look at the tab. So far, it's a baker's dozen. Heinekens."

I whistled. "In two hours?"

"Yeah, bartender says he's going to cut him off soon. Good for my story. So get ready."

It was another hour before the bartender rang last call on David Meyers. Jacobs snapped away with his Nikon as our boy lurched into the hard sunlight and stumbled on a curb cut. I heard a snicker from behind the camera.

"This guy is pissed," Jacobs said.

We watched as Meyers made his way to his car. The lot attendant was just a kid. He took the car check but didn't go back into his shed for the keys. Instead, the kid tried to talk to Meyers. The man in the suit cocked his head and listened, almost as if the kid were speaking something other than English. Then, our city exec exploded. First, he kicked his tires. After that, he slammed both hands on the roof of his car. The kid backed off, scurried over to his shed, and closed the door after him. Meyers followed, Jacobs snapping away, catching every movement for tomorrow's front page. Meyers raged at the little wooden shed, tugged at the door, pounded on the glass. Finally, the kid opened a small window. The two exchanged more pleasantries, then the kid picked up a telephone and began to dial. At that point, Meyers stuck his hand through the window and grabbed a set of keys off the counter. The kid dropped the phone and watched as David Meyers ran back to his car, got in, and started it up.

Meyers almost hit four kids in a Honda as he pulled out of the lot. But pull out he did, into a stream of busy traffic, weaving his way, presumably home. I looked over at Jacobs, who took the camera off his eye and shrugged.

"Follow him."

I pulled into traffic about five car lengths behind. Jacobs sat back and continued to snap pictures.

"Give me your phone," I said.

Jacobs looked at me and handed over the cell. I dumped in a number and waited. At the other end was Dispatch for the nearest cop shop. Jacobs watched as I read off Meyers' tag number and gave them his location. Then I flipped the phone shut and tossed it back to the reporter.

"What the fuck you do that for?" Jacobs said.

"You'll get your story. This way it's not a homicide as well."

The reporter shrugged. "Maybe you're right."

Meyers hopped onto the Kennedy heading north. The expressway seemed to sober him up. He stayed in the right-hand lane and clocked a steady sixty. We both exited at Armitage. Meyers drove another block or two and pulled into a parking garage just south of Fullerton. I didn't see a cruiser the entire time.

"His condo's a block away," Jacobs said.

"Guess he made it," I said.

"Safe and sound." Jacobs held up his camera. "Until tomorrow's edition, that is. Then his world is over."

"Yeah."

"So now you know what guys like Johnny Woods do," Jacobs said. "Does it help you at all?"

I didn't have any answers for the reporter. As I'd find out soon enough, I didn't even have the right questions.

CHAPTER 5

The next morning, I got up and ran out along the lake. It was still dark. The city lay before me, edged in light. To my left, I could feel the water, hear it rustle against the rocks. A thin line of pink was rising from a distant shore called Michigan, offering the first hint of dawn.

I was halfway home when I saw her. She was about a hundred yards ahead of me, wearing a black Gore-Tex shell over a long-sleeve yellow sweatshirt, black runner's gloves, and cap. Her stride was smooth and nice. I ran behind her for a minute or so, then pulled alongside.

"Hey."

Rachel Swenson's eyes widened a bit. She stopped and turned down the volume on an iPod Shuffle clipped to her upper arm.

"Michael Kelly."

Her cheeks were red with the cold. Underneath her hat, she looked like she might be a law student at Northwestern, getting in her miles before an early morning class in contracts. In reality, Rachel Swenson was a sitting judge for the Northern District of Illinois and a woman I had been meaning to call for at least a year. She leaned close and gave me a hug. I got my arms up, almost too late, and then hung on too long.

"How are you?" she said.

"Pretty good. You run out here often?"

"Not as much as I should. How about you?"

"I try. Gets harder when it's cold."

"Tell me about it."

On cue, a volley of wind punched in off the lake. Rachel shivered and stamped her feet. I shook out my arms and tried to think of something to say. We stepped into a pause that seemed to last an hour and a half. Rachel got us out the other side with a thud.

"I saw you the other day."

"Where?"

"I was at Graceland," she said. "Thursday morning."

Graceland was a cemetery in Chicago. Nicole Andrews was buried there. She had been a friend to both of us. Now she was dead. Murdered, actually. By a third friend.

"I sat in my car and waited for you to leave," Rachel said.

"You should have come over." A second burst of wind pulled the words from my mouth and scattered them across the lake-front. Rachel, however, caught my meaning.

"Seemed like you wanted to be alone," she said.

I shrugged.

"I waited there almost an hour, Michael. Then I left."

"Sorry," I said.

"Don't be sorry. How often do you go to Nicole's grave?"

"Not that much."

"How often?"

"Not much. Maybe once a month. I just stay awhile. Sometimes it's a good place to think."

Rachel was looking at me closely now. I didn't like it.

"You okay, Michael?"

"I'm okay."

And I was. At least, I thought so. Nicole was my best friend. Always would be. Death was just another thing to work around.

"Why don't we get together sometime," Rachel said.

"I was going to call and suggest the same thing."

The judge cocked her hip and tilted her head. "You were going to call?"

"Yes."

"And ask me out?"

"Exactly."

"Michael, it's been at least a year since I've talked to you."

"I know."

She sighed. "You got my number?"

"I got it. Told you I was going to call."

Rachel turned on her music and began to jog in place. "This is where I turn around. Call me. Drinks, dinner. Whatever. Might do us both some good."

I watched her go. It was cold, but I watched her, anyway. Then I headed home. Ripped off the last mile and a half, feeling strong, promising myself I'd call this woman, wondering how in the hell I was going to find out her phone number.

CHAPTER 6

Half an hour later, I was showered, dressed, and headed down to Intelligentsia. They'd been open fewer than ten minutes, but the queue was already five people long. I got a large coffee and opened up the *Trib*. Fred Jacobs' story played just below the fold. Five column inches with a jump to page four. Probably fewer than a thousand words in all. The career obit for one David Meyers. According to the article, the mayor would hold a press conference today and put the soon-to-be-former exec out of his misery. I imagined the mayor's niece was already redecorating her new office and turned to the sports page.

By seven a.m., I was back downtown, sitting chilly a half block from City Hall, waiting on Johnny Woods. I had never seen the guy, but Jacobs had given me a description. Even better, Janet Woods had given me a picture. Their wedding shot, actually. Janet wore a lace dress with a long veil, sweet smile, and not the vaguest idea of the mistake standing directly to her left. For his part, Woods looked like a big guy. Maybe six-three, two hundred plus. He was thick too. Thick forehead over a thicker brow. A thick smear of ears, nose, and lips. Thick arms, one stiff by his side, the other circling his bride's waist, tugging her close, daring nyone to try and take her. The one thing about Johnny Woods that wasn't thick was the hair on top of his head. That probably pissed him off. I had a feeling Woods could hit when he got pissed and I bet it hurt. In fact, I'd seen his handiwork up close. Of course, lots of guys could hit. Make the heavy bag pop in the gym. That is, until the bag grew arms and hit back. If things played out right, maybe we'd get to see about Johnny.

The mayor's fixer stepped out of City Hall at a little after nine. Woods wore a Brooks Brothers suit, red tie, and black loafers. He was freshly shaved and probably whistling. I got out of my car, dropped a few quarters into the mayor's meter, and drifted behind. Johnny strolled down Clark Street, moved to the curb, and lifted his hand. A yellow Checker pulled to a stop and Woods got in. Fortunately, I was in the Loop, amid an armada of hacks, yellow, green, blue, and everything in between. I hailed a Flash cab and told him to follow the Checker. The cabbie thought I was kidding. I told him I was a cop and shoved a couple of twenties under his nose. The cabbie smiled and followed. At a discreet distance, even.

JOHNNY WOODS' CAB threaded its way north, through Chicago's Lincoln Park neighborhood, to the corner of Clark and Webster. There, the Checker swung a left and eased to a halt. I got out around the corner and tiptoed behind. My boy found his way down the block, to a small bit of street called Hudson.

It was a nice street. Actually, it was more than nice. It was a street with the quiet, comfortable attitude of money. A grand display of two-flats and single-family homes ran down both sides of Hudson. Turn-of-the-century brick and stone spread out behind black iron fences. Big yards with trees and birdhouses. Covered garages and a BMW or two parked somewhere in the back. Starting price for a shack on this block was two million. In Chicago, folks lined up for the privilege.

Halfway down the street sat 2121 North Hudson. More cottage than house, it was half the size of its neighbors and the only building on the block made entirely of wood. A short sweep of stairs led to a small porch, supported by slender columns carved with an Ionic turn at the top. The double front doors looked to be made of oak and were heavy with beveled glass. To one side of the porch was a pair of windows, long and narrow, set with stained glass, and trimmed in lead. The house itself was covered in scalloped blue siding and accented with white. All in all, 2121 had a look of quiet elegance, with the small touches of craftsmanship you don't see today—unless, that is, you're looking at something built a long time ago.

Woods stood in front of the tiny gem and took stock. Then he stepped up the walkway onto the porch and rang the front bell. I stopped a few houses down and slouched. I was good at that. Woods tapped his hand against his side and fidgeted. No answer. He thought for a bit and took a look through the front door. Then he thought again and pushed. The door opened. My boy stepped inside.

I wasn't sure what to expect from the tail. Maybe dig a little dirt. Maybe find a quiet moment and have a chat with my client's husband. I wasn't expecting a walk through Lincoln Park and I wasn't expecting any breaking and entering. Less than a minute after Woods walked through the door, I got another surprise. Johnny came out of the house and down the stairs, head low. He glanced up. Just once, but that was enough. His face was white. Eyes wide. Body stiff. I'd seen that look before and gently turned away. Woods blew past me and hit the corner at Webster, half running. I followed quickly and got to the end of the block just in time to see him wave down a cab. Woods took a last look around, ducked his head into the back of the taxi, and was gone.

I rubbed a thumb along my lower lip and walked slowly back down Hudson. Johnny Woods had been in the house thirty, forty seconds, tops. He could have killed someone. Could have robbed the place. Could have raided the refrigerator and been done with it. None of those, however, seemed likely. I figured Johnny Woods went to the house looking for someone or something. Whatever he found inside had surprised him. And scared him. All of which interested the hell out of me.

CHAPTER 7

I took a look up and down Hudson before I approached the house. The street was empty, quiet except for a few birds having some fun next door. I slipped on a pair of leather gloves, eased my gun off my hip, and held it by my side as I walked up the stairs. The front door was still ajar. I pushed it open with my foot. Nothing. I walked inside and found myself in a small parlor, a greeting area with a coat stand against the wall. It held a trench coat on a hook and a wooden-handled umbrella. Underneath, I noticed a pair of men's boots. They were dry and looked like they'd been that way for a while. I crept out of the parlor and into a large sitting room. Sun streamed through the stained glass and threw a rainbow of color across walls washed in cream. The floor and furniture were made of lightly varnished wood, thick, shiny, and smelling of soap and lemon. To my left, a grandfather clock ticked away the morning. Softly. To my right, a mahogany banister leisurely carried a flight of stairs to the cottage's second floor. All in all, it was peaceful, pleasant, a nurturing sort of place—that is, until my eye reached the top of the stairs. It was there I saw the old man, hanging from a well-crafted bit of railing by what appeared to be a good strong length of rope.

I took the stairs one at a time, got to the top, and moved past the body. There was one bedroom and what looked like a study upstairs. Both empty. I went back downstairs, checked the kitchen and a small basement. Also empty. I put my gun back on my hip and went upstairs a second time. The old man was hanging against a run of turned balusters. The rope was looped under his shoulders and tied off back under the railing. I crouched down, reached through the wooden pegging, and turned the body, just enough to get a look at the face. It was a refined face. A face of education. Of culture. Probably the face of a grandfather. At least it had been. Now the face was tinged with blue, which told me whoever I was looking at had died from a lack of oxygen. I didn't think it was the rope, however, that did it. Mostly because it wasn't looped around the corpse's neck. Also, because the dead man's mouth was stuffed to overflowing with sand.

I hadn't seen anyone suffocated with sand before and wasn't quite sure how a detective should proceed. I sat back for a minute and considered. The corpse didn't seem to mind the wait. His eyes were open when he died. Now he just looked at me and dangled. I took a letter from my pocket. It was actually an electric bill, overdue by at least three months. The hell with ComEd. I slipped a little bit of the sand out of my new friend's mouth and into the envelope. Then I gently reached over and went through his pockets. In his shirt pocket, I found a set of reading glasses. The rest were empty. I thought about searching the house. Then I thought about Johnny Woods. Maybe he ran away. Maybe he ran to the nearest phone and dialed up Chicago's finest. I figured my work here was done and headed for the exit.

The street was as quiet as I'd left it. No cops waiting at the curb. No neighbors peeking through the shades. I decided to push my luck and took a quick turn around the yard. The back door was locked. The windows looked undisturbed. Facing into the alley, I found a garage with a Lexus parked inside. Near a corner of the building, I saw what looked like fresh scratches in the dirt. The soil underneath was loose and quick through my fingers. I pulled out the envelope and checked the sample I'd taken from the crime scene against the soil from the yard. Close, but no cigar. My victim had been suffocated with what looked like beach sand, which meant whoever killed the old man had come prepared for the job. I walked back to the front of the house and was about to step onto the sidewalk when I noticed a small plaque. It was set a few feet off the ground, just to the right of the porch. I moved close and read the inscription.

THIS IS POLICEMAN BELLINGER'S COTTAGE.
SAVED BY HIS HEROIC EFFORTS FROM THE CHICAGO FIRE. OCTOBER 1871.

I made my way back to Clark Street and walked five blocks north, to a steam shop called Frances'. It had been in business since 1938, which was long enough for me. I ordered a bowl of chicken noodle soup, the old-fashioned kind, with thick noodles, real chunks of chicken, and broth that warmed from the inside out. I loaded it up with pepper and enjoyed. When I was finished, I stepped to the back of the shop and found one of the few pay phones in existence on Chicago's North Side. I dropped a quarter and called in the body on Hudson to the police. Then I went back to my table and ordered a corned beef sandwich on marble rye and coffee. Whatever Johnny Woods was up to, it wasn't good. I didn't think, however, it added up to murder. Then again, there was at least one corpse in a house on Hudson that might beg to disagree.

CHAPTER 8

The next day I got to my office early. Broadway was being repaved for the fifth time in the past three years. The Vatican had Michelangelo, a single man lying on his back, painting a chapel. Chicago has city workers, four to a shovel, filling potholes and pulling down twenty-five bucks an hour. Either way, it seemed to be a lifetime's worth of work.

I closed the blinds in an attempt to shut out the noise. The jackhammer, however, would have its way. I sighed, put my feet up on the desk, and opened up the *Tribune*. David Meyers' afternoon at Hawkeye's had dropped to page two. The body on Hudson was buried, literally. An inch or so of column space on page thirty-four. No hint of foul play. No mention of a mouth full of sand. Just a dead guy found inside a house. His name was Allen Bryant. He was seventy-five years old and lived alone, an amateur historian with a special interest in the Chicago Fire. Bryant, it seems, was the great-great-grandson of the home's original occupant, a cop named Richard Bellinger, and kept the house as a tiny monument to the fire. I didn't know where any of this was going. Except nowhere. I also didn't know why the police seemed to be covering up a homicide. I knew, however, where I could get some answers. Or at least some creative outrage. I picked up the phone and dialed.

"What do you want?"

Dan Masters was named in the article as a working detective on the Bryant case. He wasn't exactly a friend. More like the Catullus poem I had shared with my client. *I hate and I love.* In Masters' case, it was mostly hate.

"You in the office today?" I said.

"Depends. Are you planning on coming in?"

"I was."

"Then I'm out."

"You may want to stick around."

"Why?"

"The homicide on Hudson. I read in the paper you're working that."

"I caught the call. Not sure if we're going to work it as a homicide yet."

"Really?"

"Really."

"You find a lot of seventy-five-year-old guys in their homes with their mouths stuffed with sand?"

No response.

"Didn't think so."

"Fucking Kelly. You called it in."

"I'll be over in a half hour."

"Bring your lawyer."

"I won't need one." I hung up the phone and headed out to see my pals at the Chicago PD.

CHAPTER 9

Masters was working out of the Nineteenth District, at the corner of Belmont and Western on Chicago's North Side. I got there a little after two p.m. and was ushered into a large room jammed with detectives and their desks, in varying states of decay and disarray. Cops call it the bull pen.

A woman in her early thirties was cuffed to a chair a few feet to my left. She had brown hair with paint-by-number highlights and makeup that looked like it had been put on with the lights off. Her head was slumped to her chest and her eyes were closed. She offered up a delicate yet definite burp as I sat down, mucked her lips together once or twice, and settled back into a light doze. The detective sitting across from her was somewhere north of fifty. He pecked away at a manual typewriter and seemed capable of ignoring everything and everybody in the room. That is, until the woman woke up.

"Why am I here?" she said.

The cop stopped typing and pulled a pair of half-moon reading glasses off his nose.

"You crashed your car through the plate-glass window of a Krispy Kreme." The cop checked a report on his desk. "At the corner of Paulina and Montrose."

"I know that," she said.

"That's why you're here."

"It was an accident. Is that against the law?"

"You're drunk, ma'am."

"No, I'm not."

"I can smell it on you."

"No, you can't."

"We found seven empty liquor bottles in your car."

"They're my mother's."

"You failed the field sobriety test."

"What's that?"

"When they asked you the alphabet."

"He was confusing me. I have a disability."

"Ma'am."

"Is this because I'm a woman?"

"Ma'am, we're going to administer a Breathalyzer."

Silence.

"Ma'am?"

"I have a drinking problem. It's a disease."

"Yes, ma'am."

"I want my lawyer."

"Yes, ma'am."

We were all waiting for the legal eagle to show up when Masters shouldered his way into the room and sat down at the desk.

"Sorry for the wait."

"That's okay," I said. "I forgot how much fun this can be."

"Yeah."

"This your desk?"

"I have an office now."

I hadn't seen Masters in six months and he didn't look any better for it. His face was the color of paste. His eyes were rimmed in red and full of water. His hand shook a bit as he moved some papers around, and he might have smelled of gin. Of course, that last bit could have wafted over from Miss Krispy Kreme next door, but I didn't think so.

"Anyone notice you sitting in here?" Masters talked in an undertone and swung his head around the bull pen. I swung around with him and shrugged.

"Don't know."

"No one came up and said hello."

"Don't think so."

"Okay. Let's go."

I followed Masters down a thin hallway to a solitary door with a sign on it that read ROOM NO. 1.

"Step in here."

I walked into a small room with a wooden table and a row of blue chairs on one side. There was a TV and VCR in one corner and a dry-erase board in the other. The TV was turned off and the board had been wiped clean. Masters dropped a brown file folder on the table and sat in one of the chairs.

"Sit down, Kelly."

I sat.

"You talk to the press about the body on Hudson?"

"Would we be sitting here if I had?"

Masters nodded at the brown folder on the table between us.

"This is the working file. Tell me what you know and you get a look—provided you keep your mouth shut. Offer up the usual happy horseshit and the conversation ends. Right now. I go to the county and file charges. Tampering with a crime scene. Obstruction of justice."

"They'll never stick."

Masters shrugged. "Maybe not. But you'll never get inside this file. And you want to get inside this file."

I looked at the brown file. Then I looked up at the detective.

We weren't friends, but we weren't enemies. We trusted each other implicitly, except for the times when one of us didn't. Like I said, Catullus. Right now, Masters' face was split in half with a nasty sort of grin. Not a good sign.

"You don't know what I'm talking about, do you, Kelly? How did you wind up at the house on Hudson yesterday? Let's start with that and we'll make it up from there."

Masters was right. I did want to get inside the file. I had no idea why, but that didn't make me want it any less.

"There are some things I can tell you," I said. "Some things we just have to leave alone."

Masters leaned back in his chair and slipped his feet onto the table. "I'm listening."

"I was tailing someone for a client. The person I followed was in the house for less than a minute. No way he, or she, could have been the killer."

"Because they weren't in the house long enough?"

"Exactly."

"He, or she, could have killed this guy earlier and just been returning when you picked him, or her, up."

I shook my head.

"I saw this person's face when they left the house. Scared. Shook. Didn't expect to find that body inside."

Masters dropped his feet off the table, scratched the side of his jaw, and pulled a copy of a police report out of the file.

"Start with this. I'll be right back."

He left the room, undoubtedly to talk to whoever was watching me on the closed-circuit camera secreted in the wall paneling to my right. I had read about a half page of the report when Masters came back into the room. He wasn't alone.

"Hello, Kelly."

Vince Rodriguez was wearing a soft brown Italian suit with a striped shirt and olive-green tie. He had a gold watch on one wrist and carried a second file folder under his arm. This one was thick with paper. He dropped it on the table and took a chair to my right.

"Detective Rodriguez," I said, and gave him my best profile. "Tell me. Is this really my good side?"

"Shut up, Kelly."

That was Masters. He slumped back in his chair, poured some coffee from a thermos, and offered me nothing. I had tasted cop coffee before so that wasn't a problem.

"Taken a look at the autopsy report?" Rodriguez said, and began to unpack the file on the table in front of him.

"Not yet. Why don't you give me the highlights?"

"Water found in the lungs. Appears Bryant might have drowned somehow."

"So the sand in his mouth was postmortem?"

Rodriguez nodded. "Probably staged by the killer. Why, we have no clue. Now, tell me this, Kelly. What do you know about the Chicago Fire?"

"The Chicago Fire?"

"That's right."

Rodriguez flipped open a manila folder tabbed HISTORY and began to read.

"Started on the night of October eighth, 1871. Burned for two days. Destroyed most of the city, more than seventeen thousand buildings."

I looked over at Masters, who offered the slightest of shrugs. Rodriguez kept talking.

"The fire started at 137 East DeKoven Street, current home of the Chicago Fire Academy. In 1871, it was the home of one Catherine O'Leary. The fire is believed to have started in her barn. The theory for years was that a cow kicked over a lantern and the whole thing just got out of control. Now, however, people aren't so sure."

"You mean the cow wasn't good for it?" I said.

This time it was Rodriguez who looked toward Masters. The veteran cop cracked his knuckles and grunted.

"Told you," Masters said. "Guy knows nothing. And if he knows something, it's still nothing."

The detective was right. I didn't know much about 1871. Still, I could fake it with the best of them.

"The house on Hudson predates the fire," I said. "You think there's a connection."

Rodriguez grinned thinly and held out his hand. Masters reached into his pocket and pulled out a couple of twenties. Rodriguez pocketed the cash.

"I told him you'd see it. Straight off."

"Doesn't mean it's anything," I said.

"But you see it," Rodriguez said. "Just like we did. There were only a dozen or so buildings that survived the fire of 1871. A hundred-plus years later, we have a body turning up in one of them. A guy, by the way, who happened to be an expert on the fire."

"Coincidence?" I said.

Rodriguez shook his head and pulled a single sheet of paper from the murder file.

"There's more. Best we can tell, this is the only item missing from the house on Hudson. First edition of a book written by Timothy Sheehan in 1886. Titled *Sheehan's History of the Chicago Fire.*"

Rodriguez pushed the page over so I could take a look.

"How the book fits in," Masters said. "Whether it has any connection to any of this. No real idea."

"And you guys are sitting on all this because the brass says so?"
Rodriguez nodded.

"The press would have a field day with it," Masters said. "You know that."

"Fifth Floor showing any interest?" I said.

"Why do you ask?" That was Rodriguez again.

"Just thinking that might be where the heat is coming from. No pun intended."

I smiled. Masters leaned forward, letting his bulldog features swell with blood. It wasn't pretty. Then again, it wasn't supposed to be.

"Why don't we cut the bullshit here, Kelly. Tell us all about your client. Starting with why they're so interested in Johnny Woods."

I hadn't figured on Woods' name coming out of Masters' mouth. I think he enjoyed the moment.

"So you know about Johnny."

"We know," Rodriguez said. "Again, we don't understand."

I was in a bit of a spot and my two cop friends knew it. Johnny Woods appeared to be a key to whatever was going on. Throw in the fact that he was one of the mayor's guys and the stakes rose considerably all around. Masters and Rodriguez wanted answers. I had plenty. Problem is, none of them were going to be what you might call good.

"What exactly do you know about me and Woods?"

"You've been asking about him," Rodriguez said.

The image of Fred Jacobs flickered through my head. I should have figured as much.

"Okay, I've been asking. It's a personal thing."

"Personal?" Masters said. "Just so we're all clear. You're telling us Johnny Woods had nothing to do with your presence at 2121 North Hudson yesterday."

The corner I was in seemed to be getting tighter by the minute. "I didn't say that."

Masters got up from his chair and clasped both of his hands on top of his head. "Maybe we need to take a statement from this guy, Vince."

"I don't think so," Rodriguez said, and looked at me. "I think we can get what we need and still make Kelly feel good. Right, Kelly?"

"I'll tell you what I know," I said. "You keep my client's name out of it."

Rodriguez looked at Masters, who shrugged, then smiled. "As long as Mrs. Woods is not our killer, you won't have any problems, Kelly."

"Fuck off, Masters."

"So that's it, then."

Some days you just can't win. Inside a Chicago cop shop, make that most days.

"Yeah, that's it," I said. "Woods' wife asked me to help her out, so I tailed hubby to the house on Hudson. Just wanted to talk to the guy. See what his day was like. Woods rang the doorbell. No answer. He looked around, rang again. Then he pushed the door open."

Rodriguez was taking notes now. Masters was asking the questions.

"Did he force the door?"

"No. Looked like it was ajar. He just pushed it open. Like I said, he was nervous."

"Then what?"

"He went into the house. Less than a minute later, he came out. White face, big eyes. Scared. Ran right by me. Got himself a cab and never looked back."

"Then you went in," Rodriguez said.

"I went in. Saw the body. Didn't touch anything and left."

It went on for a while longer. Details of the body. The house. The Johnny Woods angle one more time. Just to see how many different lies I could tell. It wasn't hard. Never is when you didn't do anything and are mostly telling the truth. Finally, they were done. The big question, of course, remained unanswered.

"So why was Woods there?" Rodriguez said.

"No idea."

Rodriguez held up a photocopy of the title page to Timothy Sheehan's book. "You didn't see one of these in there?"

I shook my head.

"Johnny Woods didn't walk out with one?"

"Not that I saw."

"You ever talk to Woods about his wife?" Masters said.

"What do you know about that?"

"We've had a couple of calls out to their house. Domestic stuff."

"Let me guess," I said. "No one ever filed a report."

"Janet Woods didn't want any paperwork filed," Masters said. "We accommodated her request."

I looked from one cop to the other and back. "Sounds like you know as much about my client as I do."

"Wasn't hard to figure out how you might be involved, Kelly, if that's what you mean." Masters picked up the Bryant homicide file. "Either way, when you talk to Janet Woods, you leave this out."

"Leave what out?"

"The house on Hudson. Leave it out. And don't talk to any of your friends in the press. About any of this."

Masters dropped the file back onto the table and turned to Rodriguez. "We done here?"

"Yeah," Rodriguez said.

Masters left without another word. Rodriguez and I walked back through the bull pen and out to my car.

"What was that about?" I said.

"What?"

"Masters. Laid it on a little heavy at the end there, don't you think?"

"A lot of people watching this case, Kelly. Kind of people who turn working cops into memories. In a hurry."

"So the heat is coming from the Fifth Floor."

"Yup."

"What do they want?"

"They want us to bury it. Right now, Bryant isn't even classified as a homicide. 'Undetermined cause,' I believe, is the phrase we're using."

"'Undetermined cause,' huh? And now I put one of the mayor's guys in the middle of it."

"See why you're such a popular fellow?"

"Woods didn't have anything to do with it, Rodriguez. He was just there. Like me."

"Not quite. You followed him to Hudson. But he went there for a reason. Maybe not to kill anybody. But he went there for a reason."

"So what are you guys going to do?"

"Us? Leave it the fuck alone."

"Really?"

"Absolutely. Mostly because I don't want to wind up with a kilo of cocaine in the trunk of my car some night."

"Downtown can play rough."

"You know better than most." Rodriguez lifted an eyebrow. "Besides, I got a secret weapon."

"You think I can't resist taking a shot at this?"

"Am I wrong?"

I shrugged. "Probably not."

"Here's the deal," Rodriguez said. "You take a look at the Bryant thing. Quietly."

"And if it goes sideways?"

"I'll cover what I can. Until we find out what's going on, however, it all stays out of the press."

"Fair enough," I said. "But let me ask you something. Why the interest? I mean, why get involved at all?"

We had stopped in front of my car. Rodriguez slid a foot onto the bumper and watched traffic fight its way down Belmont. It was early April in Chicago, and I could see the cop's breath as he spoke.

"You know why, Kelly. It's what she'd want us to do. Or at least try."

Nicole Andrews had been part of Rodriguez's life as well. The love he waited for, only to never have. I'd had more time with her. A childhood's worth and that would have to do.

"I'll take a look, Detective. But I don't think the Fifth Floor is behind this."

"Maybe not. But they're worried about something. Been around long enough to know that."

"The Chicago Fire? Eighteen seventy-one? Seems like a long time ago to be killing folks."

"Do me a favor. Just take a look."

I agreed and we shook hands. Then I got in my car and pulled out of the police parking lot. As cops go, Rodriguez was a good one. Straight shooter and good instincts. This time, however, he was wrong. People murder people for just a very few reasons: money, jealousy, revenge, power. They all make sense. The Great Chicago Fire of 1871? Not so much.

I took a left and headed east on Belmont. Rodriguez needed a vacation. A little R & R. I'd give his hunch a day or two and tell him there was nothing there. Then I'd move on to more pressing issues. Like how to get Johnny Woods to stop beating up his wife.

CHAPTER 10

The Chicago Historical Society sits just off Lake Michigan, at the corner of Clark Street and North Avenue. I walked in with the midmorning senior citizen crowd. The lady at the wooden desk in front had *volunteer* written all over her. She was twenty years past her prime, with enough money to make it not matter. She wore a black wool suit with big gold buttons, black pumps, and a red silk scarf with black horses and yellow chunks of chain on it.

Bolted just above her head was a set of massive radiators belching steam and pouring heat onto an unsuspecting public. The volunteer, however, refused to let it spoil her day in the city. She smiled and waved me over.

"A bit hot, isn't it?" She fanned herself with a society booklet.

"Just a little," I said.

She was beyond perspiring and now openly sweating. Her face was florid, except for her cheeks, which made florid seem pale.

"I was going to get a bottle of water," I said. "Would you like one?"

"Oh, no, thanks. I'm off in ten minutes. My girlfriends are coming down."

She pointed over to the Big Shoulders Café. It stood at one end of the building, next to a second stack of radiators that looked like something out of *Mad Max Beyond Thunderdome*.

"We're going to have lunch at the Big Shoulders."

I guessed that was a big treat in the big city. Why else would someone eat chicken salad at 200 degrees Fahrenheit? Of course, I was talking to a mature woman of about sixty years who talked about her girlfriends like they had just gotten out of high school home ec. Anyway, I liked her. Even better, I needed her help.

"I'm looking to do some research on the Chicago Fire," I said.

"That's one of our specialties," she whispered.

"I know," I whispered back. "That's why I'm here. On the Q.T. I'm with the *Tribune*. We're hoping to scoop the *Sun-Times*. Maybe I shouldn't say any more."

If it were possible for florid to fluoresce, the volunteer's face did exactly that.

"Got it." She winked. "We have an entire section of our library devoted to the fire. By the way, my name is Teen."

I shook her hand.

"Teen?"

"Short for Kathleen. A friend gave it to me in high school. Just sort of stuck. I'm sorry. What's your name?"

"Michael. Michael Kelly."

"Irish. How nice. I'm Irish too. My grandfather hailed from Cork."

I didn't know where my grandfather hailed from—besides a barstool inside an old Clark Street boozer called the Stop and Drink. So I made something up.

"That's nice," Teen said. "Now, it's the fire, right?"

I nodded. She pointed up a swirling staircase to a glass door with RESEARCH LIBRARY stenciled across it.

"The best place to start is with our research staff."

She wrote me out a pass and I trudged upward.

TEEN WAS TRUE to her word. Fifteen minutes later, I was knee deep in abstracts, clippings, and journals from the fire. It all seemed highly entertaining, not to mention highly irrelevant, when the volunteer approached again.

"How was the Big Shoulders?" I said.

"Well . . ."

Teen looked around like someone was listening so I looked around too. She looked back and we bumped heads.

"Sorry," she said.

"That's okay. Happens all the time in the journalism game."

"I told the girls I was going to skip lunch."

Teen pulled out a handkerchief embroidered with her initials and dabbed at her face.

"I wanted to come up and share something with you," she said.

I waited. She waited. So I smiled.

"Okay," she said. "There was another man here. I'm not sure who he was. But he was also interested in the fire."

"Place like this," I said, "must get a lot of people interested in the fire."

"Not like him." She peeked around again. "He looked dangerous."

"Dangerous, huh?"

Teen nodded as if we were on the same page. I was thinking maybe I could take her in as a partner. She could be like the lady in *Murder, She Wrote* and I'd be her dumb assistant.

"He asked for access to the green room," she said.

"Which is?"

"Where we keep our historical accounts of the fire and primary source materials. Not the abstracts."

"You mean the real letters and all that good stuff?" I said.

"Yeah."

"Would *Sheehan's History of the Chicago Fire* be in the green room?"

The mention of Mr. Sheehan seemed to agitate my new friend. "The other man asked about that book."

"The dangerous one?"

"Yes."

"You remember anything else about this man?"

Teen shrugged. "He was big."

"And dangerous?"

"Yes, dangerous. He wore sunglasses. Kind of hard to get a look at him."

"Did he have hair?"

"Oh, I don't know. He wore a hat. One of those stocking hats. Very warm."

"Did he sign in? On a logbook or anything?"

Teen shook her head. "I wouldn't think so. Why? Is he another reporter?"

I smiled again. "Sounds like it."

"Do you want to see our *Sheehan's*?" my new friend said.

"Is it in the green room?"

"Yes, it is."

"Seems only fair."

Teen stood up, straightened herself, and led the way. I followed.

CHAPTER 11

The green room was exactly that: green rug, green drapes, and dark green wallpaper. With a light thread of green running through it. Wooden carrels ran down one side of the room. Each had a banker's lamp, gold plated with a green glass shade. Interspersed among the carrels were leather reading chairs, green, of course, with silver studs stitched down the sides and along the armrests.

Floor-to-ceiling stacks ran down the other side of the room and contained, presumably, the collected wisdom of Chicago's history. I walked down one of the aisles and pulled out a file on the *Eastland Steamer*. In 1915 it capsized on the Chicago River, found the bottom in fewer than three minutes, and killed 844. I slid that bit of tragedy back onto its shelf and moved over to the Chicago Fire.

The volunteer had left to find the curator. That's what she called her boss: curator. I figured, Hell with the curator. If he really wanted to curate, he'd be here. Ten minutes later, I had the first set of files on the fire open when someone stepped across my light. I turned.

"The curator, I presume."

He gave me a once-over like only a man who kept files for a

living could. The badge on his lapel read LAWRENCE RANDOLPH. Like it or not, the curator now had a name.

"Why would you want to do any original research?" he said.

"It's a calling. You know, like the phone call you get in your head when you're supposed to become a priest."

Randolph just stared.

"Didn't go to Catholic school, huh?" I said.

"The material here is extremely fragile. Delicate. And some of it, highly sensitive."

"That's what I want. The highly sensitive part."

Randolph had a head that could have passed for a thumb had it not been for the ears. He plucked a pair of spectacles off the bridge of what he most likely called a nose and began to polish.

"I really don't see this working," he said.

"It's about a murder."

It usually does the trick. Most likely does the trick. In this case, definitely did the trick. The glasses went back on the nose and the flat expanse of face drew down just the slightest hue of pink.

"A real murder?"

"Sure." I flipped out my ID. "I lied to your assistant. I'm actually a private investigator. Working a case. Dead guy's name was Allen Bryant. Did a lot of research on the fire. Maybe you heard of him?"

Randolph shook his head.

"Not your century, huh?"

Another shake of the head.

"Okay. Anyway, this book popped up. *Sheehan's History of the Chicago Fire.*"

"Timothy Sheehan?" Randolph scuttled down an aisle. Rows of books towered on either side. I scuttled after him.

"The definitive work on the fire," he said, and stopped before a particularly imposing shelf. "Move out of the way."

I barely had time before a ladder, set into a metal track on the floor, came whirring down the aisle. Randolph had summoned it via a button built into the framework near my head.

"Pretty neat there," I said.

Randolph clambered up the ladder and came down with the tome. It was old and blue with gold lettering on the cover: *Sheehan's History of the Chicago Fire* by Timothy Sheehan.

"You got a lot of copies of this?" I asked.

"That's a first edition."

"Tell me what's so special about a first edition?"

"Nothing. Just worth more money."

The private investigator in me caught the faintest whiff of a motive.

"How much money?" I intrepidly asked.

"*Sheehan's* was published in 1886. They offered a very limited first printing."

The curator flipped open the cover. On the inside was the number 12 embossed in red.

"Each one is numbered. One through twenty."

"Just twenty of 'em, huh?"

"That's right. There is at least one other first edition in the Chicago area. Not entirely sure about ownership, but I believe it's in private hands."

I didn't tell Randolph that his private hands were now dead. Might make him nervous, and I didn't need that.

"The scarcity of copies," Randolph said, "obviously makes each first edition worth a considerable amount."

Randolph talked about money like it was a dirty secret. I figured I'd do the same.

"What's considerable?" I whispered.

"Two, three hundred dollars."

My motive suddenly didn't smell so good.

"You think someone got killed over a first edition of *Sheehan's History of the Chicago Fire*?" Randolph said.

"You don't buy it either."

"I don't see why," he said.

I considered the book, then moved my eyes back to Randolph.

"If you were me, what would you do?"

The curator looked at the book. Then he looked at me. "I'd read it."

So that's what I did. I was on page fifty when Randolph was there again. At my shoulder. The smell of fine and dusty typeface was heavy upon him. Or maybe it was just booze.

"You been drinking?" I said.

Randolph blinked.

"I just got to the part about the watchman," I said.

Two blinks. I took that as a good sign and continued.

"Mathias Shafer, age forty. He's sitting up in the city's watchtower on the night of the fire. Sees a bit of smoke. Rings down to the boy. Let's see. . . ."

I consulted my *Sheehan's*.

"Boy by the name of Billy Brown. Stop me if you already know all this. Billy is down in the business part of the tower. The part where all the alarms are. He's got his girl down there. Playing the guitar for her and—well, you can figure out the rest."

Randolph took off his bifocals and wiped them down.

"That's right, you got it," I said. "Billy pulls the wrong alarm and continues with the wooing. That's what they called it back then. Wooing. Same deal, just a better name. Anyway, a half hour or so goes by and Shaffer notices the bit of smoke is now a lot of smoke and a bit of fire. He calls down to Billy again. Tells him he pulled the wrong alarm. Billy zips himself up and says, No worries, boss, I'll get right to it. Except he doesn't get right to it. Another half hour goes by before the city gets its fire engines where they need to be. By then—hell, it was too late, wasn't it?"

Lawrence Randolph blinked three times, picked up the files I had been looking at, and left. Tired from my lecture, I sat back in the green leather reading chair and rested my eyes. My *Sheehan's* hit the floor with a definite thud. I started, swore, and went to pick up the book. Beside it was a folder the curator had left behind. It was labeled THEORIES ON THE FIRE'S CAUSE AND ORIGIN. I picked it up and started to read. Three articles deep, I found the first feather in what I was certain would be a wild-goose chase. Still, I couldn't resist and began to take notes.

CHAPTER 12

W hat do we know about this?"
I had made my way back to Randolph's office.
Inside I found a shapeless collection of wood and leather covered in books and papers. Behind a large desk was the shapeless man himself, eating lunch from a brown paper sack and not especially happy to see me darkening his door.

"About what?" he said.

"This *Sun-Times* article."

Randolph put down a pretty nice-looking banana, picked up the clippings file I had dropped on his desk, and gave it a look. Then he put the file down, picked up the yellow fruit again, and slowly began to peel.

"Rubbish," he said.

"Really?"

"Really."

The article was written by a reporter named Rawlings Smith. It was a weekend magazine piece from 1978, speculating on who might have actually started the fire.

"Did you notice the day the piece ran, Mr. Kelly?"

It wasn't included on the copy I had read.

"April first," Randolph said, and took a delicate bite of his banana.

"April Fool's Day," I said.

"Precisely, Mr. Kelly. April Fool's Day. This article was a joke, played on the city and two of its most illustrious families."

"So you don't believe a word of it?"

"Not a word."

"You sure?"

Randolph offered a look to the heavens, as if in silent prayer for the small tortures sent his way each and every day. Then he steeled himself and returned to schooling the great unwashed. Also known as yours truly.

"There are any number of theories as to how the fire started," Randolph said. "There's O'Leary's neighbor, Peg Leg Sullivan. Alleged to have started the fire with his pipe and an errant bit of lit tobacco. There's O'Leary's drunk tenants, the McLaughlins. Had a party that night. Supposedly a couple got, shall we say, amorous in the barn, knocked something over, and started the fire. Then there's the supernatural: a meteor hit Chicago. Lit the whole place up like a Christmas tree."

"You believe any of those?"

"Who knows, Mr. Kelly? Who really knows?" Randolph threw the remains of his banana in the trash, folded his lunch bag up into a neat brown square, and slid it inside the pocket of his jacket. Probably made of tweed.

"In my business, you are now talking about one of the Holy Grails: exploding the O'Leary myth. Finding out, definitively, who or what started the fire. It's the dream of every curator who's ever sat in this chair."

Randolph leaned back in said chair and arched his eyebrows to the right, sort of like Groucho Marx. "You see that?"

I could only assume he was talking about the painting hanging on the wall. It showed an afterthought of a man from a bygone era, captured in thin oil and what appeared to be an even thinner light. His mouth was curved in a small smile, as if he knew the joke was on him, even in the nineteenth century.

"That's Josiah Randolph. My great-granduncle. Original curator of the society. Wrote the book for this job."

"Big shoes to fill."

"Indeed. Josiah was curator at the time of the fire."

Randolph swiveled in his chair and gestured to a small leather-bound volume in a glass case behind his desk.

"I donated his diary to the historical society. It describes how the building that housed this institution burned to the ground. Josiah was the last man out and tried desperately to save a copy of the Emancipation Proclamation. Lincoln's final version, handwritten by the great man himself and the only one of its kind. Alas, Josiah failed."

We had a moment of silence for Lincoln's lost Proclamation. Then I pushed us back to the present.

"Let's say, just for kicks, that you solved the mystery. Proved beyond a doubt who started the Chicago Fire."

"Then, Mr. Kelly, I believe I might rate a painting of my own." Randolph picked up the clipping file again. "This article, however, is a joke. John Julius Wilson was our mayor's great-great-grandfather, not to mention his namesake. Charles Hume was publisher of the old *Chicago Times* and helped to rebuild this town. Two of Chicago's giants. The idea that they conspired to actually start the fire—"

"According to this article, it was part of a land swindle. Maybe a mile or so worth of city real estate."

"I can read, Mr. Kelly. The idea is pure fantasy." Randolph

dropped the clip file on his desk. "If it were possibly true, even a shred of it, don't you think someone such as myself would have put it together by now?"

"Have you ever talked to the reporter who wrote the article?" I took a look at my notes. "Rawlings Smith."

"No, I haven't," Randolph said, and got up to go.

"Might be worth a phone call," I said, and got up with him.

The curator opened the door to his office and stood aside.

"As you might imagine, Mr. Kelly, I'm an exceedingly busy man. Now, if you don't mind."

I walked out the door, Lawrence Randolph close behind.

"You think this is all crazy, don't you, Randolph?"

I walked quickly and spoke softly, allowing the words to drowse back over my shoulder. The curator struggled to keep up. Not really wanting to listen, but even more afraid of what he might miss.

"A waste of time might be a more apt description."

I stopped and turned. Ready to set the hook a final time.

"But what if it were true?"

"The article?"

"Yeah. What if it were. What if you discovered who really started the Chicago Fire. And what if it was our mayor's great-great-grandfather. Make you pretty famous, wouldn't it?"

The curator shook his head and continued walking toward the front. But not before I saw the gleam again. The bite I was looking for. Ambition, fame, fortune. The lure was universal. The flame burned hot. Even down the hallowed hallways of history.

TWO MINUTES LATER, I was standing in front of the historical society, a copy of the old *Sun-Times* article in my pocket. I wasn't especially hopeful. In fact, I wasn't hopeful at all. Timothy Sheehan's history was just that: a history; the *Sun-Times* article, as Randolph put it, pure fantasy. Still, there was no bigger, no more smug lion in the zoo than the right honorable mayor of Chicago. And I, for one, could never pass up the opportunity to reach between the bars and poke a stick in his well-insulated ribs.

CHAPTER 13

I grabbed the Red Line downtown. Got off at Lake and walked a handful of blocks to the corner of Clark and Randolph. Some people would call the pile of bricks you find there City Hall. Others might call it the County Building. Only in Chicago could they both be right. And wrong.

The east side of the building carried a Clark Street address. Inside, it was tastefully lit and quiet, full of dignified men and women in business suits, smiling and nodding, walking down mostly empty hallways. This was the center of business for Cook County, also known as the County Building.

The west side got its mail delivered to a LaSalle Street address. Inside, it was full of garish light and noise, lawyers in cheap suits with a lot of hair gel and even more cologne, entire families camped out on benches, children screaming, women arguing, hustlers hustling, the mayor's men on the muscle, a bit of shaving cream still peeking out from under the occasional ear, ducking into an elevator and retreating upstairs. This was John J. Wilson's domain, also known as City Hall.

I entered the building on the county side. An old man in a blue security guard uniform and a plastic-looking white shirt was slouched just inside the door. He had an unlit cigarette in his mouth, a gun on his hip, and was snoring lightly.

"Land Records," I said.

"Staircase on the left, two flights down."

The man talked around the cigarette without opening an eye. I tipped a hat I didn't have and headed in. The hallway was deep and quiet, the staircase made of cold cracked marble. Everything felt old, nothing more so than the county's Bureau of Land Records. It was actually three stories underground and had, as best I could tell, avoided that bane of society called the computer. For the most part, that is. There were two or three crowded up against a wall. Other than that, it was large canvas-covered books, row after row of them, documenting the comings and goings of every parcel of property in the great city of Chicago, not to mention the rest of Cook County. I wandered down one aisle, then up the next.

"They are cross-divided by section and parcel number, then organized by year. Do you have a parcel number?"

The man who spoke to me was slightly built with thin shoulders, tapered fingers bordering on delicate, and a face that looked too fragile for its own good. He had black hair with a vein of pink running through it. He wore black jeans and a shirt that fit my vague notion of turquoise. He had a gold earring in each ear and a tattoo of a yellow star on the side of his neck. He was twenty years younger than everyone else in the place and wore his air of bored indulgence like a badge of honor.

"Actually, no, I don't have a parcel number."

"Have to get a parcel number before we can help you," my soon-to-be friend said. "Top of the stairs, two doors down. Room 206. Give them the address. They'll get you a parcel number."

"I'm thinking this piece of property is not going to be in your system. At least not with a parcel number."

"All property in Cook County has a parcel number."

"I believe you," I said. "It's more a matter of when. What's your name?"

"Hubert." He said it with an edge, daring anyone to comment.

"Hello, Hubert."

I sidled him a bit out of the aisle so his boss couldn't see us. She had blue hair, gold mascara, and gold glasses on a string around her neck. She wore nothing less than a muumuu and was snapping gum and pretending to index property books two aisles away. She wasn't fooling me, however. Hubert and I were up to no good and she was determined to find out exactly what kind of no good it might be.

"Listen," I said, dropping my voice just enough to get him interested without being scared. "The listing I'm looking for is old."

Hubert was nonplussed. "Our records cover the entire twentieth century."

"Eighteen hundred sort of old."

"Before the fire?" I caught the ghost of a gleam in the young man's eye. This was sexy stuff. Relatively speaking, that is.

"Exactly."

"What did you say your name was?"

"I didn't."

For Hubert, that was even better. He pushed me down the aisle toward a gray door in the back. The last thing I saw was the lady with the blue hair, looking our way and picking up the phone.

CHAPTER 14

Through the doorway was a set of black iron stairs climbing two flights up and back, to another door of government gray. Hubert found the key and opened it. The air was like the inside of a closed coffin—if the inside of a closed coffin had any air, that is.

"This is our historical section, 1890 and before. Don't come in here too often."

Hubert found a switch and pulled it. Pale light dropped down from a single forty-watt bulb. I tried to get my bearings. Hubert was already whipping into the darkness.

"Come on. The bitch out front will wonder what we're about in here."

It was like the main room but even older. Shelf after shelf of property books, creaky and yellow. We took two lefts, a right, and then straight into a wall.

"Sorry," Hubert said. "Back this way."

We backtracked down one aisle and then across to a sagging set of shelves that ran from the floor to just below the ceiling. Above that was a long thin window, covered in wire mesh and set at what I figured to be about sidewalk level. Dirty light filtered in from the street, along with the smell of what I could only imagine to be Panda Express on a very bad day.

"Sorry. Chinese takeout has their Dumpster in the alley right outside."

I ran my finger down one of the bindings. It was covered with spider scrawl in what appeared to be quill ink.

"Not a problem," I said. "At least we can see. What does this say?"

Hubert bent down and took a closer look. "It says *Shortall and Hoard*. Then it gives a plat number and date."

"Who is Shortall and Hoard?"

"John Shortall," Hubert said. "Basically saved Chicago's property record system."

"Really?"

"Sure. The fire destroyed all of Cook County's official real estate records."

"Everything?"

Hubert snapped his fingers. "Gone. Shortall ran a title abstract company. Kept copies of almost all Cook County conveyances in his office."

"Convenient."

"Yeah. As the fire approached, Shortall commandeered a wagon at gunpoint, loaded up his records, and got them out of town."

"If he hadn't?"

"No one would have legally owned anything." Hubert shrugged. "Chaos."

"And these are the records?"

"This is them."

I pulled out a book and opened it up. Felt the creak of time as pages and ink pulled apart.

"Careful." It was Hubert, peeking over my shoulder.

"I got it, Hubert."

"Yes, but the ink is brittle. And these are the only copies."

Hubert slid the book from my hands and started peeling the long pages apart. I caught the flash of a date: 1858.

"Sorry, Hubert. This is too early for me, anyway."

"No reason not to handle it just as carefully."

"Yes, Hubert."

I hung my head for the appropriate moment of penance and reflection. Then I pulled some books from 1870 off the shelves.

"These are the ones we want," I said.

"This is the time period?"

"It's a start."

"And the location?"

"The city."

"No kidding. In 1870 there wasn't much else outside the city. Property-wise, that is."

"Just south of the Loop," I said. "Near Roosevelt and Canal."

Hubert bit the ring he had pierced through his lower lip and ran his finger along the parched spines of Chicago history.

"That's still a lot of ground. More specific?" Hubert handed me a look he probably figured passed for coy. I let him play.

"You got it right," I said. "The Irish quarter. O'Leary's barn and the whole neighborhood."

"DeKoven Street," Hubert said.

"Number 137, Hubert."

"Yes, yes. But here it will be listed by property number. Not a high property number in 1870. But they did still have them." Hubert dug a little deeper into the shelves and came up with four long books. "This covers O'Leary's barn and ten blocks on either side."

I reached for the book, but Hubert held up a hand. "We take them apart a page at a time. Each page, a moment at a time."

Four moments later, we had skimmed across forty property transfers in O'Leary's neighborhood. Fourteen of them were sold to the same person. Or, rather, to the same set of initials: J.J.W.

"Did they always use initials back then on deeds?" I said.

Hubert shrugged. "Don't know. Seems sort of weird."

The kid pulled the property register closer and squinted at the scrawl. "Actually, I think this is a company."

He pointed to a squiggle of ink. "I think that's a *Co.* at the end. Could stand for company."

I took a look. The kid was right.

"I don't suppose John Shortall kept any corporate records from back then?" I said.

Hubert shook his head. "Sorry."

"Burned in the fire?"

Hubert nodded. "All the corporate records were completely destroyed. Everyone who had a business basically had to reincorporate. Start all over again. Records-wise, that is."

"Corporate chaos?"

"I'd think so."

Hubert ran a long nail down the property register, swallowed up some courage, and posed the question I knew was coming.

"If you don't mind me asking, these initials. Do they ring a bell?"

Hubert danced his fingers off the page as I slammed the register shut. "Shut up, kid."

"Yes, sir."

I slid the book back to its place on the shelf. "And forget about those initials. Make your life a whole lot nicer."

"Yes, sir."

I looked at the dark wall of books surrounding us. Thought about John Shortall. Getting his wagon loaded up at gunpoint.

Saving Chicago's real estate market. Probably making himself a bunch of dough in the process. Seemed just about right. Then I thought about the initials I'd found scattered throughout the old property records: J.J.W.—as in John Julius Wilson. Also known as the mayor's great-great-grandfather.

"Let's go back downstairs," I said. "Before your boss misses us."

"Okay."

Hubert began to pick his way back down the dark aisles.

"FYI . . ."

"Yeah?" I said.

"My boss . . . she's the mayor's cousin."

"The lady with the blue hair?"

"That's what they say."

"And she runs this place?"

"Yep."

I scratched the side of my head. "You gonna lose your job, Hubert?"

"Nah. I'm gay, so she's scared stiff of me." The young man's words floated back on a cloud of nonchalance. "I'll tell her you made a pass at me or something. She'll love that."

"Thanks, Hubert."

"Don't worry. She won't believe it. Just give her something to talk about. That's all it takes. Besides, working in Land Records isn't exactly my life ambition."

"Let me guess. You take classes at Second City."

Hubert turned and smiled. "Stereotype. No, I'm a hacker."

"Computers?"

Hubert wiggled fourteen rings, scattered across ten fingers. "Given the time and the money, nothing I can't get into."

"Really?"

"Scary real. You want to buy stuff online, let me set up your computer first. Save your credit cards from getting scammed."

The kid slipped me a business card, red with yellow stars: HUBERT RUSSELL. "Gotta get back," he said.

"Thanks, Hubert. Name's Michael Kelly."

"No problem, Mr. Kelly. It was fun."

We shook hands. Hubert went back downstairs. I waited a minute and followed. I could feel Hubert's boss tracking me as I walked through the bureau. The kid fell in step halfway across the room and spoke in a voice plenty loud for anyone who wanted to listen.

"Sorry I couldn't help you, sir. The property you want was actually not even platted back in 1840. Chances are no one technically owned it. At least, not anyone who could produce a legal deed. Like I said, if you want to find out more, you might try the Chicago Historical Society."

Hubert winked and opened the door to let me out. Then I was alone again, in the cold marble corridor, walking back in time. To 1871 and a gang of land thieves, also known as Chicago's founding fathers.

CHAPTER 15

How did you get in here?"

I wandered back to my office on Broadway at a little after two in the afternoon. The girl sat in the same chair her mother had. She had the same hair touched in red. Same elegant lines for nose and chin. Same pale skin, stretched tight over high cheekbones with dusky points of fatigue underneath. Like her mom in just about every way. Except she didn't have the black eye. Not yet, anyway.

"You left the door open," the girl said, and threw a look behind her.

"I don't think so."

She smirked, in a way that made me feel suddenly slow. Suddenly old. "Okay, so I'm good with locks."

I made a mental note to get the locks changed and took a seat behind my desk. My notes from the historical society and the County Building went into a drawer. Then I booted up my Mac and checked my e-mails. I could feel the girl waiting, watching, assessing. I thought she might get a little antsy. I was wrong. After a minute or so, I looked up and across the desk.

"Let me guess," I said. "You're Taylor Woods."

"How did you know?"

"You look a lot like your mom."

Taylor held up the volume of Catullus I had shared with her mother less than a week earlier. "I borrowed a book."

I got up and walked over to the shelf by the door. Felt for the Smith and Wesson, a .38 caliber snub nose I kept in a space behind the *Iliad*. The gun was still there. Loaded and, thankfully, not in the hands of a teenager. Then I sat back down behind my desk.

"I showed that book to your mom the other day."

"She told me," Taylor said. "I study Latin in school."

"What grade are you in?"

"I'm fourteen. Freshman in high school."

"So you can translate?"

"A little bit." She looked down at the title and then back to me. "*I hate and I love.* That's pretty easy."

"You like Catullus?" I said.

Taylor weighed the pros and cons of a poet who wrote two thousand years before she was born. Took all of five seconds.

"Seems pretty cool. Kind of romantic."

I could have told her all about romance. About how it was sometimes better read than lived. But I figured people, even fourteen-year-old people, had to figure some things out for themselves.

"What's up, Taylor?"

"My mom told me you were going to help us."

"She did?"

"Yeah. She told me if there was trouble, I should come find you."

Taylor held out my business card. A name, address, e-mail, and phone number. Not much more than that to a business card. Until it's in the hands of a kid. Until it offers you up as a savior.

"Does your mom know you're here?"

She shook her head and hair fell over the lower half of her face. She pulled the tresses back behind her ears and settled herself in her chair.

"You came on your own?"

"Yes."

"Where's your mom?"

"At home, I guess."

"So she's not in trouble right now?"

"No. Is that what I have to wait for? I mean, before we can come and see you?"

"No, Taylor. It's okay to come and see me whenever you want."

We sat for a moment and I thought about things. Taylor picked through the pages of Catullus, then looked around the room. Waiting, apparently, for my plan.

"Who's that guy?" she said. I followed her finger to a couple of old volumes that sat on the edge of my desk.

"That's a Greek playwright by the name of Sophocles. Ever heard of him?"

She shook her head. I picked up a book titled *The Oedipus Trilogy*.

"He lived in the fifth century B.C. Any thoughts about the fifth century B.C.?"

Taylor just looked at me so I kept going.

"Sophocles wrote three plays known as the Oedipus trilogy."

"What were they about?"

"That's a big question." I opened the text and found a line from Sophocles' *Oedipus at Colonus*.

κακῶυ γὰρ δυσάλωτος οὐδείς

"What's that?" Taylor said.

"Ancient Greek." I pointed her to the translation: "Man is born to fate a prey."

"Is that supposed to be a puzzle?"

"Sort of. Sophocles believed each man was born to a destiny he couldn't escape. And that anyone who thought otherwise was a fool. Like Oedipus."

"Oedipus was a fool?"

"Oedipus was a king. A man who thought he was the master of his fate. A man who thought he could solve any problem through the force of his own intellect."

"Let me guess," Taylor said. "That didn't work out."

"Oedipus asked a lot of questions. Problem was, he didn't always get the answers he wanted."

"Was that the point of the play?"

I smiled and closed the book.

"There are a lot of points to the Oedipus trilogy, but, yeah, I guess that's one of them. Don't ask a question unless you're sure you can handle the answer."

Taylor ran her hand across the frayed cover and pulled it across the desk.

"Mind if I take this one too?"

"Suit yourself."

I showed her the book's layout. Where the English translations were for each Greek passage. How the comments in the back of the book worked. She took it all in, then stacked Sophocles on top of Catullus.

"Thanks. I kind of like this stuff."

"Me too," I said. "Makes you think."

"Want to know what I was thinking just now?"

"Shoot."

"I was thinking, *I wonder if he has a girlfriend?*"

"How interesting," I said.

"So do you?"

"Do I what?"

"Have a girlfriend?"

"What did I just tell you about asking questions?"

The girl smiled. For the first time since she sat down, she seemed 100 percent kid.

"What do you want to know?" I said.

"Why don't you date my mom?"

"Excuse me?"

"She says you two used to go out."

"Your mom's married. For the second time."

"Yeah, we know about that."

"Move on, Taylor."

Now she laughed a little. Bounced a bit in her chair. I noticed a tattoo on the inside of her wrist. Looked like some kind of fruit. Maybe a peach, but I couldn't be sure.

"Want to know what she said about you?" the girl said.

"We're old friends."

"I know. Want to know what she said?"

I tipped forward in my chair and slid my elbows onto my desk. "No, I don't want to know. How about you, Taylor? You got a boyfriend?"

The girl dropped her eyes to the floor and pulled the two books I'd given her close to her body. The part in her hair was straight down the middle of her scalp. Just like her mom.

"I don't mix too well," she said.

I knew I shouldn't have asked the question. As usual, about ten seconds too late.

"You got friends," I said.

"I have people I talk to every day."

"What do you call them?"

"I call them *people I talk to every day.*"

Her eyes crept up toward mine. There was a touch of annoyance in her voice and hard color rising in her cheeks.

"I like to be left alone. Sort of like you."

I looked around the office. "Like me?"

"Sure. You're not married. You work by yourself. Looks to me like you're alone a lot."

I wasn't sure if she was attacking me. And *if* she was, whether it was out of spite or just plain old hurt. Either way, it was okay. She was a kid. And I'd been alone long enough to deal with any accompanying sting.

"Looks can be deceiving, Taylor. Let me ask you something else."

"Go ahead."

"You like ice cream?"

"Yes."

It was a reluctant yes. But a yes, all the same. Ice cream usually helps to turn the page for kids. Adults aren't so easy.

"There's a great spot down the street," I said. "Best hot fudge sundaes in the city."

I got up. The girl got up with me, Sophocles and Catullus in tow. I turned out the lights and we left. We were halfway down the hallway when Taylor spoke again.

"You forgot to lock the door."

I almost swore but caught myself. Instead, I went back down the hall and locked up. Then the two of us headed out for some ice cream.

CHAPTER 16

The Bobtail sits at the corner of Broadway and Surf. It's a throwback place with a long marble counter, soda jerks dressed in white out front, and hand-cranked ice cream made in the back. Taylor ordered a chocolate ice-cream soda. The guy behind the counter took a glass with a Coke logo on the side, fitted it into a metal holder with a handle, and cranked a good amount of chocolate into the bottom. Then he dropped in three scoops of ice cream, filled the glass with seltzer from a black-handled dispenser, and stirred with a long spoon. Real whipped cream and a cherry went on top and the whole thing was slid down the counter. Taylor pulled the paper wrapping off a straw and, for the second time, looked like a kid.

"Aren't you going to get anything?" she said.

I ordered a scoop of vanilla ice cream in a cup. Taylor seemed happy with that and dug into her soda. Three minutes later, she hit bottom with her straw. I got her a spoon and she scooped ice cream from the depths of her glass.

"Pretty good," she said.

"Told you."

Taylor pushed her glass away and turned toward me. "Are we going to talk about my mom now?"

"Sure."

I got up and walked us over to a table by the window. We sat in chairs made of thin white wire. The fourteen-year-old with the ice-cream soda got left at the counter. Taylor Woods was back. A kid with the problems of an adult.

"You think your mom's in some kind of trouble," I said. "Tell me about that."

"Mom said you knew."

"About your step-dad?"

"Yeah."

For the first time, I sensed a crack in the façade. It ran like a shiver through her voice and across her lower lip, finding a home in her eyes as her gaze slid to the floor.

"You like your step-dad?" I said.

A narrow set of shoulders offered a single shrug that said enough.

"You scared of him?"

She shook her head.

"You scared for your mom?"

Nothing.

"It's okay to be scared for your mom, Taylor. And it's okay to be scared for yourself."

"I didn't say that."

"Okay."

"I'm not scared of him. You wouldn't understand."

I thought about the guy who once called himself my father. The death of quiet inside an apartment. A footfall on the doorstep and voices down a hallway. A quiet, dangerous sort of rumble. Something you developed an instinct for. Ten years old and creeping through the kitchen as the voices got closer. Out the back door and into the fading sunlight. Melting into the streets, into the safety of the neighborhood. I'd wait until well past midnight before heading home. Marking time with whoever was around. Listening to Bruce, walking the streets, drinking beer as I got older, fighting anyone and anything. Believing it was just another day of normal. I understood more about "Dad" than anyone would ever want. More than the kid in front of me probably ever needed to know. At least, that's what I thought.

"What's he doing to your mom, Taylor?"

She looked out the window and onto Broadway. A couple walked by, arms linked, a stroller filled with a baby in between. They looked pretty happy, but I didn't think it registered with my young friend.

"He's killing her, Mr. Kelly. Bit by bit, he's beating my mom to death and there's nothing anyone can do to stop it."

Taylor wiped at a tear as it slid down her cheek and seemed angry over it.

"When was the last time?" I said.

She pulled at a napkin. I looked across at the ice-cream guy behind the counter, another teenager, this one on his cell phone and in another world.

"It's all the time. Every day, sometimes. Then it's quiet for a while. Then it's bad again."

I wanted to reach out, maybe touch the girl's hand. Instead, I settled for more conversation.

"Okay, Taylor, go on home. Don't say anything to your mom. I'll come by and have another talk with her."

"When?" The tears had stopped as quickly as they started. She dried her cheeks, folded up the napkin, and put it on the table.

"When is he gone?" I said.

"He'll be gone next week. Wednesday or Thursday night, for sure."

"How do you know?"

"He's staying downtown. Some city event for the mayor. My mom is supposed to go with him, but she's too sick."

"What does that mean?"

Taylor narrowed her eyes and never looked more like her mother.

"It means he came home last night and busted her face open. Now she can't be seen with him and his work pals."

"How bad is it?"

"I'm here, aren't I?"

I nodded. "Okay, I'll stop by next week. We'll get a plan together."

"I already have a plan," she said.

"What's that?"

"You kill him." The girl looked up as she spoke, and I felt a chill.

"No one is killing anybody, Taylor. You got that?"

"You're not inside that house. You don't know."

I pulled my chair a little closer and muscled into the girl's space. "You think it's that easy to kill someone?"

A shrug.

"Trust me, it's not. Have you told your mom any of this?"

A shake of the head.

"Okay, I'll talk to her next week. Till then, we just let things lie."

I thought she was going to cry again. Or embroider her case for putting a bullet in Johnny Woods. Or maybe both. Instead, Taylor got up and walked out onto the street. I paid for the ice cream and found her waiting at the corner. There wasn't much more to say so I put her in a taxi. Gave the cabbie her address and the fare plus twenty. Then I wandered down Broadway. Thought about my young friend and her developing taste for murder.

A lot of folks wouldn't see the threats of a fourteen-year-old as anything but idle. I wasn't one of those folks. A kid can pull the trigger just as smooth and easy as anyone else. Sometimes even easier. I knew that, mostly because I'd lived it. Or close enough.

The worst times were always late at night. The times I'd make the mistake of falling asleep and he'd get home, come looking for me. It was better when my older brother, Phillip, was there. Even if he'd been kicked quiet.

Either way, the old man would eventually get to it. Stand me up in the living room and take a good look. Close enough so I could smell the liquor—what I know now was liquor. Back then it just smelled like a beating. Mingled with cigarettes, sweat, and fear. My old man was afraid of most every big thing in life. That's why I was out there in the first place. In the living room. At three in the morning. No fear here for Dad. Only control.

He'd pick a topic. Didn't matter what. Maybe it was just the way I looked at him when he pulled me out of bed. Didn't matter. I'd try to stand tough. He'd walk back and forth. Ask me questions.

Did I think I was a tough guy? He'd show me tough.

Did I think I could get away with the bullshit I pulled with everyone else?

I wasn't that goddamn smart and he damn well knew it. School. Sports. Whatever. I half-assed everything. Goddamn faker.

He'd move close on that last word and wait for me to flinch. Who the Christ did I think I was fooling, anyway?

Didn't matter the question. Didn't matter the answer. There was no right answer. Nothing, nobody worth answering to. I knew that. Still, the questions got louder. The old man got closer. Finally, I'd try something, some sort of response. When I got older, I realized that was a mistake. Just what he was waiting for. He'd stop pacing, hover close.

"What did you say?"

From the corner of my eye I could see my mom, virtual rosary beads in hand, half praying, half asking my dad to go to bed and forget about it. Not much fucking chance. I'd answer again. And wait. I knew it was coming, but it never failed to amaze. The speed. The ferocity. Whip-fast. Loud and fierce. In my ears first, then exploding across my face, slamming my eyes shut, scorching white bursts just underneath the lids. It was just an open palm to the face. But it was the first shot and it always shocked me, scared me, hurt far more than whatever followed. When I was nine, I cried. When I got a little older, I just stood there and took it. Either way, it didn't matter. Whatever my reaction, he always followed up with another shot, probably so he didn't have to think about the first either. It was usually a half-closed hand to the head. Then he'd bring his fists to the party. Once, twice, as much as it took until I went down. After that, it was okay. The old man was sated. He'd grumble something to my mother and go to bed. My mom would come over and ask if I wanted a cup of tea. I'd say no. Then I'd go down the hall and get back into bed. I'd hear him next door, breathing already heavy, nothing else between us save a layer of drywall and a lifetime of regret.

No one would talk about it the next day. Or the day after that. None of us, not even Phillip. Instead, we'd just wait. Until we were old enough where we could leave. Or kill him. It was the last part that stayed with me today. The killing part seemed real to me back then. It seemed real to me now. Maybe even a little bit right. I'd take what Taylor said seriously. And do what I could to make sure she stayed a kid.

CHAPTER 17

I woke up the next morning, looked at the clock, and allowed myself a smile. Then I picked up the phone and dialed.

"What?"

Fred Jacobs sounded like he might have been asleep all of five minutes.

"Wake up, Fred."

"Kelly?"

There was a fumble as he dropped the phone. Followed by a curse or two. Then my favorite reporter came back on the line.

"Seriously, what the fuck is wrong with you?"

"What?" I said.

"It's six-thirty on a Saturday morning. People like to sleep on Saturday mornings."

"Get out of bed, Fred. Take yourself outside for a nice run."

More fumbling, then the line cleared.

"What do you want, Kelly?"

"Vince Rodriguez and Dan Masters."

Jacobs didn't respond. I allowed the silence to thicken and congeal before I continued.

"Saw them over at Belmont and Western the other day. Asked me what I knew about Johnny Woods."

"You think that was me?"

"I know it was you, Fred. No one else knew I was looking at Woods."

Fred Jacobs could lie with the best of them. At six-thirty on a Saturday morning, maybe not so well. "Okay, Kelly. It might have slipped out."

"I bet."

"Sorry."

Across the line I could hear the scratch of a match followed by a smooth inhale. Jacobs had lit up his first heater of the day.

"What do you expect?" he said, and blew smoke through the receiver. "You know how this stuff works. Besides, you love being down there."

"You think so?"

"Hell, yeah. You got the itch, Kelly. Just no badge anymore to scratch it with."

"Thanks, Fred. I'll write that down. Next time, just try a little harder to hold up your end of things."

"Don't worry about that." Jacobs' voice puckered at the mere thought of his not living up to the journalist's code of ethics. A code he had just admitted to trampling not ten seconds earlier.

"Okay, Fred. I need a little more info."

"Knew that was coming."

"It's painless. An old *Sun-Times* reporter named Rawlings Smith. You know him?"

"This have to do with my story?"

"Could be."

Jacobs thought about that for a second. Trying to figure out how he could get his scoop without waiting on me.

"He's in Joliet," the reporter said. "Working at a paper called the *Times*."

"Never heard of it."

"Not exactly *The New York Times*. In fact, it doesn't even rate in Joliet. And that ain't good."

Another draw on the cigarette and a gurgle in the lungs.

"How'd he wind up there?" I said.

"Not sure."

"You heard things?"

"I always hear things."

"Bad things?"

"If they were good, a guy like me wouldn't hear 'em."

"No details, huh?"

"You going to see Smith?"

"Thinking about it."

"Ask him yourself. I don't know the guy, so I'll stay out of it."

I figured that was decent of Jacobs. Or as close to decent as this reporter was likely to get. "Thanks, Fred. I'll let you know when I have something."

I punched off and called directory assistance for Joliet, Illinois. There was no listing for Rawlings Smith. I called down to the *Joliet Times*. A sleepy female picked up on the fifth ring. I told her a reporter named Smith had left me his card and wanted to interview me for a story. She told me the guy I was looking for worked weekends and would be in at nine. I smiled for a second time, got out of bed, and got dressed.

JOLIET IS ABOUT forty miles outside of Chicago. Famous for nothing except its prison. Remember Joliet Jake from the *Blues Brothers*? He did his time inside Joliet's Stateville lockup, home to two thousand of Illinois' worst. I cruised past the big walls and kept moving. The *Joliet Times* was located in a storefront downtown. At the back of the empty newsroom was a cubicle. Inside it, the old crime reporter I was looking for.

"Call me Smitty," he said.

So I did.

"Smitty, thanks for taking the time."

I had called ahead and told him I wanted to talk. He didn't ask why, so I didn't offer. Now he was here. Waiting for the other shoe to drop.

"Not a problem, Mr. Kelly. What can I do for you?"

I could see the reporter thirty years prior, brown hair, eyes sketched in blue, sharp features and intelligence everywhere. Now it had all gone to booze and cigarettes. A life swallowed up in a matter of newsprint and missed deadlines.

"I'm here about an article you wrote."

"Been a reporter a lifetime, son. Wrote a lot of articles."

From his bottom drawer Smitty pulled out a can of Bud and poured it into a water glass. It was more warm foam than beer, but that didn't diminish his enthusiasm. Smitty tipped the glass my way and took down half of it in one go.

"Management doesn't seem to care much on weekends, so I indulge. You?"

"No, thanks. How did you get here, anyway?"

"You mean paradise?"

"I'm sure it has its moments."

He poured the rest of the beer into his glass and watched it settle. I watched with him. Then he continued.

"Not exactly the happily-ever-after you plan on, is it? I was thirty-two years old. Hell, that was more than thirty years ago."

Smitty moved forward to the edge of his seat. One disinterested leg crossed over the other. His foot dangled at the end, bobbing time to a beat only he could hear.

"Thirty-two. My own byline at the *Sun-Times*. Phone calls from New York. *Newsweek* had its eye on me. Did you know I was short-listed for a Pulitzer?"

He looked over, a bit of challenge in his eyes.

"No, I didn't. Congratulations." I said it neutral, enough to keep the conversation moving. The old man wasn't stupid. He knew I didn't really care about his would-be Pulitzer. He also knew I had to listen, so he sunk into it.

"A seam corruption out of the First Ward. Alderman's name was Frank Raymond."

I'd heard the name but not much else.

"Before your time," the reporter said. "A throwback guy. Big cars, silk suits, cigars, the whole thing. First Ward was filthy with the bent-noses. Still is, I assume."

I nodded. Smitty ignored me and plowed ahead.

"Anyway, Frankie liked sex. Problem was, he liked it with little girls."

"Hold on. I remember that."

That got a cackle. "Figured you might."

"Maybe 1975, around there?"

"That's right. Even got a picture of him with a kid. 'Course, back then we didn't use photos the way they would today."

"I bet."

"Look up the clips. Story ran on the front page for two weeks. First, it was the sex stuff with Frankie. Then he started talking and they took down the largest child pornography ring in the Midwest. Wound up passing new laws on child prostitution as a result of that story."

The old man's gaze crept up and over my shoulder. I let him sit with his memories. After a while, he came back.

"They sent Frankie away for two years. I thought it was light time. One of those country-club pens."

"What did Frankie think?"

"Never got a chance to ask him. He took a slug of bleach a month into his sentence."

Smith coughed up a bit of phlegm. He spit it into a napkin, looked at it, folded the napkin, and put it in his pocket.

"That's the way it goes, you know. Highlight of my career. At the time I thought it was just the beginning. But it turned out to be the end."

"How'd you wind up down here?"

It was the second time I had asked the question. This time I got the glimmer of an answer.

"I rode high for another year or two. Downtown loved me. Mostly because they thought they owned me. See, Wilson's men gave out the tip on Frankie. Not the Wilson you know. This was his old man. Alderman out of the Tenth Ward."

"I've heard of him."

"Sure you have. Red face, white hair, and pinkie rings. Never made it to mayor, but he ran Chicago's City Council in the seventies. Anyway, he wanted to put one of his pals in the First Ward chair but couldn't move on Raymond."

"So he dropped a line to the press."

"To me, in particular. I checked it out. All true. So I ran with it."

I nodded and thought about Fred Jacobs: his green pants, white socks, and two Pulitzers. In Chicago, most things never change.

"You were tight with the old man?"

"No one was tight with old man Wilson. Never really wanted to mingle, that guy. Nothing like the son. Still, for a while I had a number to call. Then I got on the wrong side of the books. Didn't know it, but managed to, anyway."

"How?"

"You won't believe it."

"Try me."

"It was the fire. The big one, 1871."

Somewhere a coin dropped.

"I've heard of it," I said.

"Course you have. Here, let me show you something."

The reporter unfolded from his chair and shuffled down a linoleum corridor. In a back room were some boxes and a wooden filing cabinet that looked like it came from the public library of my youth. Smitty opened up the second drawer and pulled out a folder.

"This article right here. Read it and weep. My ticket to Pa-lookaville."

The clip was bound up in a plastic binder. It was the same clip I had pulled out of the Chicago Historical Society, the reason I had come down to Joliet. I felt the society's copy in my pocket and read the headline aloud.

"FORGET O'LEARY'S COW. DID A WILSON BULL KICK OVER THE LANTERN?"

Underneath was a short blurb.

Two historic families linked to Chicago Fire conspiracy.

"Seemed harmless enough," Smitty said, and lit up a cigarette. "Just an old story I got onto. Crazy theory. Started by Mickey Finn, of all people."

"Mickey Finn? As in slip-him-a-mickey Mickey Finn?"

"Sure. Finn was a Chicago guy. Didn't you know that?"

I shook my head. Smitty exhaled a cloud of blue velvet and picked a piece of tobacco off the tip of his tongue.

"Guy was five feet nothing. In the 1890s, he ran a place called the Lone Star Saloon and Palm Garden Restaurant. Nice name, huh? Down at the ass end of old Whiskey Row."

"Whiskey Row?"

"Today it's known as home to the Chicago Public Library.

Back then, Mickey offered his own sort of education. Taught the local kids how to lift a wallet. Then he'd set them loose on his customers after they'd had a few."

"Mickey got a cut, of course."

"Like something out of *Oliver Twist* was Mickey. Little bastard invented a special drink. Called it the Mickey Finn Special. When one of his waitresses saw a big billfold, the customer got himself a Special as his next drink, whether he ordered it or not. Guy would wake up in an alley somewhere, wallet and money gone. And that was if Mick was feeling generous."

"Sounds like Chicago," I said.

"Crazy town." Smitty took in another lungful of cancer and offered up a smoky chuckle in exchange. "Jesus, I do miss it sometimes."

The reporter dropped his cigarette to the floor and rubbed it out with his foot. "Enough of that. You want to know how Mick fits into the article I wrote."

"Be nice."

"Okay, it goes like this. Around 1895 or so, Mickey Finn began pushing a story around town. Claimed Charles Hume started the Great Fire. Hume was the editor of the *Chicago Times*. Heavy hitter around town. Last name like Kelly, you gotta be Irish, right?"

I nodded.

"So was Mickey Finn. I'd pour us some Jameson now if I had any. But those days are long gone."

I got us a couple more warm Buds from the reporter's desk. Smitty liked the idea and produced a bottle of Ten High bourbon. It didn't have a cap, but that didn't seem to bother Smitty. He poured it on top of the Bud and screwed it straight down. I lifted my glass and drank. The reporter waited until I was done before he continued.

"Hume hated the Irish. Do you know he actually wrote an

editorial suggesting Chicago should hang its Irish from the city lampposts. Be a nice decoration, according to Hume."

"Sounds like a real visionary. How did the Wilson family fit in?"

The reporter held out a hand for patience. "Our current mayor's great-great-grandfather. Man he was named after. John Julius Wilson."

"Seminal seed of the clan."

"One and the same. In 1870 he's a shanty Irishman just off the boat. Like tens of thousands of others. But not so. According to Mickey Finn, Wilson finds himself a friend in Mr. Charles Hume. A powerful friend who suggests Wilson dabble in real estate."

"And . . . ?"

"Wilson was the straw man. Winds up buying a flock of land for Hume and the *Times*. In the Irish tenement section of Chicago."

"Where O'Leary's barn was located?"

"Exactly. So they bought this land low—"

"Planned to burn out the area, clear the land, and sell it high."

The reporter smiled. "That was it. Burn out the Irish. Hume hated the Irish. Did I tell you that?"

"You did. And it's duly noted. Of course, John Julius Wilson was Irish himself."

"That wasn't the color green old man Wilson's heart went pitter-patter for." Smitty tapped out a bit of rhythm on the birdcage he called a chest and hauled out the rest of his story. "October eighth, 1871. The plans are laid and the match is lit. One problem."

"Wind?" I said.

"You know your fire, young man. Yeah, wind. Forty miles an hour's worth. Whole city goes up like the fucking stack of kindling it was. Burns to the ground. But these guys, they come out smelling like a room full of roses."

"Wilson and Hume got rich?" I said.

Smitty shrugged. "Finn was a little soft on his figures, but he thought they may have taken in over a million dollars each."

"That would make them . . ."

"In Chicago? In 1871?"

"The foundation for an empire," I said.

"Witness the empire." Smitty pointed to a picture of the Chicago skyline, tacked over a hole in the corner of the room. "So that's the story I wrote in 1978. Leaving out specifics on the money, mind you. A weekend piece, sort of a soft feature. Figured it might be good for a laugh."

"You didn't believe it?"

"Believe it? We ran it on April Fool's Day. City editor thought it was a neat joke."

"Not so much, huh?"

"I never talked to anyone downtown before it ran. Never even checked to see whose toes I might be stepping on." Smitty pulled at the plastic and rubbed the yellowed edge of his old clip.

"How did they come for you?"

The old man's smile broke off at the edges and crumbled into a sigh. "I was coming home off a late shift at the paper. Stopped at a light near Chicago and Halsted. All of a sudden, there are flashers in my mirror. Cop says I'm drunk. Gets me out of the car and searches it."

"Dope?"

The reporter shook his head. "I drink beer and whiskey. Maybe too much as I get closer to a hole in the ground. I cheated on my wife. Once. Lasted less than six months. But drugs? Never had a joint in my hands. Not once. Would have been a tough thing for them to sell."

Smitty muscled up as best he could for the last part. I held his eye and gave him enough of a nod to continue.

"I'm in the slam when this weasel of a prosecutor comes in. Now he's the head asshole."

"Gerald O'Leary?" I said.

"You got it. He's carrying a Saturday night special in a plastic bag. O'Leary says they pulled it out from under my seat. Matched it to a strong-arm robbery and rape reported less than three blocks away. Of course, the victim had already picked me out of a photo lineup. I found out later she was a working girl. Imagine she was easy to convince."

"He offer you a deal?"

"Oh, yeah. And he let me know why too. Said I should have kept my nose out of the fire. Didn't belong there. And now I got burned. Then the fucker smiled. Thought that was funny as all fuck."

I pictured a young O'Leary, making his bones with the city's power brokers, stretching out Smith's hide on the wall.

"I quit the *Sun-Times*; they dropped the charges. Course they made sure my wife knew all about it. Walked out on ten years of marriage with my two kids. I packed up my typewriter and hit it. That was the deal. Flush one life down the tubes."

"What about the other big papers?"

"There was a saying on the Fifth Floor back then. *When old man Wilson hates, he hates good.* They put out the word. I was untouchable. No one would hire me. Finally sneaked under the wire here. Don't know why, but I didn't ask any questions. Thirty years later, the check still clears. I drink my beer, defrost dinner, and watch ESPN. That's about all I want out of life."

"Hell of a story."

"Make a great movie," Smitty said. "Unless you have to live it."

"Why'd they do it?" I said.

"Well, that's the kicker, isn't it? The whole lot of them running scared from nothing but a rumor. Mickey Finn's fucking fairy tale."

I lifted an eyebrow. "You sure about that?"

Smitty shrugged. "Who knows? Who cares? Long time ago. What was it you came down here for, anyway?"

The table between us was now full of old records, clippings, and handwritten notes. Somewhere in there was a threat. Heavy enough to scare someone important. Heavy enough to ruin the career and then the life of the man before me. I pulled my copy of his article from a pocket and laid it on top of the pile. Smitty looked at it and then me.

"So you knew about this all along?"

I nodded. Then I told him about the old land records and the corporation bearing Wilson's initials.

"The corporate records were destroyed in the fire?" Smitty said.

"That's what my guy told me."

Smitty rubbed the back of his thumb along his lower lip. I could feel the reporter's instincts beginning to stir.

"Convenient," he said. "If any of it's true, they would have dumped all the property into different hands immediately after the fire. Never reincorporated J.J.W."

"And the whole thing would have disappeared."

"Could be. There must have been a hell of a lot of confusion after the fire. Here, grab a seat."

Smitty pulled up two chairs near a computer terminal and began to type away.

"I can access the corporate records for Illinois. Let's run a search on your company."

Smitty typed in the initials *J.J.W.* The wait was not a long one.

"The only J.J.W. I get was incorporated in 1983. Looks like they sell rugs."

"Not our guys."

"Nope." Smitty turned from the terminal. "Your company seems to have disappeared." He was breathing a bit harder and reached for the cup of booze to settle himself.

"You okay?" I said.

"Sure. Just haven't had the thrill in a while. Nothing in the world like sniffing out a story."

"Fun, huh?"

"More dangerous than fun, son. Least from where I sit."

Smitty put his cup down. "Let me ask you a question," he said. "Why are you digging all of this up? I mean, if it were true, it'd be a hell of a story."

"But you think there's more."

Smitty nodded. The air felt suddenly close. As if something was being offered. Something that, once accepted, could never be undone.

"You really want to know?" I said.

"Someone's dead, aren't they?"

"You think they'd kill over this?"

Smitty licked his lips dry and pressed his palms flat against the side of his pants. "Come on."

He led me back to his cubicle. The newsroom was almost empty, a single reporter tapping away on his computer halfway across the room. Smitty put the whiskey away, found a key, and unlocked his bottom drawer. I looked inside and saw the black butt of a .38 with gray tape on the grip.

"Illegal and unregistered," Smitty said. "Year in jail, mandatory, just for having it. But I carry it with me everywhere I go. Had something like it with me ever since I left Chicago."

"Thirty years ago?"

"The boys who saw me out of town suggested it might be a good idea. Don't know if they were doing me a favor or just trying to keep me up nights." Smitty nodded down at the gun. "But there it is."

He slammed the drawer shut and locked it. Like that might be the end of it. The past, however, doesn't go away that easy.

"Got one more thing to run past you, Smitty." I pulled out a scrap of paper. "Ever hear of this book?"

"*Sheehan's History of the Chicago Fire.*" The reporter scratched the side of his jaw and shook his head. "Can't say I have."

I nodded and we stood there. If Smitty was wondering how the book fit in, he didn't ask.

"Thanks for the help," I said, and stretched out a hand. Smitty took it and we shook.

"No problem, son. You need anything else, let me know."

"Really?"

"Sure. I just ask two things. First, keep my name out of it. Like I said, all I want is a comfortable hole in the ground and the dignity to go there without much of a fuss."

"And the second thing?"

"If you go after the Fifth Floor, don't go halfway. Otherwise they'll eat your balls for breakfast and laugh when they're done."

Of all the things the old reporter told me, the last was one of which I had no doubt.

CHAPTER 18

I got back into the city at a little after four p.m. A woman was sitting in my lobby. She had a long blue coat on and a brown bag of groceries by her feet.

"Rachel Swenson."

"I got tired of waiting. Besides, my number's unlisted."

"I would've found it."

"Yeah, right."

I picked up the bag of groceries and led the way through my lobby. "How are you?" I said.

"Cold, tired, and hungry."

"How'd you find out where I live?"

"I'm a judge, remember? Thought we'd make some dinner. Maybe you could figure out the rest of the night for yourself."

"Really?"

"No, not really, Michael. You think your life gets that great?"

I looked back over my shoulder and found a smile. Thought that was good but had no idea why.

"We need to talk," Rachel said. "I was giving you ten more minutes, then it was going to be a phone call. Now open up the door and let us in."

I fumbled for the keys to my apartment, trying to remember

the exact state of disarray on the other side. The images I had were not good, but that couldn't be helped. I took a deep breath and pushed in the door.

"Not bad, Michael. Not bad."

Rachel took a quick and kind look around. Then she moved past me. I kicked clothes, shoes, newspapers, and at least one Giordano's pizza box under the couch. A beer bottle rolled out the other side. I grabbed it and put it on the coffee table. Then I followed the judge back toward my kitchen. She stood in profile, coat off, bag of groceries on the counter, and a couple of cabinet doors open.

"You know where anything is back here?" she said, without looking my way.

Rachel was wearing jeans and a pale blue sweater. Her eyes matched the sweater. Her teeth were white and her hair carried a hint of honey. She had some sort of shiny lipstick on and a touch of blush across her cheekbones. Her nails were hard and clear with white tips. They tapped a tattoo on my kitchen counter and waited.

"That's a refrigerator," I said, and pointed in the general direction of the large white box growling silently behind her. "It's got some beer in it, if you're interested."

Rachel closed the cabinets and turned her attention my way. "You ever cook for yourself?"

"Actually, Judge Swenson, I do." I moved past Rachel and pulled the cabinets open again. "Breakfast is my specialty. I can make an omelet out of just about anything." I stopped and looked at her. "Seriously, anything."

"I don't think I want to know."

"Don't knock it until you've tried it. I can burn a steak with the best of them. Spaghetti, the occasional meatball. That kind of thing. You know, when the mood strikes."

"How often does the mood strike?"

"Not very."

"Well, I invited myself over, so I'll cook tonight."

"Fair enough."

I grabbed a couple of Goose Islands from the fridge and sat up on the counter. Rachel pulled some onions, garlic, and olive oil out of her bag.

"Glad you like pasta, because that's what's on the menu."

I gave her a thumbs-up. "Meatballs?"

"Sausage," she said, and took a sip of beer. "And the best on-the-fly red sauce you ever tasted."

"Red sauce. You sound like Tony Soprano."

Rachel smiled. "Actually, I got this recipe from one of Vinny DeLuca's bagmen."

Vinny DeLuca was about a hundred years old and the head of Chicago's Mob. He'd like someone like Rachel. She was tough, smart, and stood her ground. He'd like her a lot. Unless she got in his way. Then he'd kill her if he had to, stick her in a trunk, and put her in remote parking at O'Hare. Nothing personal.

"You know Vinny?" I said.

"No, but I headed up a federal probe we did a few years back."

"Didn't know you were a prosecutor."

Rachel pulled a chef's knife from the drawer. "You think I've been a judge my whole life?"

She cracked a couple of cloves of garlic with the flat of the knife and began to chop. I went into the living room and slipped on a CD of Charlie Parker. The Bird's genius floated through the flat. When I got back to the kitchen, Rachel had heated up some olive oil in a pan and thrown in the garlic. I moved close. She was humming along to the music and tapping her foot. It was nice.

"So how did you get the recipe?"

She tumbled some onions into her saucepan. The sausage followed.

"This guy named Tommy Tata. Low-level guy we were looking at for wire fraud. For some reason he loved to talk to me."

"I bet," I said.

Rachel washed her hands and opened up a can of tomatoes.

"One day he slips me a piece of paper as we walk in for a hearing with the judge. I had been talking to Tommy about maybe working a deal. Take some years off for information on DeLuca."

"And you thought this was the payoff."

Rachel dumped whole tomatoes into a pot and began to crush them with a wooden spoon.

"Yeah, well, I open the note up at counsel table and what do I get?"

She pointed to the stove with the spoon.

"Tommy's twenty-minute red sauce?" I said.

"You got it. Tata pulled down fifteen years and never said a word. I got the recipe. So let's enjoy."

I watched as Rachel worked on her sauce. A little salt and pepper. Oregano, basil, a finely grated carrot, and some low heat.

"That's it," she said. "Now we let the sauce simmer for a bit."

I pulled another beer out of the fridge and opened it up. The judge and I walked back into the living room and sat down.

"Okay, Rachel."

"Okay, Michael."

"I must come to the unfortunate conclusion that you're not here to jump my bones. At least not until I get you a little drunker."

Rachel tipped her bottle my way and winked. "Don't be so sure."

"Really?" I felt a flutter at the back of my throat. Rachel picked her words with a careful sense of grace.

"Nicole used to talk about you. A lot. Then I saw you at the grave."

"That's not such a big deal."

"Yes, actually, it is. When I ran into you again at the lake, I don't know. Thought it might be kind of fun."

"Might be more than fun."

"You think?"

I moved closer and kissed her. Hadn't planned on it, which was usually the best way. She closed her eyes and kept her arms at her side. Then she moved her cheek against mine and gave me a chill.

"We do need to talk, Michael."

"Better be good."

She pushed back against my chest. I let her go. She reached for her beer and took a sip.

"I don't know that *good* is the word. A friend of mine took a call yesterday."

"And this friend works where?" I said.

"He's a special agent for the FBI."

"I'm impressed."

"Don't be. One of his colleagues works a lot with City Hall."

"Taking out the mayor's trash?"

"You know how that works."

I thought about Fred Jacobs and Hawkeye's. "Seems a lot of folks help the mayor with his problems."

Rachel folded her hands together and considered her perfectly sculptured nails. I got a bad feeling and waited.

"As of yesterday, you became one of those problems."

"How so?"

"My friend claims the mayor's office floated your name."

"They float names, do they?"

"Sure. People to keep an eye on."

"And what does the FBI do?"

"Sometimes they take a look. Run a background check. Pull up financials. Depends on the tip."

"Nice to know Big Brother is alive and kicking. Tell me, how much did I make last year?"

"My guy says they took a pass. Didn't feel it was worth their time."

"I'm devastated."

"Thought you would be. Anyway, there's your comforting moment for the day. Now, would you like to tell me what you've done to get our good mayor so pissed off?"

"Paranoid is more like it."

"Whatever. Want to talk about it?"

"Probably not."

Rachel shrugged. "Your call. Just remember what the mayor can be like."

"You're not a fan?"

"Of the evil empire? Please. The man is genetically ruthless, morally bankrupt, and a dictator."

"Ah, but a benevolent one."

"Right. As long as you don't threaten him. Something you, apparently, have managed to accomplish."

I took a sip of beer. "You find that at all exciting?"

She moved a little closer. "It'll do. For now."

I laid my palm against hers. Then my fingers. One tip at a time. Our lips brushed together, then brushed again, and we both swayed a little. Even while seated, we swayed. On the couch. In the middle of my living room. Moving to a rhythm neither of us anticipated or necessarily understood. Still, it was nice. Like there was a lot to look forward to and no need to rush. I felt her put her bottle down on the table behind me. I thought I should pull the blinds down on my front windows. Then she moved again and I didn't think about that anymore.

CHAPTER 19

First the sauce bubbled, then it burned. We didn't care. We ate cereal afterward. On the rug, in my living room. She wore one of my shirts and drank coffee. I had tea. It seemed good. Like it fit together. At least for now.

"You think this will work between us?" she said.

"Work as what?"

"Good question."

"How about we see where things go and enjoy it for whatever it's worth?"

She wrapped both hands around her mug and blew on coffee that wasn't hot to begin with. Then she spoke again. Slowly, softly.

"You know about me?" she said.

"What do I need to know?"

"Well, I was engaged a few months back. Kind of a quick thing. Actually, kind of a stupid thing."

"Didn't know that."

She peered out at me from under her newly revealed past. "Now you do."

"So I do. Didn't work out, I take it?"

She held out her left hand, five digits devoid of any significant jewelry. "Not exactly."

"You want to talk about it?"

"Not especially."

"You okay now?"

"I hope so."

"Look at me."

She looked up.

"You look okay to me," I said.

"Thanks."

"I *was* going to call, you know."

"I believe you." She smiled, leaned over, and kissed me. "I just beat you to the punch."

"Yeah, well, you might regret that."

"How so?"

"The stuff we talked about earlier."

"The mayor?" Rachel said. "He doesn't scare me. Does he scare you?"

"He gets my attention."

"Good. He's someone who should get your attention. Especially if he's asking around about you. I told you, he's a ruthless man who has got to go."

"I thought judges weren't supposed to be political beasts."

"We're not, generally speaking. But there are exceptions. Thing is, in this town we've never had any good alternatives to the mayor. He keeps the streets clean, taxes low—or at least someone else's fault—and rules with an iron fist. So everyone shuts up."

"And now?"

"Now we have someone. A real alternative."

"Let me guess. Mitchell Kincaid."

Mitchell Kincaid was fifty-three years old, black, and good-looking. He graduated from Northwestern Law School, which, in academic circles, made him very smart. He was also about to launch a run for mayor, which, in Chicago circles, made him incredibly stupid.

"Mitchell is what this city needs," Rachel said.

"And you really think he can take down Wilson?"

"I've gotten to know Mitchell pretty well. Been on some boards. Fund-raisers. He's transcendent."

Rachel glowed when she said it, in a way I found both exciting and disturbing. Exciting because she was in my apartment, wearing nothing except a pin-striped button-down oxford. Disturbing because she was glowing for another man, one who wasn't even in the room.

"Transcendent, you say?"

"I'm serious, Michael. He's a good man. And an honest man. He can unite and he can lead. You'd like him."

"You think so?"

"Yes. And he'd like you. In fact, I'd like the two of you to meet."

"Not right now, I hope."

Rachel stretched her body against mine. "No, Mr. Kelly. Right now, I'd like you to show me the rest of your place."

"You mean the bedroom?"

She got up with a smile. Led the way like she'd been there before. I followed. Willing to go pretty much wherever.

CHAPTER 20

My eyes snapped open just as my alarm clock clicked over. From 3:03 to 3:04 a.m. Rachel's body was warm against mine. Her breath, rhythmic and even. I slipped out of bed. My piece sat in its holster, draped across a chair. I pulled the gun out softly and looked over. Rachel hadn't moved. I slowed my breathing and listened into the night. Someone was in the flat. I knew enough to know that, almost before I woke up. It's a sixth sense. Comes maybe from being a cop. Or maybe from creeping enough places myself. Either way, someone was in the flat. The only question remaining: Did they know I was awake?

The door to my bedroom was open about a foot. A crescent of light carved up the floor. I held my gun in two hands, muzzle up, and came up on the dark side of the door. I watched the light as I moved. There was a creak from the living room. Might be a random sound. The stuff you hear only when it's quiet and you're about to fall asleep. I didn't think so.

I went in quickly, slipping open the door and shouldering into the room. I sensed a body to my right, just as something exploded next to my ear. I fired once, heard the tinkle of broken glass and then footsteps. Whoever I had shot at was not exactly dead.

Instead he was running down the hallway toward my kitchen. I gave chase. He hit my back door, went down the stairs, and into an early morning that was still night. I was about to follow when I heard my name. I turned. Rachel was in the hallway, naked, holding her chest. I caught her before she hit the floor and felt for a pulse. Nothing. Rachel had been shot. I hit my cell phone and began CPR.

CHAPTER 21

I sat in my bathrobe on the living room couch and drank coffee. Vince Rodriguez sat in a chair and looked out my front window. It was a little after five in the morning. Still dark out, but there were signs of life: a *Trib* van dropping off bundles of papers, a green garbage truck, the occasional jogger.

"Going to need to get the window fixed," the detective said.

I grunted and rubbed my palm across my forehead.

"What was he looking for?" Rodriguez said.

I looked around the flat. The intruder had gone through my desk and bookshelves. Nothing seemed to be missing.

"Whatever it was," I said, "he didn't get it. Think we can keep this quiet?"

Vince looked over at me. "Is that what you want?"

"Yeah."

"What about her?"

Rodriguez looked up as Rachel Swenson came out of the bedroom. She had insisted on getting dressed in her own clothes before talking to us about anything. I told her Vince had seen everything there was to see when he arrived. She didn't much give a damn.

"How're you feeling?" I said.

Rachel rubbed her chest where the rubber bullet had struck her.

"Hurts like hell."

"Supposed to," Vince said.

"Left a big bruise."

"Supposed to."

"Stopped my heart."

Vince shrugged. "Nothing's perfect. I got here in less than ten minutes and your vitals were fine."

"Thanks, Detective."

Rachel sat down and sipped at the hot whiskey I had made for her. I wasn't sure if she was more pissed at getting shot, being seen naked by one Vince Rodriguez, or having said detective know she and I were shacked up. At least for a night. I had the feeling it was an unhappy combination of all three. Rodriguez turned back to me.

"I can keep things quiet, Kelly. The question is why?"

"Let me answer that," Rachel said. "I'm a federal judge. Maybe you haven't noticed that, Detective. Probably not a great idea to be found naked, shot with a rubber bullet, at three a.m. in the home of a private investigator. Agreed?"

Vince nodded toward the judge. "Agreed, ma'am. None of this goes any further. And I'm sorry. Now, let me ask you this. Either of you get a look at the guy who broke in?"

I shook my head. "Only thing I know is that he was big. Six feet. Maybe a little more. Carried what looked like a revolver in his right hand."

Rodriguez looked over at Rachel, who shrugged.

"All I know was he shot me."

"Either of you cut yourself?" the detective said. Neither of us had.

Rodriguez picked up a couple of small yellow envelopes and held them in front of his face.

"I pulled a print off the sill. And a smear of blood. Guy must have nicked himself running out of here. Probably not enough points on the print for a legal match. But there it is."

"What about DNA?" I said.

"If you want to run it, yeah, you could get a profile. Problem is, you don't have a suspect."

Rodriguez slipped the envelopes into his pocket and waited.

"Whoever he was," I said, "he thinks I have something valuable. And was willing to take a risk to get it."

"Which means what?" Rachel said.

"Which means," Rodriguez said, "Kelly thinks he has someone on a hook. Just needs to reel him in. Of course, there's always the chance Kelly's the fish that winds up in the bottom of the boat."

Rachel held the mug up close to her cheek as she spoke. "Enlighten us, Michael. What, exactly, are you trolling for these days?"

I sipped my coffee. Rachel jiggled her foot and waited.

"Whatever we talk about stays here," I said. "At least for now. Agreed?"

The judge looked at Rodriguez, then back at me and nodded.

"Just a guess," I said, "but it probably has to do with the body on Hudson."

"What body?" Rachel said.

I looked at my friend the cop, who picked up the thread.

"We asked Kelly to help us out with a death we're investigating."

"A murder?" Rachel said.

Rodriguez held his hand flat and then tipped it back and forth, ever so slowly. "Could be. Probably."

"Definitely," I said. "Guy's name was Allen Bryant. Looks like he was drowned. Then had his mouth filled with sand."

I jerked my head in Rodriguez's direction. "These guys are getting a lot of heat from the Fifth Floor to bury the case. Vince and Dan Masters asked me to step in and take a look. Unofficially."

"Which brings us back to tonight," Rodriguez said. "And the reason why people feel the need to break into your home and shoot the judge here with a rubber bullet."

"Yes," Rachel said, and took a sip of her whiskey. "I'm all ears."

So I told her what I knew. About Janet Woods, her husband, and the boxing match they called a marriage. About Johnny Woods' trip to the house on Hudson and the missing *Sheehan's*. About the Chicago Historical Society and the curator who wanted to be a star. Then I pulled out a copy of the article I had copied, originally published as an April Fool's prank. Rachel read through the clip, handed it to Rodriguez, and turned back to me.

"You think there's something to this?" she said.

"I spent Friday afternoon in the County Building. Pulled some land records from 1871."

"They go back that far?" Rachel said.

I nodded. "Title abstracts. Still a little foggy, but it appears a lot of the land around O'Leary's barn was owned by a corporation with the initials J.J.W."

I could hear Rodriguez click his teeth together. The judge leaned in as she spoke.

"J.J.W.? As in John Julius Wilson?"

"Very good, Your Honor. Unfortunately, any corporate records were destroyed in the fire."

"No way to figure out who the principals were?"

"No," I said. "I also spent some time with the reporter who

wrote this article thirty years ago. Guy named Rawlings Smith. Claims the piece spooked the Wilson clan. Bought Smith a one-way ticket out of town."

"And you believe him?" Rachel said.

"I believe I do."

Rachel shifted her eyes to Rodriguez. "Detective?"

Rodriguez's face was cast in shadow, but I could still see his hands, long, veined, impassive, folded together loosely and draped across his knees.

"Officially, no comment. Unofficially . . . no comment."

"You're a big help."

"Your Honor?"

"Best I can see, you put him onto this wild-goose chase."

"Vince had nothing to do with it," I said. "I found the body at Hudson. I decided to help out. On my own."

"Blundered into the whole mess," Rachel said. "And now you figure whoever killed Mr. Bryant thinks you have whatever it is they want. Shot me tonight to get it."

"It is a circle full of circumstance, Your Honor," Rodriguez said.

"Fuck off, Detective."

"Yes, Your Honor."

I held up a hand. "That's not exactly what I think, Rachel."

"It isn't?"

"No. The person who killed Allen Bryant wasn't the guy who shot you. At least, I don't think so."

"Explain." That was Rodriguez, sitting up now, curious.

"The person who broke in tonight carried a gun with rubber bullets," I said. "Why? If it was Bryant's killer, he'd be packing the real thing. After all, what's another life? No, this was a different guy. A thief, yes. Just not up to the job of killing."

"Which means what?" Rachel said.

I got up and stretched. "Which means there are at least two groups involved in this. One is willing to take a life. The other is still working up the courage."

"Does that bring us back to the mayor?" Rachel said.

"Maybe," I said. "Maybe not. But if my great-great-grandfather burned down the city and lined his pockets in the process, I'd be worried. Maybe even worried enough to kill."

CHAPTER 22

Rodriguez left my flat at a little after five-thirty. Rachel and I sat in the living room. I listened to the wind blow through the hole in my window. Rachel hugged her knees to her body, drank my whiskey, and stared straight ahead. After a few minutes, I got up, went into the bedroom, and got dressed. Rachel had her coat on and was waiting by the door when I returned. I drove her home. It was still quiet on the streets. Even quieter in the car.

"I'm sorry about all this," I said.

Rachel wasn't crying. Too tough for that. She was, however, close. And that probably made things worse.

"What the fuck, Michael. Jesus Christ. I'm goddamn naked, out cold on your living room floor, and you decide to have your cop buddy over."

"I thought you were dead."

There wasn't much more to say so I drove. We pulled up to her house, a Gold Coast graystone a block from the lake. It was still mostly dark out. I turned the car off and listened to the engine. It didn't have much to say either.

"Good night, Michael."

"Good night, Rachel. I'm sorry."

"Sorry for what?"

"For tonight."

"Don't be. Just pretend it never happened."

"Including the date?"

"None of it."

"That what you want?"

She looked out the window in a way that would give any man pause.

"Maybe this is a bad idea," she said.

"Yeah?"

"Maybe."

"Fair enough."

An awkward hug later, she was out of the car. I waited until she got inside her front door, cursed at the empty street in front of me, and pulled away. Halfway down the block, I saw a rust-colored Dodge Monaco parked in front of a hydrant. I pulled up alongside.

"Following me, Detective?"

Dan Masters was blowing on something hot in a Styrofoam cup. He spoke without looking at me. "Get in the car."

I parked, legally, behind him and slipped into the passenger seat.

"You watched her get in the front door," he said. "That was nice."

"You think so?"

"I think it was a good idea."

"Makes her feel safe, right?"

Masters snorted and turned the engine over.

"Is that what you were going for there, Kelly? How about the 'she just got shot while she was naked and left for dead in my apartment' feeling. How about the 'I better do anything I can possibly fucking think of or I'll never see this woman on whose radar I don't belong in the first place ever again' feeling. Think you might want to be addressing any of that, lover boy?"

The detective shook his head, took a sip of his joe, and slapped his lips together. Then he put the car in gear and pulled away from the curb.

"Rodriguez told you what happened?" I said.

"Sure, he told me. I was checking out the block while he was inside with you and the judge."

"Find anything?"

"A guy getting a blow job in an alley."

"Is that supposed to be interesting?"

"He was a Chicago alderman."

"Okay."

"The married kind. His date was a working girl."

I looked over at Masters, who sipped and smiled. "I got him a cab home."

"Nice chit to have."

"Yes, sir. You need some breakfast? I need a breakfast. Let's go over to Tempo."

Tempo's been around for a lot of years. Its business plan is simple. Stay open all night and be within staggering distance of Rush Street. Folks coming out of the late-night bars aren't too picky about what's on the plate. If it's not moving, put some ketchup on it and eat it. We got a booth near the front. I ordered scrambled eggs. Masters ordered toast and another coffee.

"You aren't eating?" I said.

"Nah. Lost my appetite."

The detective played a toothpick across his teeth and looked out the window. The last of the taverns had flushed an hour earlier, and the street was filled with the wretched refuse. Four frat boys stumbled to a corner and headed our way.

"Nice lady," Masters said. The waitress brought our coffee and the detective's toast.

"Excuse me?"

"Your friend there. Judge Swenson. Nice lady."

"About that. We need to keep tonight quiet. Especially the part about Rachel. Totally quiet."

"Mum's the word, Kelly."

Masters buttered some toast and let his coffee cool. The frat boys shuffled into our diner and began asking for a table. One waitress brought me a plate of eggs while another took the college kids into the back. Masters watched them settle in and then returned to our conversation.

"The Bryant murder."

"It's a murder now?" I said.

"Whatever. Rodriguez told me you think this Chicago Fire connection is legit?"

"The more I look at it, the better it gets."

The detective poured sugar into his coffee. Did it the old-fashioned way: held the spoon over his cup, filled it up with sugar, and then dropped it in. His hand holding the sugar shook a little. The spoon was worse. He finished with the coffee, stirred three or four times, and took a sip.

"Seems like you might be stepping on some toes downtown, Kelly."

"That bother you?"

"Not at all."

The detective's response came too fast. Fear does that to a person. Does it to old reporters in Joliet. Does it to tough detectives in Chicago. The waitress wandered over and gave us a refill. Masters waited until she left before continuing.

"Thing is, I'm a year and a half from my twenty. Full pension. Wouldn't want to screw that up."

"I hear you."

"Do you?"

"I think so. You don't have to be in this, Masters. Same for Rodriguez."

The detective gave a single nod and looked away. His face was still old-school. Square jaw, blue eyes, and a wire-brush police academy haircut. A cutout from a police recruiting poster circa 1970, one that had been put up on a wall and left there too long. Now it was curled at the corners and yellow, torn in too many places to count, and held together with pieces of dried-up tape.

"How you feeling, Dan?"

"I look like shit, right?"

I shrugged.

Masters slid a look across the booth. "What did Rodriguez tell you?"

"He told me you were going through a tough time."

"Nothing else?"

"He seemed a little worried."

That earned me a laugh. "Good."

Chicago had passed a no-smoking ordinance for all its restaurants. I guess that didn't include the detective's Marlboros. He lit up and cupped his cigarette in his hand as he drew the cup of coffee to his lips.

"How're the eggs?" he said.

"Awful."

Masters nodded and exhaled smoke through his nose. It floated across the table in soft pillows. I inhaled as much as I could. Surgeon general be damned. I loved smoke: firsthand, secondhand. Didn't matter much to me.

"Rodriguez didn't tell you my story?"

"No, he didn't."

"Rodriguez knows," Masters said. "One of the only ones who does."

"We don't need to do this."

It was too late. Dan Masters was ready to talk. And I was ready to listen. Whether I was ready or not.

"It was maybe six months ago." Masters grimaced at the date and showed me all of his teeth for the first time. Middle-of-the-road caps, gums receding, edged in black.

"Actually, it was six months, four days, and"—the detective glanced down at his watch—"about four hours ago. I was supposed to work a double shift. At least, that's what I thought. We have this duty roster for detectives. Swear the fucking thing is from the sixties. A bunch of colored magnets on a metal board. Tacked to a wall. Tells us our shifts. Sometimes the magnets don't work so well. This was one of those times. A yellow magnet fell off and I thought I was doing a double. Working straight through till nine in the morning. I really got off at one."

"So you got home earlier than you thought."

"Earlier than my wife thought."

Now I knew where this was going and liked it even less. Not after all that had already gone on. Not in the Tempo restaurant. Not at six in the morning.

"We had a nice place in Lincoln Square. One of those new developments near Welles Park. You know the place?"

"Sure."

"So I got home at a little after two. We lived on the second floor. I figured Michelle would be sleeping so I was quiet coming up the stairs."

Masters took another sip of coffee. The waitress came by with the bill. He waited for her to leave.

"You know what I remember most, Kelly?"

"What's that?"

"You remember your wife, the wife you've had for twenty-two years. Saying some guy's name. Saying it like she meant it. That's what you remember. That's when you step outside of yourself and realize your life will never be the same. Realize this'll be it, the sounds, the smells, the moment by which everything else will be reckoned. Your life happened before or after this moment. Nothing else matters. Everything else pales."

The detective twisted a wedding ring on his left hand. Except there was no ring there. Just a patch of pale white skin where the gold used to be.

"What'd you do, Dan?"

Masters took a final draw on his cigarette, until the red cinders scorched his lips. Or at least it seemed that way. Then he dropped the remains into his cup.

"That's what Rodriguez asked me. 'What'd you do?' Must be a cop thing. Thinking about the gun."

Masters thumped his weapon onto the table. It was a heavy thing, forty caliber, blue steel, covered in a rich coat of oil. A weapon that was cared for, ready to go.

"I stood in the kitchen," Masters said, "and listened. Michelle and the guy were still in the bedroom. I had the gun in my hand. Looking at the door. Thinking about going through it. Then I just got cold inside. Walked back down the stairs. Sat in my car until he left. It was a little after five in the morning. I gave her another ten minutes and then I went in. She took one look and knew. Never said a word. Just started to cry."

Before I could respond, there was another noise. The college kids again. Screaming for their orders. Masters closed his eyes. He had a couple of days' growth of gray coloring his cheeks. A small muscle twitched along the line of his jaw, and he opened his eyes again.

"I sat down at the kitchen table and put my arms around her.

She still loved me, but that wasn't going to carry the day and we both knew it. After a while, she stopped crying. Asked if I wanted any breakfast. I said no. She asked if I wanted to sleep. I said no. Never went in that bedroom again."

He looked across the diner at the college kids and kept talking.

"Later that day we went downtown and filed papers. Two months after that, we were divorced. I gave her everything. Really, all we had was the condo, but it was no good to me."

"Where do you live now?"

"LaSalle Street. One of those furnished jobs."

"How is it?"

Masters shrugged. "What do you think? Excuse me for a minute."

One of the frat boys had made his way to the waitress station. He was wearing a collared shirt under a cranberry-colored sweater and a pair of tan chinos. The waitress asked him to go back to his seat. The kid wanted to talk about an order of pancakes. She told him to go back to his seat again and turned away. He wasn't used to being ignored. Certainly not by the help.

He'd just put a hand on the girl when Masters arrived. A cuff to the back of the head knocked the kid against the wall and to the ground. Before anyone could move, Masters had back pressure on the kid's wrist. He was on his knees and swearing up a storm. Masters increased pressure on the wrist, a practical demonstration in how the cooperation-to-pain ratio worked. The kid wasn't dumb and decided to shut up. The rest of the frat boys were nailed to their seats. No heroes there. I wandered over. Just in case.

"These guys pay their bill?" Masters spoke to the waitress, who hovered somewhere between the kitchen and hysteria. She fumbled in a pocket on her apron and came out with a slip of paper.

"I was just about to give it to them."

Masters shooed her along with a wave of his free hand. "Get the money, ma'am."

She moved forward. A suddenly sober trio in the booth threw some bills at her. I guess their buddy on the ground was going to get a free meal. Seemed only fair.

"You got it?" the detective said. The waitress nodded. Masters released the kid, who hadn't uttered another word. Probably an honors student.

"Now, the four of you, get your coats on and get the fuck out of here. Not just this place. This neighborhood."

Masters shoved a thumb my way.

"This guy's a police officer. He sees you around here, it's in the back of the cruiser. Now get out. And I don't want to hear a word from any of you."

Two minutes later, we were back inside our booth, the frat boys just a memory.

"They're okay," Masters grumbled. "Just young and drunk. Nothing wrong with that."

Our check still lay on the table. In a green leather binder with TEMPO in gilt-edged lettering across the front.

"Let me get this," Masters said, and stuffed some money into the binder. The waitress tried to refuse, but the detective insisted.

"Sorry for the sad story, Kelly. Not sure why that all came up."

"You going to be all right?" I said.

"Day at a time. I remember now why I told you."

"Why?"

"You like being alone?"

I shrugged. "Don't think too much about it."

"You should. Not something you want to get used to. The judge is a good lady. Something else you should think about."

"Yeah?"

"Yeah. The good ones are hard to spot. Even harder to keep. You need to try harder."

We walked outside and stopped at the corner. Masters offered me a ride home, but I said I wanted to walk for a bit.

"Suit yourself," Masters said, his breath steaming in the early morning chill. "Keep me in the loop. On the City Hall thing."

"Gonna pay a visit to the Fifth Floor," I said. "Take a meeting with Johnny Woods. Probably this week."

The detective nodded and unlocked his car. "Just keep me in the loop."

Masters pulled away from the curb and drove three blocks, to his furnished apartment on LaSalle Street. He'd lock himself inside and pour out a glass or four of happy morning gin. Day would dwindle into night. He'd read the paper, watch TV, and wonder whatever happened to the girl he knew named Michelle. He might go out for dinner. Probably not. Easier to cook something from a can. Then he'd get into bed, close his eyes, and sleep. Only to get up tomorrow and do it all over again.

I felt for Masters. Decided I needed to keep closer tabs on him. Then I thought about my apartment. My own life. Maybe not quite as empty. Not yet, anyway.

CHAPTER 23

The fifth floor of City Hall looked a lot like the fourth and even more like the sixth. The difference lingered in the shadows. There you could catch a glimpse of ambition, the faintest whiff of avarice, and the footsteps of those who curried favor. Sometimes lost, sometimes won, but always curried. Because that's what the Fifth Floor was all about. A court of intrigue, inside a building of stone and a city of red blood and muscle. At its center sat the only door along the entire hallway that mattered. A plain and simple door. Brown and wooden. The exact same door closed off the Office of the Bureau of Planning on the fourth floor and the Assistant Commissioner of Water on the sixth. Here on the fifth floor there was no such ornate title. Just simple letters, gold leaf, five in all, hammered into the wood with tenpenny nails. Five letters that spelled MAYOR. Anyone who needed any more of an introduction to this door need not bother stepping through its crooked portal.

I got off the elevator and turned left, away from the door and down the hall. There, if you knew how to find it, was an archway of sorts, leading into a cubbyhole that was more hole than cubby. A green metal desk was pushed up against a beige wall. The desk's occupant had his back to me and was leaning over a filing cabinet.

"Hey, Willie," I said.

The mayor's unofficial assistant straightened up and spoke without turning. "It's not who I think it is."

"Turn around," I said.

"Be happy to. Once I hear your boots backing down the hallway."

I took the only seat available, a folding job with one leg that was missing its rubber stopper, and tilted back.

"Nice chair, Willie. Come on. Turn around. You know I'm not going anywhere. Or maybe you'd rather I pay Himself a visit."

Willie Dawson turned and looked. Not in a way that made me feel fuzzy and infused with civic warmth.

"Kelly."

"Willie."

I hadn't seen Willie in more than a while. Time had not been unkind. Mostly because it didn't need to be. Willie Dawson was somewhere between forty and dead. His skin was black to the point of shiny and stretched tight over his skull. He was mostly bald and specialized in dandruff, a blizzard of white flakes drifting down onto his shoulders, desk, and environs. Environs now including me.

On most days the layer of scurf only enhanced Willie's wardrobe. Today was no exception. His suit was light brown, of the leisure variety, and worn through in all the proper places. His shirt was yellow, although I doubt its hue was of natural origin. His tie smacked of maroon, with little yellow figurines on it. I squinted and the figurines morphed into Marilyn Monroe. For the first and probably last time during my visit, Willie smiled.

"Sure it's Marilyn. Like it, huh? Actually I can plug it in and she takes her clothes off. But, you know."

Willie looked around. I nodded. Willie actually wasn't a bad guy. In fact, he was a good guy. Good as in connected. In fact, if you dressed like Willie did, there was more than bad taste behind it. It was Willie's way of telling all the Giorgio Armanis to park their asses and pay attention. Simply put, if Willie could dress like that and still carry water to the mayor . . . well, Willie could carry water to the mayor.

"What's the problem, Willie?"

Dawson gave his head a shake and turned back to his filing. "You know what's the matter. It's been what—two, three years and he can't even stand the mention of your name."

"When has my name been mentioned?"

"Never."

Willie turned around and leaned across his desk. The smell hadn't gotten any better. Cheap cigars, bad teeth, and something like Vitalis. If they still made Vitalis. If not, Willie probably had some stashed away.

"And it's not going to get mentioned," he said. "Not by me, anyway."

"Got an election coming up."

"Thanks for the news flash. Mayor got eighty-six percent of the vote last time out."

"Mitchell Kincaid wasn't the other name on the ballot."

Willie chuckled and shuffled some papers. "Mitchell Kincaid. Fuck Mitchell Kincaid. He's a nobody."

Willie Dawson was black. Mitchell Kincaid was black. Kincaid, however, didn't sign Willie Dawson's checks. The mayor did.

"Is that what you came up here for? Talk to me about Mitchell-fucking-Kincaid?"

"No, Willie, this isn't about Kincaid. Just a feeling I got."

Willie had stacked and restacked all the paperwork he could find. Now he sat down, propped a pair of green Converse high-tops on his desk, and stared out a window he didn't have.

"A feeling, huh?"

"Yeah, a feeling."

The first line of sweat decorated Willie's upper lip. He wiped it away, pulled his feet to the floor, and angled closer.

"Your last feeling, half the sheriff's office went upstate."

"Six guys, Willie. There were a lot more should have been with them."

"Six was enough, Kelly. Six senior guys. Joe Dyson, two months from retirement. You know what he's doing now? Let me tell you."

Willie's chair creaked and his voice dropped to a hiss. "He's pissing through a tube and crapping into a bag. Know why? He had a stroke. Second month in the joint. A stroke. Paralyzed. No bodily functions. Doing his five years in a fucking prison hospital. Not that it matters."

I'd heard about Dyson. Even felt bad about it. But not bad enough. The back of my neck began to burn a bit. I pulled a pen and a pad of paper from across Willie's desk and began to write.

"This is the address of Kim Bishop. She lived over on the West Side. Henry Horner Homes. Joe Dyson sat her husband, Ray, on a radiator. Inside a prosecutor's office. Ray confessed to three separate murders. Hell, he would have confessed to killing Jesus Christ himself. See, Willie, his flesh was cooking. And it was going to cook until he talked."

I pushed the pad back across the desk.

"I was there when they gave Ray the needle. So was Kim. The needle for three murders Ray had nothing to do with. Thanks to Joe Dyson, a cop who just wanted to get ahead. You go tell Joe's story to Kim. Maybe you two can go to church together."

Willie ripped out the page and threw it into a wastebasket under his desk. Then he turned his back on me again. The burn subsided, the pulse slowed. I had overplayed my hand.

"Listen, Willie, I don't expect any warm welcome up here. I'm just telling you, there's something going on you want to know about. You didn't listen last time. I'm telling you now."

Ever so slowly, the chair turned. Willie was nothing if not shrewd. He didn't have to like me to be that.

"Could be bad, Willie. Worse than Dyson. Could be flat-out murder."

"Coming out of the Fifth Floor? Murder? What, the mayor is whacking people now?"

"Willie, listen."

"No, Kelly. You listen. What is it with you? Every time you come around, you got a hard-on for the mayor. What did he ever do to you? You think you lost your badge 'cause of him? Wrong. You brought that on yourself. He didn't necessarily want you out. That was the county's call."

"He didn't stop it."

"Not the fucking point," Willie hissed. "So you do have a hard-on for the mayor. You know what, get the hell out of here. You could be wearing a wire right now, for all I know. Murder. Get the fuck out before I call downstairs."

Willie stood up. I had worn out my welcome, which wasn't the worst thing in the world.

"I need to see Johnny Woods," I said.

"So go see him. He's not my fucking problem."

"Where's his office?"

Dawson gestured down the hall.

"Thanks, Willie. I'll see you around."

I left Dawson in his cubbyhole, head again deep in his filing cabinet. Willie's mind, however, wasn't on his paperwork. He was thinking about murder. An election. And the mayor. Pretty soon Willie would start talking. Probably about all three. Sometimes, that was all it took to get things going.

CHAPTER 24

I was halfway down the hallway when Johnny Woods came around the corner and nearly ran into me. He was carrying a folder in one hand and a cup of coffee in the other. A small woman, curly brown hair, perfume, and curves, followed in his wake. Woods stopped short and saved his coffee from spilling on both of us.

"Whoa, sorry about that, fella."

Johnny gave me his best guy smile. I gave him one right back.

"That's okay, Johnny. I was just coming to see you."

Woods gave the woman a quick nervous look. "We know each other?"

I offered a hand. Out of reflex, the mayor's man grasped it.

"No, but we have some mutual friends," I said. "Name's Michael Kelly."

I could see Woods trying to place the name. Then he did. And didn't like it at all.

"What can I help you with, Mr. Kelly?"

"Maybe we could go into your office?"

Woods gave a halfhearted nod and led the way. His office consisted of white walls and a blue carpet. His desk was standard issue, gray gunmetal. The credenza behind him was filled with pictures of Woods and the mayor, signing bills, cutting ribbons, breaking ground. All the usual bullshit stuff politicians take pictures of. I sat on a metal chair with red padding. Woods had a nice leather one and eased himself into it.

"I assume you're the same Michael Kelly who got himself booted off the force a while back?"

"I'm a private investigator now."

"I know. You took down Bennett Davis last year, if I recall."

"You recall well."

"That was quite a high-profile thing."

"Murder usually is. Especially when the killer is also a county prosecutor."

Woods straightened some papers and adjusted a silver picture frame facing him on his desk. I caught a glimpse of Taylor. She was holding what looked like a good-size muskie. Woods had an arm around his stepdaughter. Seemed like a man who liked his life. At least, for that moment in time. Then the snapshot disappeared and the city fixer cleared his throat.

"So tell me, Mr. Kelly. What can I do for you?"

"It's about a house on Hudson. Number 2121. Lovely place, turn of the century, stained glass, wooden floors, and a dead guy hanging off the second-floor railing."

The blood in Woods' face drained into his feet. He looked past me to see if his door was closed. Fortunately for him, it was.

"Ring a bell, Johnny?"

"I don't know what you're talking about."

"You don't?"

"No, I don't."

"Maybe this is something I should take to the police. Or, better yet, the press."

I dropped a small black memory card onto the desk between us.

"Know what that is, Johnny?"

Woods didn't say anything. Just looked at the card. I thought he was having one of those out-of-body moments they talk about on *Oprah*, but I couldn't be sure.

"That's a memory card from my digital camera," I said. "It's got about nine shots on it. Time-stamped. Of you walking down Hudson. Into the house and back out again. I'm afraid you look a bit rushed on the way out."

The card was actually empty. Johnny didn't need to know that. He'd been inside the house on Hudson and knew it. Now he knew I knew. That was all that mattered.

"What do you want, Kelly?"

"Why?"

"Why what?"

"Why the house on Hudson? Why Allen Bryant? What the fuck does the mayor's hatchet man want with all of that? And murder on top of it?"

"Jesus, Kelly. Enough already. The boss is five doors down."

"I assume this was a job for him."

"Don't assume anything. That's rule number one. As for murder, like you said, I was as shook as anyone when I walked into the goddamn house. Christ, I'd never seen anything like that."

Woods reached for a pitcher of water on his desk and poured himself a glass.

"Never seen a dead guy, Woods?"

"Honestly? Outside of a funeral home, no."

"Who did you tell?"

"About me being inside Hudson? Nobody. Not yet. Been trying to figure it out."

I figured Woods was telling the truth. At least, as far as he went. There was more, of course. There was always more.

"Have you talked to the police?" Woods said. "No, you

couldn't have. Otherwise you wouldn't be here. What is this? Blackmail? Jesus Christ, I got nothing."

"I'm not here to blackmail anyone, Johnny. If I wanted to do that, I'd take my memory card five doors down. I told you what I want to know. Why did you go to see Bryant in the first place? What's the connection to downtown?"

"I can't get into that."

"No, huh?"

Woods shook his head and gave me the look of someone who didn't know what he was made of inside and was deathly afraid of finding out.

"Let me explain something to you, Johnny. When you walked into that house, you walked into a murder. When you fled the scene—and you did flee the scene. I have some great shots of you getting into a Checker. Even got the tag number so we can track down the cabbie. Anyway, when you fled the scene, you became suspect number one. By my count, there is no suspect number two. What does all that mean? Even you can figure it out. Whatever you were doing there, it won't matter. I go public and the Fifth Floor drops you like a bad habit. Police arrest you and it's over. Your career, your life. Everything except your picture on the front page and a steady diet of prison sex. They'd enjoy a beefy guy like you, by the way. That's your future, Johnny, and it's all just a phone call away. So you figure out if it's worth it to play the stiff-upper-lip routine for the mayor. Of course, maybe he'll stand by you when it goes bad. What do you think?"

Woods looked at me. Then out the window. Then back at me.

"You're a real motherfucker, aren't you? I mean, I heard about you but, hell, I'm just doing a job here."

"If it wasn't a dirty job, you got no problems."

"Christ, Kelly, it's politics. What the fuck do you expect?"

"Tell me about it. If I can keep you out, I will."

Woods hesitated, but not too long. Sometimes when you look inside, it doesn't take that long. I think this was one of those times.

"Okay, I'll give you some details, but not here. Not now."

"When?"

"Give me a number. I'll call you."

I scribbled down my cell number and shoved it across the desk. "Don't wait too long, Johnny."

He nodded.

"And make sure you have a story ready about why you met with me this morning. The mayor will want to know."

Another nod.

"And make sure your girlfriend outside backs you up. They're the ones who always get you."

This time Woods just looked at me. Moved his lips and nothing else. "Close the door behind you."

I did. The person with the curves was sitting at her desk, trying hard to pretend she wasn't trying hard to listen through her boss's door. It was a thick door. I figured she got every other sentence. Tops.

"Your boss wants to see you," I said.

She got up, swift and stiff, head down, eyes averted, and slipped inside Johnny Woods' inner sanctum. I was twenty feet down the hall and could still hear Johnny when he started to yell. Maybe the door wasn't so thick after all.

CHAPTER 25

I was waiting for the elevator and thinking about lunch when the door with the word MAYOR on it swung open. Three men came out and checked the hallway. A moment later, the man himself walked out. Through a tangle of arms and legs I could see the lean frame, long arms, and pale, heavy-wristed hands. A body shifted and I caught the mayor's face in profile. A dark brow crouched over darker eyes. Below that lay a blunt expanse of nose, long, pockmarked lines for cheeks, and thick lips the color of uncooked sausage. The mayor's surname might be Irish, but his features carried more than a touch of Poland, from his mom's side. The mix was not one to win any beauty contests. In Chicago circles, however, it was every bit the potent political offering.

The mayor checked his watch as his minions circled in a tight orbit. Then Wilson's eyes traveled down the hall, flicking over me like a cold shadow before returning with a bit of interest. The mayor leaned his head an inch or so to the left and whispered into the ear of the man next to him. It was his cousin Patrick Wilson, also known as the brains of the family. Not that the mayor was dumb. Just simple. Like a shark is simple. Single-minded. Relentless. Looking for an easy meal.

"Michael Kelly." The mayor's cousin stepped forward and offered a hand. I took it.

"Hi, Patrick."

Patrick Wilson was easy to like. He loved to smile, shake hands, and talk about "win-win situations." I believe that was the phrase he used just before they flushed my career as a cop. In the parlance of the Fifth Floor, Patrick was known as the velvet glove. The hammer stood just behind him.

"Nice to see you," Patrick said.

I heard a grumble. Or maybe it was a snort. Or maybe the mayor just scratched himself somewhere private and liked it. Whatever it was, the secret signal was given. Patrick Wilson immediately flared to the left. The mayor's other two henchman spread out to the right. I stepped into the semicircle as the elevator behind me chimed. No one took any notice. I shook the mayor's hand as his crew checked me out from a variety of angles. This was always how it was with the mayor. Sort of like an audience with a Mob boss, only we were standing in a corridor of City Hall.

"Michael Kelly," the mayor said. "What brings you up here?"

"The view."

The mayor offered the bottom half of his upper teeth in what I guessed to be a smile and turned to his cousin.

"He likes the view, Patrick. See, I told you this was a good thing."

The mayor turned back to me.

"My cousin just came back from working in one of those big law firms. Forty-first floor of the Hancock. Floor-to-ceiling windows. Seven hundred fifty dollars for an hour of his time."

The mayor glanced back at Patrick, who looked appropriately chastened.

"Now he's back with us. Working for the people. Except this

morning, I hear he complains about his office. Can't see the lake from his window."

The mayor shrugged.

"I brought him into my office. Let him look out the window for a while. No one can see the lake from City Hall. Just a lot of buildings."

"And the people," I said.

"Exactly. The people. That's what we're all about. The people. You get it, Patrick?"

Little cousin nodded.

The mayor grunted. "Come inside for a second, Kelly."

Mayor Wilson turned and went back into his office. I followed. Everyone else knew enough to stay outside. The door closed behind us. Wilson took a seat behind his desk.

"Take a look at this."

On a low table beside his desk, the mayor had a small-scale model of a park set up, complete in all its details, right down to miniature lampposts, benches, and trees.

"Is that a dog?" I said, and pointed to a miniature canine lingering suspiciously near a miniature fire hydrant.

"Springer spaniel," the mayor said. "Best kind of dog God ever made. Got three of them. You know what all this is?"

I shook my head.

"This is Anderson Links," the mayor said, and smiled.

Anderson Links was once Chicago's most exclusive golf course, one hundred acres of soft-limbed trees and butterflies spread out along the lake and two minutes' drive from the Loop. Anderson was old-school, one of those private clubs golfers lust after because they can't buy their way in. To play at Anderson, you had to know somebody. Preferably somebody with old money, white skin, and the political compass of Nelson Rockefeller. The club itself had operated for the better part of a century under what was described in the press as a 999-year lease with the city. That is, until one night when the mayor decided he'd had enough of the North Shore bluebloods and fired up Chicago's road graders. The next day the city awakened to pictures of well-tended fairways bulldozed into oblivion, and Anderson's clubhouse padlocked shut. The mayor held a press conference. He was terminating the lease and taking the property back for the city. Now he was telling me why.

"The birds have nowhere to go, Kelly. Geese alone fly from the upper reaches of Wisconsin all the way to Mexico, some of them. They need places to rest."

"Okay," I said.

"This will be a stopover." The mayor checked a memo on his desk. "An Audubon stopover. That means a bird resting place."

"Okay," I said again, as it seemed to do the trick.

"It will also be a park for the people. Here, take a look."

Now the mayor took off his coat and got down on his knees so he was level with the model park. I shrugged and squatted down beside him.

"I'm planting seven different types of trees. This section right here will be the Japanese maples."

The mayor slipped the thin tip of a tongue between his lips and began to move trees and park benches hither and thither.

"These benches will be made of red oak. I want them facing east so people can sit there in the morning. Watch the sun rise over the lake."

"So the *people* get a lake view," I said.

"Exactly. The average guy. No charge."

The mayor stopped moving benches and looked over at me. Our faces were close enough that I could feel the faint wheeze of mayoral exhaust.

"What're you doing up here, Kelly?"

"Just visiting a friend."

"A friend, huh?"

The mayor got up and returned to the soft chair behind his big desk. I found my way to a hard wooden seat.

"You don't have any friends up here, Kelly. You understand that?"

"Business, then."

"Business. Okay."

The mayor hesitated, smooth eyelids closing to half mast, considering my fate. I didn't say anything.

"It's not that I don't like you," the mayor said. "Not at all. In fact, I admire you. Know why?"

"Why?"

"Good question. 'Cause you got balls."

The mayor held his hands in front of his face, palms up, like he was holding a couple of casaba melons. At least that's the way I saw it.

"Big fucking balls. Sure, you got taken down off the force. No more needs to be said. But you didn't whine and complain. Didn't go to the press. Didn't file another fucking lawsuit to make me puke. You took it like a man, understood it for what it was. And you came back. You're a player again. Not with a badge, no. But you're someone people talk about. Someone people fear, just a little fucking bit. So when I see you on my floor, I wonder. What is Kelly with the big balls doing here? Does he have a problem with me? Does he think I destroyed his career? Is there something here I need to attend to?"

I smiled. Carefully.

"Mr. Mayor, I'm not out for you. Or anyone else. Like you said, what's done is done. I understand that. On the other hand, you're right to be concerned. A guy like me has nothing to lose. Been ruined once. Won't hurt so much the second time."

Wilson pointed a long finger my way. "Exactly. Which makes you a dangerous person. You hear about my Olympic bid?"

I shrugged. "Who hasn't?"

"Got a conference room across the way. Have the entire village laid out in miniature. Next time you come back, I'll show it to you."

The mayor made a move to get up but stayed put behind his desk. "You didn't answer my question, Kelly."

"Sir?"

"Am I having a problem with you?"

Wilson tipped forward as he spoke, eyes slitted again, mouth slightly open, circling his object of interest, trying to decide if what he saw was a threat or just another meal. To be honest, I wasn't sure myself.

"All I can promise is, I'll play it straight," I said. "Right down the line."

"And let the chips fall where they may?"

"Something like that, Mr. Mayor."

Wilson's chair squeaked as he leaned back in it. "Don't suppose you'd come work for me?"

"Don't suppose I would."

The mayor offered a chuckle that dried up and died from a lack of enthusiasm. Then he got up from behind the desk.

"My old man would have loved you. Don't really give a damn who you tell to fuck off. And you're even polite about it. I envy you."

The mayor moved to the door of his office. I was just on his shoulder when he turned.

"I hear you know some Latin."

I nodded.

"Took some myself," the mayor said. "Even remember a phrase or three."

I waited. The black eyes were busy, crawling over me, taking stock.

"*Verbum sapienti satis est.* You know what that means, Kelly?"

"A word to the wise is sufficient," I said.

"That's good. They told me you were a smart fuck. Guess they were right. I could find out why you were up here today. But I think I'll let it lie. For now. A word to the wise, however. Stay the fuck out of my way. I might like you, but I'll still cut off those big balls and broil 'em up for breakfast."

"A friend suggested that was a distinct possibility, sir."

Wilson jiggled a jowl at that one and seemed about to pursue the matter. Instead, he opened the door to his office and walked out. I followed. Two minutes later, I was on the elevator, a Wilson aide on either side, sinking fast toward the street.

CHAPTER 26

Janet Woods lived in a section of Chicago known as Sauganash. On the northwest edge of the city, Sauganash was more suburb than city, more Irish than WASP, and tight-knit to the point of incestuous.

A lot of cops lived in Sauganash. A lot of firemen. A lot of people like Johnny Woods. People who worked for the city and had to live there in order to keep their job. Homes in Sauganash rarely went on the market. When they did, prices started at a half mil, which was okay since no one got to buy in the neighborhood unless they "knew" somebody. Like I said, a tight-knit group.

Johnny and Janet lived at the squared-off end of a neat block of colonials. The lawns were green, the streets clean. Kids played basketball in the driveway and probably had nice teeth. All in all, the place was safe. Boring, yes. And everyone seemed to look alike. Still, it was Sauganash. A daily celebration of a certain kind of life, preserved under glass and, in the minds of its residents, the only state of mind in which to live. Unless, of course, you could afford Winnetka.

I parked around the corner with a view of the front door. It was just past three on a Thursday afternoon, and I needed to have a word with my client about her daughter. The same daughter who wanted me to kill her step-dad. I had thought about calling ahead of time but decided against it. Sometimes, it was better to just show up.

I was about to get out of the car when I saw a black Saab back out of the driveway. Janet was behind the wheel, wearing a scarf and sunglasses. I was going to flag her down. Instead, I turned the engine over and followed.

A couple of minutes later, we were out of Sauganash and into the grit along Lincoln Avenue, past two blocks' worth of Korean restaurants, a couple of motels that rent rooms by the hour, and an all-night bail bondsman. Ten minutes after that, Janet Woods pulled to the curb inside the 1800 block of West Winona. She got out, took a quick look behind her, and headed for a place called Big Bob's Saloon. I didn't know much about Big Bob's except that it sponsored Chicago's only live turtle races. They happened every Friday night. Six turtles with numbers on their shells, a man with a microphone, and a hundred or so screaming fans. You could bet on a turtle, win a pitcher of beer, and basically get hammered as the green guys crawled across the floor. I had gone once with a woman. Won seven of eight races and lost my date halfway through. All in all, not a bad night.

I pulled up to the curb and watched the afternoon sun paint shadows across the tavern's front windows. Janet walked in and took a seat at the end of the bar. A moment later, the man pouring booze shifted his bulk her way. He fixed her up some sort of drink and lingered. The two talked, heads together, like they'd done it before. The talk continued for the better part of ten minutes. Then the bartender moved away and my client sat alone, sipping her drink and looking straight ahead. I locked up the car and walked into the tavern.

At four in the afternoon, the race track wasn't quite what

I remembered. Looked more like a dump, with a long narrow bar made of thin plywood, cracked Formica tables, and the faint smell of dead rodent wafting from somewhere near the bathrooms. Up close and personal, the bartender looked like an ex-jock from a very local high school, maybe six feet and long gone to fat. He was wearing a 1985 Bears Super Bowl sweatshirt with cutoff sleeves, and inhaling an order of Chinese takeout. The rest of the place was filled up with an old man at a dark corner table, nursing a bottle of Miller High Life as if it were the champagne of beers and staring at his life from the wrong side.

Janet drank from a plastic cup and was almost done when I walked up. She still had her sunglasses on, and the scarf bunched around her neck and lower face. She watched me approach in the mirror behind the bar.

"You come here a lot, Michael?"

"Been here for the turtle races."

Janet sniffed at that and rattled the ice in her cup. The barkeep got up with a groan, dumped some ice in another cup, and filled it up with ginger ale. He slid the drink in front of Janet, took a look at me, and asked what I wanted. I ordered a Bud and sat down without being invited.

"This guy know you?" I said.

The bartender returned with my beer, grunted back to his stool, and exhaled into a another mouthful of soft noodles. The Cubs game came up on a TV in the corner. It was the bottom of the fourth and they were losing twelve to two.

"I come here now and again," she said.

I took a sip of my beer and pretended to look around. "Yeah, you fit right in."

"They leave me alone. Give me some space to think."

"You come in here to do your thinking?"

"Sometimes. If that's okay with you."

Janet took off her glasses as she spoke. The eye had healed nicely, which was good because the scarf was covering a cheek and jaw that were ruined.

"He hit you with a fist?" I said.

Janet pushed the scarf up close to her skin. I pulled it back.

"Started with an open hand, didn't he?" My fingers traced the edge of her jaw and the soft bruises she called lips. "Lip's cut on the inside. Teeth probably went right through when he caught you. Had to be with a fist. That's why it's all swollen."

The bartender was edging his eyes my way. I wondered how much he knew about my client's bruises. I wondered why he cared.

"Put some ice on it if you haven't already," I said. "It'll help. Still, I wouldn't get rid of the scarf."

"Thanks. Is that all you came in here for?"

"Taylor came to see me the other day." I dropped it in without missing a beat and looked straight ahead. I felt her head swivel, her focus tighten.

"My Taylor?"

I nodded.

"What did she want?"

"She wanted to talk about her step-daddy. About how we could maybe figure out a way to kill him."

I caught her eyes in the barroom mirror, then they swam away.

"How do you feel about that?" I said.

"How am I supposed to feel?"

"I don't know. Sick? Scared?"

"Taylor's a kid. She's upset and angry."

"That it?"

"She doesn't know what she's saying."

"You sure about that?"

"Kill Johnny? You can't think she'd ever seriously consider . . ."
Janet dismissed the notion with a shake of her head. "No one's
going to hurt Johnny, if that's what you're worried about."

"I'm not worried. Just thought you might want to talk to your
girl. Explain some things to her."

"My kid's not a murderer."

"That's not what I said."

"Fine. I'll talk to her."

Janet sank her eyes into her drink. I scratched at the label on
my bottle of beer. The old man in the corner leafed through a
Sun-Times. He read it from back to front, two fingers played up
the side of his face, a lit cigarette dangling there. He moved his
mouth to the smoke without ever taking his hand from under his
chin and turned the pages slowly.

"You think I'm making a mistake, don't you?" Janet said.

"I told you what I think."

"The face isn't as bad as it looks."

My client's reflection played like some sort of cruel joke above
the row of bottles behind the bar.

"It isn't?"

Janet slipped the glasses back over her eyes and folded the rest
of herself back into the scarf.

"No, it isn't. Besides, I get my pound of flesh." She said the last
part with a measured cadence, a rhythm, soaked in some sort of
very private satisfaction.

"And how does that work?"

I didn't expect a window into how or where my client took her
marital pound. I wasn't disappointed.

"Not now, Michael. When I have it together, I promise, you'll
be the first to know."

She turned as she spoke, and I could see a splinter of myself
reflected in the dark lenses. I wanted more from my client, but I

wasn't going to get it. I could walk, but that didn't play for me either. Never did.

"Let's get out of here," I said. "Take a ride."

Janet tilted her head toward the street. "My car's here. How about I make us some dinner? Taylor's at a friend's for the night and Mr. Charming is staying downtown."

I finished my beer and threw down some money. The bartender kept his eyes glued to the set. Maybe Lou's team was really that interesting this year. Being a Cubs fan myself, I knew better.

CHAPTER 27

Dinner was roasted chicken and some salad. Afterward, we sat at the kitchen table with a bottle of wine and cigarettes. That's when my client decided to tell me how it started.

"He took a dozen eggs out of the fridge." Janet nodded her head as if I didn't believe her. I hadn't said a word.

"We were married less than a month. It was a Saturday morning and I had to take Taylor to a soccer game. Told him I didn't have time to pick up his dry cleaning."

She topped off her glass and offered the bottle to me. I shook my head.

"He comes downstairs. Hungover like a dog. Asks me what I said. So I told him again that I couldn't pick up the dry cleaning. He goes to the fridge and gets the eggs. Grabs me by the back of the neck and sits me down at the table."

"You try and stop him?"

"Honestly, I didn't know what was going on. Besides, he was stronger than I knew. At least he was then. So I sat right here. And he cracked an egg. Over my head. Right down my face."

Janet turned at an angle and took a hit off her cigarette, a single eye fixed on me as she blew a stack of smoke into the space between us.

"He didn't say anything. Just held my shoulders and head and cracked the egg. First one, then another. Probably about a half dozen in all. Then he left. Went back upstairs to bed. His way of telling me who was boss."

"What did you do?"

She laughed and I caught a flash of her eyeteeth. "Hard-ass Janet, right? Should have left, run for the door? Well, I didn't. Mostly because of this."

Janet waved her glass around the house in Sauganash.

"I didn't want to lose all this. For Taylor, I told myself. So I cleaned up and I stayed. Course it got worse. The eggs were just the message. After that came the pushing. Yelling. Slaps turned into fists. Rough sex, whenever and however he wanted. You know how it goes. You've seen it."

I took a sip of wine and the two of us sat with things. However they were.

"I knew someday he'd be done with me," she said. "Then he'd go after Taylor."

"So it is like that."

My client nodded to herself and something moved behind her eyes. "Not yet, but it could be. Anyway, I couldn't take the chance. Couldn't just wait around."

"So you came to see me. Almost a year ago."

"You were a friend. Okay, once we were more than friends." She took a cautious look up from under her bruises. "You thought any more about that?"

"About what?"

"About us. About what I told you."

"I try not to."

"It never would have worked, Michael. You know that."

"There might have been other options."

She began to speak, then settled for a hard grimace.

"Let's not get into this again," I said. "What's done is done. In your next life, just tell the guy."

She shook her head. "It was my body. My decision."

"Then why do I have to live with it?"

It was a selfish question. One without an answer. One that, once asked, couldn't be undone.

"We're talking more than fifteen years ago, Michael. I was a kid. And I was scared."

I nodded. "Yeah, you were a kid. We both were."

"You think there's something more to it?"

"I think you had plans."

Janet toasted her plans. "You mean I was about the money. That's why I hooked up with Taylor's dad right after you. Mr. Board of Trade. Then, Mr. City Hall. Thought a guy with a little bit of green would take care of all my problems. Get a house, nice car. All that security."

"Not so secure, huh?"

"Take a look around. From now on, I take care of my own."

"Is that why you looked me up after all these years?"

"You were always strong, Michael. Even when I finally told you about it."

"And once you told me, I might be more likely to take you on as a client?"

"Is that what you think?"

"You tell me."

Her eyes had hardened into bits of emerald, polished and shining. "I thought you needed to know what happened. Even if it happened a long time ago. As for the rest of it, if you could help me find some answers to the thing with Johnny, yes, I wanted that."

"And now?" I said.

"Now, the answers are all there. It's the questions I need to face up to."

"In the meantime, we all wait."

She reached over. Her hand was like leather and cold to the touch. Or maybe it was just me.

"It's not perfect, Michael. But I can promise you this. When we're ready, I'll walk away with my kid and never look back."

I moved my hand off hers. "Just don't wait too long."

"I won't." She stood up and stepped close. "We okay?"

I nodded and thought I meant it. She leaned over and ran her lips across my cheek. Then she started to clear the table, as if that would somehow change her life. I watched for a while before wandering into the living room. Mitchell Kincaid's run for mayor was the second story on the ten o'clock news. Janet came in with the rest of the wine and sat down.

"I saw him speak," she said. Fox News rolled tape of Kincaid, smiling and shaking hands at a rally.

"What did you think?"

"Honestly?"

"Sure."

"I thought it must have been what Bobby Kennedy was like."

I looked at the screen. The crowd around Kincaid was mostly white, mostly young, and mostly female. A little like being at a Beatles concert back when Paul and John shaved once a week.

"That good, huh?"

A college-age woman, hair dyed red and braided tight to her head, jumped in front of the candidate. She wore cargo pants, a white shirt, and a black bomber jacket. The girl lifted up her shirt to reveal a ripped set of abs. Kincaid smiled and signed her stomach as all the other women screamed.

"I didn't say I'd vote for him," Janet said. "Remember who my asshole husband works for."

I picked up the remote and froze the image on the screen. Kincaid was caught in profile, his hand reaching out to tousle the head of a young boy in the crowd.

"You think he could win?"

Janet snickered. "Going up against Wilson? Please. Barack Obama is one thing. He was only running for president. Kincaid wants to be mayor."

"In Chicago."

"Exactly. Wilson's got all the big money and unions in his back pocket. And if, by some miracle, Kincaid doesn't run out of cash, then they'll get nasty."

"How so?"

"I don't know for sure, but Johnny hinted that they were working on some stuff. He had that little glitter in his eye."

I took another look at Chicago's would-be savior. To Mitchell Kincaid's left was his security aide. Large and young, muscled and black. It was a face that bothered me, one I thought I recognized. Or maybe it was just the simmering anger that seemed so familiar.

"Let's see what else is on," Janet said, and plucked the remote from my hand. She ran through some channels and settled on Letterman. "You like Dave?"

"He's okay." I looked at a small clock on the wall. It was coming up on eleven o'clock. "But I gotta go."

"I told you, Johnny won't be back tonight."

"That's not really the point."

Janet held up a hand. "He gets a room downtown. Takes a change of clothes and goes right to work in the morning." She turned the hand over, palm facing up, and looked back at the tube. "So what else is new?"

"You think he's got a girl down there?"

Janet kept her eyes on Letterman and shrugged. I thought about the brunette at City Hall. The perfume and the curves.

"Sorry," I said.

"Doesn't matter." Janet smiled brightly at the flat screen. "Really doesn't. Just don't worry about running out of here. At least because of him."

She turned up the volume on the TV. Enough to drive our conversation into early retirement. I leaned back into the couch. It was soft. Dave was funny. He had Billy Crystal on. I liked Billy Crystal. Reminded me of a throwback sort of comedian. Didn't need to get into the bathroom to get a laugh. Class.

I took another sip of my wine. Janet laughed at a joke and I relaxed some more. Pretty soon my feet were up on the couch. Then I stretched out.

I WOKE UP in a hurry, four hours later. The house was dark. The house was quiet. It was three-thirty in the morning. There was a pillow under my head and a blanket over the rest of me. I was alone and apparently tucked in for the night.

I knew Woods was going straight to work in the morning. Still, it was better to leave. Just in case a Papa Bear named Johnny decided to come trundling home. I told myself I'd just rest my eyes for another thirty seconds. Then I leaned back into the pillow. Very white. Very soft.

CHAPTER 28

Sunlight cut across the living room, found my eyelids, and pried them open. For a moment, I wondered where I was. Then I sat up and remembered. I swore at myself in as many ways as I could think of. That took a while. After that, I crept quietly to the front windows. It was just starting to lighten. The block was still and empty. I walked into the kitchen, turned on the tap, and ran some cold water over my face. I thought about scribbling a note for Janet. Then I thought about Taylor stumbling on it. Even better, Janet's husband. Maybe a note wasn't such a good idea.

I went out the back door, found my car at the end of the block, and slid behind the wheel. So far, so good. I looked in the rearview mirror and saw the face of Johnny Woods, smiling back.

"Have fun, Kelly?"

I ducked and heard the crack of safety glass. A black tire iron had gashed my windshield. Woods was halfway into the front seat, trying to pry it free. Fortunately, he wasn't having much luck. I scooted a bit lower to the floor as Woods swung a paw south, hoping to catch some part of my anatomy. After that, he abandoned the tire iron completely and came after me, face first.

A proper head butt is akin to a work of art. The head should be held forward and low. You want to aim anywhere below the brow: eyes, cheeks, teeth. Nose is best. Lovely pop and hurts like hell. Johnny Woods was no exception. Blood all over the front seat and a moment's peace for yours truly.

I got my hand on the driver's latch and opened the door. Woods had one hand on my leg, the other still pressed to his proboscis. That was pretty much how we got out of the car, sprawled on the corner of Kirkwood and Hiawatha.

I scrambled to my feet as Woods swung again. Missed by a lot. He was still bleeding pretty hard, breathing even more so. Johnny might have been a fighter in his day, but that was a long time and a lot of doughnuts ago. I held my fists on either side of my head, elbows in and tight to the ribs. I didn't try to turn or move. Just stood there and let Woods come. At first, he was tentative. A couple of swings I caught up high off my shoulders. When he saw he wasn't getting hit, Woods got a lot bolder. Began stepping into his shots. Rights, then lefts. He was windmilling, losing most of his power on the way in, each swing punctuated with "fucker" or "motherfucker." I ducked and weaved a bit. Woods telegraphed his punches, and they were easy to pick off. I caught some with my forearms. The body shots I let in. Allowed them to bury in my side and ribs. He could hear me grunt as they landed. I think Johnny enjoyed that. I didn't blame him. From his point of view, I had just spent the night with his wife.

After twenty seconds or so, Woods realized something. Fighting is hard work, even when you aren't getting hit. Sixty seconds in, he was pawing more than punching. Thirty seconds after that, he was done. Woods hadn't really hurt me. Maybe a tweaked rib or two, but nothing more than a light spar. Johnny, on the other hand, was spent.

I put out a hand and pushed against the soft body. Woods fell back against my car, slipped down the side, and nuzzled up to the grille. Leaking oil in more than a few spots and looking at me over his shoulder. Still trying to swear but not getting the words entirely right. He was pissed. Just too tired to do much more about it.

"Take it easy, Woods. You can take another run when you get your breath back."

Johnny took my advice and sat back against the bumper. I leaned against a tree and waited. Part of me wished he could actually hit, make it worth my while to hit back. But that part wasn't going to make Johnny Woods any tougher, any more or less of a man than he already was. Besides, the guy spent his spare time beating up women. He was lucky I didn't take a swing or three just for fun. He'd have more than a busted nose to worry about.

"Fucking tough guy, huh, Kelly?"

"Not tough. Just trained. If you don't know how to do it, hitting people can be a hard job."

"You enjoy tagging my wife."

"Let it go, Woods."

"I don't fucking think so."

"I do."

I dropped to a knee and got close enough so even Johnny would understand.

"Your wife's got a face full of pain. And it's not the first time. She's been documenting every beating you put on her. Now she's going to take her little girl and get the fuck away from you. And you know what? You're gonna let her go. You know why?"

I held two fingers close to his face.

"Two reasons. First, 'cause if you try to stop her, she goes public. One press conference, and the mayor dumps you quicker than the sack of steaming horseshit you actually are. Second reason is even simpler. I don't like cowards. And I especially don't like cowards who beat up women. Anything from you, anything at all, and I find you. No matter when, no matter where. I find you and I beat you till you beg for the gun. And that's when you get it. I bust your teeth open with the butt, put the barrel in until it hits the back of your throat, and pull the trigger. Last thing you see is my face. You got it?"

He didn't say anything. Just sat there, looking at the ground, wiping at the blood as it dripped off his face.

"Take a look at me, Woods."

He did.

"Just give me a reason. I won't think twice about it, and I won't miss a minute's sleep afterward. You understand?"

Woods nodded. Once, twice, three times. Then he paused. First it was the lower lip. After that, the chin began to tremble. He jammed his eyes into his fists, sniffled, and sobbed. The pity party had started. Looked like it was going to take a while so I stood up and considered my ruined windshield. A mom walked by with her kid. Probably heading off to school. I smiled. The two of them took a look at us and kept walking.

"Why did she have to do that?" Woods spoke with an after-taste of sorrow that was as self-serving as it was considerable.

"Do what, Johnny?"

"You know what."

Woods didn't care about my threats. And he certainly didn't care about his wife's bruises. It was the role of cuckold that Woods couldn't stomach. The idea that his wife would take another man. In his own house, even. Cowards, especially ones who prey on women and kids, always have the biggest egos. The mayor's man was no exception. Just the latest and sorriest example.

There was a steadier trickle of cars coming down the block now. A few more people on the street. Most of them were notic-ing us. Some talking. I knew it was just a matter of time before the police showed up.

"Nothing happened with your wife, Woods. She hired me because she wants to be rid of you. We were talking last night and it got late. I slept on your couch. Believe me or don't, I don't much give a damn. Now get in the car."

I got behind the wheel. Woods probably figured he wasn't making the greatest impression on his neighbors and found his way to the passenger door. The glass was spidered halfway across my side, but I could see well enough. We drove to a White Hen. I bought a bag of ice, a bottle of water, cotton, and bandages.

"Here, clean yourself up."

Woods washed off the blood. I took out a handkerchief and wrapped up some ice.

"Press this on your face. Keep the swelling down."

Woods took the compress and swung the rearview mirror his way.

"How's it look?" he said.

I swung the rearview mirror back.

"Your nose is fucked, so forget about it. Unless you want to go to the hospital and have it set."

Woods had the ice on the side of his cheek and shook his head.

"Good idea," I said. "Leave it the way it is. If you want to breathe better, they can break it and reset it later."

Johnny rolled an eyeball my way. Guess he didn't like the idea of rebreaking a part of his face.

"Relax," I said. "I had my nose busted six or seven times. Never went to the hospital. Not a big deal."

Woods pulled the compress away and felt his face. Carefully. Then he put the ice back in place and leaned back against the headrest. I turned on the radio. Woods decided he wanted to talk some more.

"Where'd you learn to fight, Kelly?"

"We didn't fight."

"How do you figure that?"

"You fought. I didn't throw a punch."

"That's what I mean. Man kicks my ass without throwing a punch. Tells me he knows how to fight. Where did you learn?"

"Here and there," I said. "Growing up."

"You fight for fun?"

"Never fun. Not if you know how to do it. It's work. And it's mean. And it's for keeps."

"Which means what?"

"Which means it's usually for money."

"So you're a pro?"

I glanced at the edge of my reflection in the driver's side mirror. "Used to be," I said.

"So I didn't have a chance."

I looked across the car and shrugged. "Fighting's like anything else. You go up against a man at his profession and you're probably going to lose. You may get lucky. More likely you get your head busted in."

I clenched and unclenched my fist, settled it back against the steering wheel.

"Moral of the story," I said. "Know who you're fighting. And don't raise your hands unless you're willing to go all the way."

Woods didn't say much after that, which was okay with me. I turned up the volume on the radio. *Mike & Mike* was on ESPN. Talking about how they bickered off air like an old married couple. Then they proceeded to bicker about that for half a minute, just like an old married couple. I kept waiting for them to talk about sports. Just a mention. In passing, even. I looked over at Woods.

"This sound like sports radio to you?"

He didn't answer. After a few minutes, I gave up and turned it off. Then I started up the car as Woods spoke again.

"So what have you found out, Kelly?"

I turned off the car. "About what?"

Woods' face looked better now, cleaner. He laid a bandage across the bridge of his nose and smoothed it down with his fingers as he talked.

"The thing on Hudson Street. What we talked about in my office the other day. What have you found out?"

His voice had softened and carried a subtle edge. The cuckold was gone. In his place, the mayor's fixer. Inside his comfort zone. The world of Chicago politics. Leverage and power. Shadows, bluff, deceit. That was okay. My investigation into Bryant's murder thus far had turned up nothing more than nickels and dimes. I needed someone with some expertise. Someone who could turn my loose change into real money. Someone who might be scared enough to talk.

"I know about the Chicago Fire," I said. "I know the mayor's great-great-grandfather probably started it. Helped along by the guy who ran the *Chicago Times*."

Woods yawned at my initial bombshell, stretched his arms, and cracked his knuckles. Then he craned his neck from side to side and resettled in his seat.

"Sounds like a good movie to me, Kelly. Got any proof?"

"Property records. Tying John Julius Wilson to the land. Maybe along with Charles Hume."

I thought the names might bother Woods. I was wrong.

"It's not a crime to own property. That all you got?"

"I also know about the *Sheehan's*," I said.

Woods flinched at the book's mention. Just a single movement along the left side of his upper lip. But it was enough.

"I know you went to the house on Hudson to get the book, and I know Allen Bryant was killed for it."

"I told you, Kelly. I had nothing to do with Bryant. He was dead when I got there."

"What about the book, Woods? Was that gone too?"

Whatever bluff the mayor's guy had been hoping to play was crumbling pretty quick. I was getting dangerously close to some version of the truth, and Woods needed to get his side out.

"I told them this was a bad idea," he said, and shook his head. "I fucking told them."

"Told who?" I said.

Woods' fingers were as overweight as fingers could be. One wore a gold wedding band. Another had a Claddagh ring squeezed onto it. He looked at them for a long time. Didn't see anything he liked and looked back at me. I don't think he saw anything he liked too much there either, but what the hell.

"Fuck you, Kelly. You know who."

"They want the book pretty bad."

"Yeah."

"Is it true?" I said.

Woods looked up again.

"Is what true?"

"John Julius Wilson. The Chicago Fire. Is it true?"

"Oh, Jesus. Are you going to talk about this?"

"I told you, Woods. I'm only about the murder. Allen Bryant was found dead inside his house. His first-edition *Sheehan's* was the only thing found missing."

"Shit."

"That's one way to analyze it. What I need to know from you is how the book fits into this whole thing. I know about Hume. I know about John Julius Wilson. I know about the land scam and the fire. Now tell me about the *Sheehan's*."

Woods smoothed his eyebrows and massaged the skin at his temples. I started up my car and began to drive. Maybe a change of scenery would help things along.

"There was supposed to be a letter," Woods said. "Have you heard about that?"

He moved his eyes across the car. I flicked my head. Neither yes nor no. Just enough to tell him I was in control and was going to get everything he had. This morning. Right now. Woods looked away and kept talking.

"Hume and Wilson supposedly drew up a letter after the fire. Laid out the whole thing: the plan to burn out the Irish; the land grab; how it all spun out of control. Then they signed it. Each kept a copy."

"Why?"

Woods chuckled, as if he understood this part of the story all too well.

"Fuckers didn't trust each other for nothing. The letter prevented either from talking."

"The letter was protection for Wilson," I said.

"Probably. He was the poor Irishman. Needed a handle on Hume."

"Shrewd," I said.

"Runs in the family."

"So what happened to the letters?"

"That's the thing," Woods said. "This is all rumor. Urban legend. Who the fuck knows. But the Fifth Floor believes it. So they sent me out to track them down."

"The letters?" I said.

"Yeah, the letters. At Hume's request, all his papers were burned at his death. Supposedly his copy of the letter was burned then."

"Why?"

"Maybe he figured it wasn't his problem anymore, so fuck it."

We were back in Sauganash. Woods cracked a window and

watched his neighborhood slide by. I turned onto a street called Keene and pulled up to Queen of All Saints. The sign out front said it was not just a church but a basilica.

"What's so different about a basilica?" I said.

"You Catholic?"

"All my life."

Woods shook his head and grunted. "Jesus Christ. A basilica's a big church. Sometimes it contains a crypt, a place in the church where they keep the bones of a priest or a saint."

"Huh."

"You better get some religion, Kelly."

"You think so?"

I parked in front of a large green lawn, stretching out and away. Toward the basilica's twin spires, soaring, and its granite façade, impressive. Beyond that, a flourish of marble steps. Expensive. Inside the church, presumably, salvation. Or at least a chance to contribute some cash.

"What about Wilson's copy?" I said.

"Of the letter?"

"Yeah, Johnny. Wilson's copy of the letter."

"What about it?"

"That's the one you're looking for."

"If it ever existed. The mayor claims he knows nothing about it."

"Officially," I said.

"That's right," Woods said. "Unofficially, it goes something like this. The year was 1920-something. One of the mayor's horny ancestors went into a cathouse over on Skid Row."

"This was before the Wilson family had taken up politics?"

"Just before," Woods said. "They were just filthy-rich pig-fuck land barons. Anyway, this guy is in there with one of the lovelies. They have a moment between rounds and he pulls out the letter.

Showing off or some fucking thing. Just about then Chicago's finest raid the place. All hell breaks loose. Did I tell you the Wilson guy was married?"

"I'm shocked."

"I'm sure you are. Anyway, he jumps out a second-story window, half naked."

"And leaves the letter behind?"

Woods cocked a finger my way and fired. "Bingo. He went back the next day but the girl had skipped town. Family never saw or heard about it again. Over time, everyone forgot about it."

"Until recently?"

"Yeah, recently. No one is sure where the rumor started but it's out there. The letter is legit and the mayor is nervous."

"Tell me how the *Sheehan's* fits in."

Woods held out a hand. "I'm getting there. You know the first editions are numbered?"

I nodded. "One to twenty."

"You've done your homework. Four's the lucky number. The first edition of *Sheehan's* numbered four contains information as to the location of the letter."

"*Sheehan's* number four, huh?"

"That's what they say. There's a clue in there somewhere."

"And you believe all this?"

Woods grunted again. "My bosses do. That's all that matters."

"You keep talking about rumor, Johnny. But I don't believe it. There's a source here. Someone is making you guys believe."

"You think so?"

"I think so. And I have a picture in my pocket. A picture of you running from a murder. A picture that tells me I'm gonna get his name. Probably sooner than later."

"Piss off, Kelly."

"Not a problem, Johnny, once I have your source. Someone put you guys onto the letter and the *Sheehan's*. Probably offered to read the tea leaves once you got the book and parse out the clue. Am I right?"

No response.

"Let me ask you this. Did he put you on to Allen Bryant's trail?"

Woods cut me a look at that one. "I found Bryant myself. Tracked down six other first editions before I found him."

"Bryant had the number four, didn't he?"

Woods nodded. "I met with him the night before he was murdered. He told me he had the book at his house and would give it to me the next morning. I showed up . . ." Woods shrugged and shook himself free. "He was dead, Kelly. I saw the body and split."

We sat in the silence of the moment. Each with our own set of problems.

"Does the mayor know about Bryant?" I said.

"Not from me. On the other hand, there isn't much he doesn't know."

"Is anyone else interested in the letter?"

"Mayor's got a lot of enemies," Woods said. "Love to get their hands on something like that."

"But would they kill to get their hands on it?"

Johnny smoothed out the wrinkles in his suit, took a little water, and washed some blood off a cuff.

"These people are civilized, Kelly. Political types."

"Doesn't answer my question. Would they kill to get their hands on the letter?"

"Absolutely not." Woods swiveled his head my way and offered up a narrow smile. "Unless, of course, they thought they could get away with it."

"Who's your guy on the letter?"

"Not going to let that go, are you?"

"No."

I thought I knew the answer but wanted to be sure. Woods shrugged.

"Fuck it. He's a little weasel, anyway."

I nodded. "The curator at the Chicago Historical Society."

"Now I *am* impressed," Woods said. "You got it. Lawrence Randolph. He's the one who pushed this thing on the mayor. Convinced him the letter from his great-great-grandfather might be real. Might be in play."

"And the *Sheehan's*?"

"Way I hear it, Randolph was the one who thought the *Sheehan's* was worth getting. Just to take a look at."

I thought about my friend the curator, sitting behind his desk. Pulling strings and moving pieces around the city. Probably got a big charge out of the whole thing.

"What does Randolph want?" I said.

"What else? Power. He wants to be the first curator for the City of Chicago. Official fucking historian or something. Mayor promised him all sorts of things. If we get the letter."

"And bury it?"

"Right. Bury it. If you ask me, the thing doesn't even exist, but there you go. In my world, sometimes the things that don't exist are the most dangerous. Now you know everything I do, Kelly. Keep me the fuck out of it."

"Or else?"

"Or else you have another enemy downtown you probably don't need."

"You worried?"

"To be honest, no. Word is you play it straight up. I figure my chances are pretty good I come out clean."

"If you're telling me the truth."

"Like I said, you know everything I do. That's all I can offer." Woods checked his watch and nodded toward the basilica. "I'm gonna slip in the back. Catch the eight-thirty mass."

He reached for the door latch. I put a hand on his shoulder.

"Just so you understand, Johnny. What I said about your wife, I meant it. Anything. Even a little bit of hurt, for her or the girl, and it all comes down on you. No talk. No bullshit. Just you and me and no happy endings."

Woods pulled out of my grip, rolled his shoulders, and ruffled up his dignity.

"Don't worry about it, Kelly. You can have her." He cracked the door to my car, put a foot outside, and leaned back toward me.

"Final word of advice, pal. Whatever she's selling, take a pass. Janet's all about Janet. Always will be. Now leave me the fuck alone. I gotta go to mass."

With that, Johnny Woods got out and walked across the grass, toward his God. An old priest in a red and purple hat was waiting at the top of the stairs. They shook hands and Johnny disappeared inside. The priest turned and looked back my way. I knew he couldn't see into my car, but I felt his weight, anyway. Being Irish Catholic will do that to you. I pulled away and put the basilica in my rearview mirror. The domestic problems in Sauganash would have to wait. There was still a murderer or two afoot. Not to mention the matter of the Chicago Historical Society and a weasel named Lawrence Randolph.

CHAPTER 29

Randolph was sitting behind his desk, holding what looked like an elephant tusk in one hand.

"Know what this is?" he said.

I didn't.

"It's an oosik."

The curator offered me the object but I wasn't interested.

"Know what an oosik is?" he said.

"Tell me."

"It's the bone from a walrus' penis."

I looked again at the object. Two feet long and seven inches around. "Congratulations to the walrus."

Randolph chuckled and laid the walrus' pride and joy on his lap. "I have a poem on the wall over there," he said. "It's called 'Ode to an Oosik.' Want to take a look?"

"I want to know about the *Sheehan's*. First edition. Number four, to be exact."

Randolph ran one hand down the side of his oosik and took some time in formulating a response. When it came, it wasn't much.

"Number four, you say?"

"Yeah, Randolph. Number four. The first edition you have the mayor's people chasing. The key to finding a letter . . . about a scandal you told me never happened."

Randolph's eyes moved back and forth across my face, looking for a lever to pull, an angle to push. After a while he gave up and decided to play it out.

"You know about the letter?"

"Johnny Woods told me."

"Okay, so I think there's a chance that Wilson's copy might exist. So what? I have no obligation to discuss that with you."

"You got the mayor's people going on this, didn't you?"

"Sure, I pushed it along. If true, it's a major bit of history. I'm a historian. So, why not?"

"Got a person killed. How's that for starters?"

"I know the mayor's men. They're not going to kill anyone over this."

I shrugged. "Who else would be looking for the letter?"

"As far as I know, it's just Wilson and his inner circle."

"Those are the only people you talked to about this?"

"Yes. And, as I understand things, Allen Bryant was going to give them the book. So why kill him?"

"So you knew about Bryant?"

"Woods called me on the morning you showed up at the society."

"You're a weasel, Randolph."

The weasel was back to petting his walrus. He held up the oosik and pointed it my way. "We still have a deal?"

"Fuck off. And put that goddamn thing down before I stick it somewhere."

The curator did as he was told. He could be bullied, but only to a point. If the man had cards to play, he was in. To the last hand.

"I can help you," Randolph said.

"How?"

"Get me the book. It will take us both to the letter."

"And, presumably, Allen Bryant's killer."

"That's your business. I just want the letter."

"And to get that, you need the book."

"Yes, I believe so."

"I don't have it, Randolph. So I don't have to think about cutting deals with you."

I got up to go. The curator remained seated. "Not yet," he said. "If you get your hands on the *Sheehan's*, however, you'll be back."

"You think so?"

"If you suspect it might help solve your murder, you'll work with me."

Randolph was probably right. That bothered me.

"Whoever has the book," Randolph said, "doesn't know how to use it. Otherwise, we would have heard about it by now, don't you think?"

"Probably."

"Precisely. I'm guessing the *Sheehan's* is still out there. Maybe Mr. Bryant hid it somewhere. Who knows?"

"And if it's out there, I'll track it down. Right?"

"That's what I'm betting on, Mr. Kelly." Randolph shifted comfortably in his seat. "In fact, I'm counting on it."

CHAPTER 30

I pushed out of the historical society just after five p.m. and drove north on Stockton Drive. Randolph was proving to be a hard guy to get a handle on, which surprised as much as bothered me. I flipped open my cell and punched in Fred Jacobs' number. It took four rings, but the reporter finally picked up.

"Kelly, not in jail yet? I guess there's something to be said for that."

"Thanks, Fred. I got another favor to ask."

Lightning flickered silently over the lake. I rolled down the window. There was a high wind moving through the trees and it smelled like a cold rain.

"Where's my story?" Jacobs said.

"It's there, Fred. Just needs a little push."

"What kind of push?"

"Hardly nothing. If you're any good, shouldn't take you more than a half hour. And you don't even have to leave your office."

Something I had seen on TV at Janet Woods' house was scratching at the back of my mind. Something I needed to nail down. I told Jacobs what I wanted. When I finished, the reporter sat on the other end of the line and breathed. It didn't sound like anything close to healthy, and I wondered how many cigarettes the man smoked every day.

"Where the fuck you headed, Kelly?"

"Sounds good, doesn't it?"

"Sounds dangerous."

"High profile, Fred, high profile. So you want that third Pulitzer or what?"

I knew he'd agree to do it. It was easy enough for a guy like him and too damn tempting not to. I went over the specifics twice and hung up. Then I held my breath and dialed up a friend.

"Look what the cat dragged in."

"Hey, Rachel."

"Hello, Mr. Kelly. I hope you're not inviting me for another overnight." Her tone was amused. A detached "had a fling with this guy once" sort of amused. I didn't especially like it.

"I thought we might get together tonight," I said. "Grab a beer."

"Why?"

"Maybe I just want to see you."

"Maybe not. Last time I was with you, I got shot."

"I know, Rachel. That was messed up and I'm sorry."

"Me too." A pause. "Listen, Michael, tonight doesn't really work. I already made plans."

Convenient word, *plans*. Great weapon. Women use it especially well. Tells the poor bastard at the other end of *plans* she's on a date without ever actually saying it. Twists the knife and preserves the veneer of deniability. Also rife with the possibility of sex—again, something the poor bastard hearing about her *plans* is not going to be any part of.

"Plans, huh?"

"Yes, Michael. Plans. No breaking and entering. No guns. No possibility of cardiac arrest. Just dinner. Plain old boring dinner. Really, it's all my heart can take."

I smiled at my windshield, but it didn't seem to do much good. "Fair enough, Rachel. Maybe we can do this over the phone."

"Do what over the phone?"

"You remember the guy who broke into my apartment?"

"Could I forget?"

"I got a hunch as to who it might be."

"Okay."

"Gonna run the guy's prints against the lift Rodriguez pulled off my windowsill."

"That was only a partial. Not going to get you very far."

"There was blood as well."

"Why are you telling me all this?" she said.

"If this hunch pans out, I might need your help."

"What kind of help?"

"Mitchell Kincaid."

There was nothing for a beat. Then her voice came back, brittle to the point of angry.

"What would Mitchell Kincaid have to do with any of this?"

"It's complicated."

"It usually is. Let me guess. The mayor is involved."

"Could be."

"Mitchell's not going to grab at a rumor about your break-in and try to smear Wilson with it. That's not how he works."

"I know, Rachel. That's not what this is about."

"Then what is it about?"

"I can't tell you right now. I just need to know. If I wanted you to take a message to Kincaid, would you do it?"

More silence collected at the end of the line.

"What's the message?"

"I don't know yet."

My soon-to-be-distant memory of a romance that never was had heard enough.

"You want me to get involved, Michael, tell me what's going on. Otherwise pick up the phone and dial the man yourself."

"Can't do that. Not until I run these prints against the partial."

"Then we have nothing to talk about. I gotta go."

Rachel gave me half a goodbye and hung up, off to her *plans*, which undoubtedly included a lot of wonderful sex without yours truly.

I flipped my phone shut and cursed on behalf of clueless men everywhere. Then I drove until I found a Kinko's, one with an Internet connection and a printer. It took a while, but Fred Jacobs was as good as his word. A little after nine, I left with the set of prints I needed to test my theory. Now I wanted a place to think and drink. Not necessarily in that order.

CHAPTER 31

Joe's on Broadway opened at six a.m. and sold cans of beer for a dollar and a quarter. I sat under a sign that hung from the ceiling and read SORRY, WE'RE OPEN. The bar was full with its evening crowd, which meant there were five people in the place. Four of them were talking to themselves, which was okay because that meant they wouldn't bother me. The fifth was the bartender.

"Yeah?"

He spoke without taking his eyes off the screen. Bob Barker was playing the plip-plop game with an overweight housewife I'd be willing to bet was from Ohio.

"A Bud," I said.

"Yes."

The bartender made a fist and pumped it once. Onscreen, the housewife hung on Bob Barker's neck as he described the recreational vehicle she had just won.

"Isn't that on during the day?" I said.

"Actually, it's not on at all. We taped the old shows and watch them back-to-back all night."

I didn't have a whole lot to add to that and took my cold can of booze to a stool by the window. The beginnings of a

Chicago rainstorm knocked politely against the glass. A homeless woman sat on a bench near the bus stop. I tipped the Bud her way. She shuffled over to the window, stood in front of me, and held out her hand. I walked outside and gave her a couple of bucks. Then I went back inside, took a seat at the bar, and pulled out the booking photo and prints Jacobs had sent me. The picture was more than a decade old, but I recognized the face. Remembered the anger.

I slid the prints and photo back into the envelope and pulled out some notes from my conversation with the volunteer named Teen. I needed to talk to her. But not tonight. I took a sip of beer and wondered if it was too late to call Rodriguez. Probably. On TV, a woman from Pharr, Texas, won Bob Barker's grand show-case. I toasted her success. Then I took a glass of Irish and another beer. It was warm inside the bar, and the whiskey tasted all the better with rain pounding against the awning outside and washing the streets clean. I decided things could wait until tomorrow and was about to order a microwave pizza when a friend scraped into the empty stool next door.

"Drinking alone. Not good, Kelly. Not good."

Willie Dawson shook the rain off his shoulders, lifted a finger, and ordered himself a water glass full of Johnnie Walker Red.

"What brings you in here, Willie?"

The bartender measured out the drink and pushed it across the bar. Willie took a taste and smacked his lips.

"Nothing like whiskey on a night like this. Nothing close. But I don't need to tell you that."

I waited. Willie took a look around the place and then back at me.

"You spend a lot of time here, Kelly?"

"What's up, Willie?"

Dawson glanced toward the front windows and beyond. I

could see smoke from a tailpipe, a wink of red, and the metallic black flank of a car, idling under the streetlight in front of Joe's.

"He wants to have a word."

I wondered how the mayor had tracked me to a dive bar on a Friday night. Even better, why? The former question would probably remain exactly that. The answer to the latter, however, was just a few feet away. I finished my Irish and nodded to the inch and a half of booze left in Willie's glass.

"Finish up, then. Don't want to keep Himself waiting."

A CHIME BEEPED as I opened the back door to the Town Car. The mayor was bundled into a corner, gazing out over Broadway, his face half lit by an interior light. I climbed into the seat across from him. Willie slammed the door shut and got into the front beside the driver. I caught a final glimpse of the back of Willie's head before a partition slid across, sealing the mayor and me in back.

"Thanks for taking the time, Kelly."

The mayor talked without taking his eyes off the street. He wore a tuxedo under the cashmere of a gray overcoat, and white calves peeked out from where his pants rode up too high. Or maybe his socks were just too short. Either way, the mayor seemed uncomfortable with the whole lot of it.

"You like wearing the monkey suit?" I said.

The mayor pulled his eyes off the street and flicked at the silk scarf tucked under his chin.

"This fucking thing? Hate it. You want a drink?"

I shook my head. The mayor leaned forward and poured himself a vodka over ice from the minibar at his elbow.

"You think I like any of this shit, Kelly?"

"I think you like being mayor, Mr. Mayor."

Wilson took a sip of his drink. "You mean the power, right?"

"I think it's a rush for you," I said. "Just like it would be for anyone."

"You say that like you'd exclude yourself," the mayor said.

I shrugged and felt his eyes measuring me from across the car.

"My mother's maiden name is Sviokla." Wilson washed his mouth out with his drink. "Polish. Southeast Side."

"The old steel mills."

"That's right. Ironworkers and Old Style. People who worked paycheck to paycheck and knew when it was time to die."

"Excuse me?"

The mayor bared his teeth and laughed like a horse. If a horse could laugh, that is.

"A lot to be said for knowing when to die, Kelly. Heart attack, stroke. Whatever the fuck it is, get on with it when you hit sixty-five and make some room for somebody else. You know what I'm talking about?"

I nodded, just because it was interesting as hell.

"Today people want to live forever," the mayor said. "Expect it, for chrissakes. But here's the question. Who's gonna pay for it all?"

"The government?"

Wilson dropped his head and grunted into his chest.

"That's exactly right. The fucking government. I'm a Democrat. Don't get me wrong. But let me ask you, how does a city pay for all that? People can't live until they're eighty, ninety years old. It just isn't natural. You don't want a drink?"

I shook my head no. The mayor freshened his own.

"Anyway, that's me. Still live in the bungalow neighborhood I grew up in. Sure, it's a bigger house than the rest of them. But still the same neighborhood. Same tavern at the end of the street."

"It's your power base," I said.

"And I won't stray too far from it, right?"

"Why would you?"

Wilson shrugged. "Know where I was tonight?"

"Fund-raiser?"

"Kid's name is Jeffrey Dobey. Has MS. Muscles like fucking Jell-O. Tough life, right?"

I nodded. The mayor took another sip of his vodka.

"So I run into this kid fourteen, fifteen years back, at a campaign stop. One of those meet-and-greet deals. Jeffrey's mom is in front with the kid. No wheelchair 'cause they can't afford one. Instead, the kid has braces on his legs. Like you see in those pictures from the fifties. Remember those pictures?"

"Polio," I said.

"Exactly. That's what I was thinking. Those braces. Where the hell did the kid get those braces? And why is he propped up against the building with his crutches and his mom at one of my rallies? Jeffrey is a black kid. Did I tell you that?"

"No."

"So I had one of my aides go over and get his story. Turns out the mom has seven kids, four different fathers. Lives in the Green."

"And Jeffrey's dad is long gone."

"As are all the others. Anyway, long story short, I pull a few strings. Get Jeffrey into the Rehab Institute. Get rid of those fucking braces. Get him a wheelchair and some doctors who give a damn."

"After you talked to them."

"Excuse me?"

"They all give a damn after you talk to them, sir."

The mayor blinked. "Tonight, I spoke at a ceremony for the Collegiate Scholars Program. Honors our top public school kids.

Jeffrey was the highest ranking senior. Spoke before me. Know what the best part of his speech was?"

I shook my head.

"He walked across the stage to give it. Kid walked across that stage, and I helped. Not a lot. Not as much as his mom or his doctors. But I helped a little bit. That's a good feeling. Good thing about this job."

The mayor sat back and pushed his eyes out the window again. No one in the media or the public had ever heard of Jeffrey Dobey. Never would. That's because Wilson didn't do it for the press, or the politics. He did it because he cared. About the kid. About his people.

"Nice story, sir."

"You think so." Wilson stretched his neck as he spoke. "I pulled some strings. Threatened some people. Cut corners. Hell, I probably booted some vet out of a bed at the Rehab Institue to make room for this kid."

"Still, the kid walked."

"That's right, Kelly. The kid walked. And that's the bottom line. In life, everything has its price. Or maybe you already figured that out."

"Every day is an education, sir."

The mayor's shoulders bounced under their cashmere cover as he chuckled. Just once and stopped.

"Cheeky motherfucker. Just think about all that. The good and the bad. Not so easy to tell the difference sometimes."

We hadn't moved from in front of Joe's, which told me that whatever else Wilson had to say was going to be on the short and, hopefully, sweet side. I figured now was as good a time as any.

"What do you need from me, Mr. Mayor?"

"You think I need something?"

"I think you tracked me down for some reason. Wanted to

deliver a message. Wanted to do it personally. And I don't think it was just about Jeffrey."

Wilson creaked forward in his seat. Close up, his face was pitted and raw; his eyes, dead as ever.

"It's never personal, Kelly. Understand that."

"Okay."

Wilson leaned back again. "It's about your friend. The judge."

"You mean Rachel Swenson?"

"Nice lady. Not my cup of tea politically, but, then again, she probably feels the same way about me."

A small smile nipped at the corners of the mayor's mouth and I wondered if he wasn't sitting in my flat a week back, listening to all the bad things Rachel had to say about him. Of course, he wasn't. But the mayor knew, anyway.

"What is it you want to tell me about the judge?" I said.

Wilson placed his drink on a little ledge that had popped out from a panel in the car door. Blunt fingers circled the contour of cut glass as he picked out his words and fashioned them into a threat.

"Rachel was involved with a man. This was maybe eight months, a year ago."

My ears grew suddenly full with the thunder of my heart, beating a tattoo in the hollow of my throat. I searched for words between the echoes.

"She was engaged to this man," the mayor said. "Thing is, there were some problems."

A small black folder materialized from a seat pocket by the mayor's feet.

"Take a look at this, Kelly. Between me and you."

I ran a hand across the folder but didn't open it.

"Man's name is Sean Coyle," the mayor said. "Irish fuck

from Indiana. Feds swept him up last month in a sting. Seems the guy's been buying up flophouses in Cicero and Berwyn for a dime on a dollar, burning them out, and collecting on the insurance."

Wilson flicked his fingers toward the folder. "It's all in there. Three or four dummy companies, couple of adjusters on the take. Guy even hired muscle to make sure none of the buyers got cold feet once he made his 'offer.'"

"Let me guess," I said, my voice tight and small. "Coyle was doing all this while he was involved with Rachel."

The mayor nodded again toward the folder. "Coyle might have dropped her name in a couple of spots, but it doesn't seem like she knew about any of this or was personally involved. We're all hoping it stays that way. Feds are going to keep Coyle's name out of the press. In return, he's giving them the rest of it."

"The rest of it?"

"The muscle Coyle used came from Vinny DeLuca."

"So the feds think Coyle's operation was being run by the Outfit?"

Wilson shook his head. "Who can tell? But you know how it goes. Feds hear DeLuca, they want to take a look. Anyway, Coyle gets his deal and it all stays quiet."

"Especially for the judge," I said.

Wilson offered up a gaze that was prairie flat and just as interesting. "Just thought you'd want to know, Kelly."

He didn't need to tell me the rest. I was shaking the Wilson family tree, looking for connections to a fire that burned Chicago to the ground. If I somehow succeeded, somehow hurt the mayor or his own, the folder I held in my hands would find its way to someone like Fred Jacobs. And Rachel Swenson's career on the bench would be over. I thought about the toll it might take on her personally. That seemed even worse.

"Thanks for the update, Mr. Mayor."

"Not a problem. Like I said at the office, I like you. Want to keep you and your friends happy. Safe."

I held up the folder. "Can I keep this?"

Wilson waved a hand. "Take it. That's why I brought it here."

"That it?"

"That's it. Glad we found some time to chat."

The mayor offered two fingers' worth of handshake. I stepped out of the car and watched it slip from the curb. Then I took the folder back into Joe's, ordered another beer, and thought things through. I didn't like being on a hook with the Fifth Floor, even less when that hook had Rachel Swenson's name on it. I drank some more beer and was about to get angry when my cell phone rang. I looked at the caller ID and then my watch. It was a little after eleven.

"Hello?"

"Mr. Kelly, it's me."

"Taylor?"

"You need to come. Right now."

"Where are you?"

"You need to come now."

"Where's your mom?"

"She's here."

"Put her on the phone."

"I can't, Mr. Kelly. Please."

"Tell me where you are."

Taylor did. I told her to stay there. Then I drank off the rest of my beer and headed out into the night.

CHAPTER 32

Three blocks removed from the house Johnny and Janet Woods called home was a building site. I pulled up a little before midnight. The thunder was close now, and constant. Dark rain moved across the lot in cold, drenching sheets. I buttoned my coat and ducked under a couple of sawhorses that were supposed to keep the public on the sidewalk.

The site was crisscrossed with patterns of light from the street. I skirted a big hole in the middle of the lot. Bullets of rain peppered the foot or so of water that sat in the bottom. I walked to the back of the lot, to a one-story wooden building waiting for sweet release from the wrecking ball. The abandoned shack sat on wooden posts with a front porch and no front door. Underneath the porch was a crawl space, about five feet high with dirt for a floor. Taylor met me at the entrance. Her hair hung about her face and her cheeks were streaked with mud. She didn't try to hug me. Didn't try to talk. She just took my hand.

I ducked my head and went under the house. Janet Woods was laid up in the back. It looked like he'd been at her with a piece of steel.

"He hit you with something this time. Something more than his fists."

Her eyes followed mine. A slight nod.

"Okay," I said. "Can you move?"

No response. I opened the coat Taylor had wrapped her mom in. Underneath was a bathrobe and flannel nightgown, soaked wet with mud and ripped in a few spots. I leaned close and listened to her breathing. Didn't sound good. Then I noticed the spots of blood. Bright red stuff. The kind that came straight from inside.

"Have you been spitting up blood?"

A nod.

"He hit you in the chest or the sides?"

Another nod. I leaned back into the night and took stock. I wasn't a doctor, but I knew enough to know my client might die while I figured out what to do.

"Okay, Janet. I think you have some cracked ribs. Maybe something broken inside too. Not sure what, but that's where the blood is coming from."

She tried to open her eyes but seemed tired and closed them again. I let her drift and kept talking.

"I'm going to get an ambulance. Get you to a hospital."

She was shaking her head no, eyes still closed. I ignored her.

"Have to, Janet. We'll be discreet. No press. No charges filed. Just the hospital. Get you fixed up and then we'll figure it all out. Okay?"

Her mouth curved into a soft smile. I moved a piece of hair off her forehead.

"Don't worry about it. Just rest easy while I make a call."

I walked out from under the porch. The wind had picked up, lifting the rain almost horizontal. I huddled against the side of the building and punched in Dan Masters' number. The detective seemed to know a little bit about Johnny Woods, his wife, and the history between them. I figured he might help. Even better, he might be discreet. We talked for a minute or so. Then I headed back toward the crawl space.

"Is she going to live?"

It was Taylor, stepping out from the shadows behind the house.

"She'll live. We just have to get her to a hospital. I called a friend. Someone you can trust."

The girl moved toward the porch and a little shelter. She sat down on the steps and shivered. I sat down beside her.

"What happened, Taylor?"

"What do you think happened? Exactly what I said. He came home, late and drunk. I was asleep and heard the noise downstairs. She must have decided to have it out. Or something."

I thought of my last conversation with Janet. Her plan for dealing with Johnny Woods.

"By the time I got downstairs," Taylor said, "he was already gone. She was on the floor. I thought she was dead."

"And you took her here?"

"I had to get her out. So, yeah, I come here sometimes. Smoke cigarettes. Stupid stuff like that."

Taylor hugged her knees to her chest and dropped her forehead. "I thought she was dead, Mr. Kelly. I swear she was dead."

"She's gonna be okay, Taylor. But you have to stay with her tonight. You understand?"

The girl stared at the wooden angle of steps walking away from her and nodded. "Okay. But we have to do something."

"We will."

"We have to. Now. Tonight."

I could hear the flicker of a siren and see the red shadows of an ambulance converging on the lot. Masters hadn't wasted any time.

"You think your step-dad's at home?" I said.

Taylor's eyes jumped in her head. From me to the approaching shadows, her face caught in a contour of sharp and angled light.

"If he's not there, he will be. Sooner or later."

I stood up. The girl remained seated.

"All right, Taylor. You stay with your mom. Don't mention me to anyone. I was never here. Okay?"

"Okay."

I slipped behind the house, toward the back of the building site. Taylor's voice surged from the darkness.

"Mr. Kelly?"

I stopped. The girl crept close. A final time.

"Are you going to kill him?"

I felt the gun on my hip, the cold rain in my mouth, lashing against the side of the old house. Beyond that were voices, washing in from the front of the lot, and a spray of flashlights heading our way.

"Go help your mom, Taylor. Leave the rest to me."

And then I left the young girl and her mother. Hoping they would survive the night. Hoping I would as well.

CHAPTER 33

I looked at the revolver in my hand, then down and into an expanse of palate, gums, and teeth that was the inside of Johnny Woods' mouth. He was sitting in his kitchen, on a wooden captain's chair, legs splayed and arms hanging to either side. His mouth was wide open to the ceiling and his eyes saw nothing as a fan blew the breeze around his head. He had three small holes, two in the chest and one at the base of the throat. Woods' bowels had let loose after he was shot, and his pants were soiled along the inner leg. Johnny didn't seem to care. When death came, it was all business, with neither the time nor the patience for vanity.

I pressed my fingers to the short barrel of the gun and felt a bit of warmth as it leeched from the blue steel. I tried, but could sense no human soul as it left the room. No feeling of Johnny Woods, passing into memory, passing into dust. Maybe if he was a better person—maybe if I cared—it might be different. Maybe not. Right now, the city fixer and wife beater was an inert bag of blood and guts. Decomposing as I sat there. And, if I didn't get moving, my ticket to a life behind bars.

That last fact got my attention. That and the soft sound I heard in the distance. Police sirens. Fading, then returning. Now a bit louder. A neighbor must have heard the shots. I looked at the snub-nosed Smith and Wesson. That's how it falls sometimes. I pocketed the gun and made my way through the house. The red fog inside my head was slowly beginning to lift. I could hear the cruisers clearly now. Sounded like more than one. They'd set up out front and seal off the back. I didn't hurry, but I didn't dawdle. Instead, I was just about deliberate as I jumped over the fence and into the alley behind the Woodses' house. I wondered where Janet was with her kid. I saw a curtain twitch at the window to my left. Fucking neighbors. I turned up the collar on my coat, slipped over one fence, then another, threading my way through backyards, heading away from the corpse.

I surfaced a half mile away, on the 5900 block of North Kilpatrick. I walked lightly down the street. My car was parked on Ionia, a block or so from the body. I hoped the cops didn't canvass the area and take down tag numbers. It would be a big job for the uniforms. Then again, the dead guy did work for the mayor.

I'd taken twenty-five good steps down Kilpatrick when I knew things weren't going to work out just so.

"Excuse me, sir."

The voice came from my left. It belonged to a cop. He stepped out from the shadow of a brick three-flat, gun drawn and at his side. I could hear his partner, moving in the yard behind me. He'd have his gun out and up, trained on my left ear. That's where I would aim and I wouldn't be messing either.

"Yes, sir," I said.

"Where're you coming from, sir?"

I figured the neighbors had gotten a look at me. Described a man in a dark overcoat, wearing gloves with a black knit hat. Couldn't be too many of those in the neighborhood. Especially carrying a recently fired Smith and Wesson revolver. One that would happen to match the slugs pulled from a corpse two blocks north. I lifted my hands and turned, slowly, toward the man in blue.

"There's a gun in my coat pocket, right side. Another on my hip."

I felt his partner grab me from behind. Felt the steel cuff slip around one wrist, then the second. The snub nose was taken from my pocket. The two cops looked at it, looked at me. One of them slipped it into a clear plastic bag. The other took the nine millimeter off my belt and began reading me my rights. Like I said, sometimes things don't always fall just right.

CHAPTER 34

I was alone in my cell. Not quite alone. The snub nose was there. At least, in my mind. Last time I saw it was on a bookshelf in my office. Behind a copy of the *Iliad*. That bothered me. More than anything had bothered me in a long while.

A buzzer rang and my cell door slid open. Three-hundred-plus pounds of black man in an orange jumpsuit creaked into the bunk below me without a word. The cell door slammed shut and we were alone. I could hear voices from somewhere down the hall, harsh angry sounds, the buzz of violence humming just underneath. A metallic lock turned over and a second door slammed somewhere close. Then it was quiet again. I stared at chunks of grayish plaster curling off the ceiling and wondered how much of it was asbestos. A long slow bout with cancer, however, was the least of my worries.

"White meat."

The voice came from the depths below. It was a voice without malice, without anger. Just a lethal sort of boredom.

"Name's Kelly," I said and tried to slow down time as much as I could. If I had to fight, I'd fight. That was how it went inside. Unless you preferred a shank in the stomach, that is.

"Kelly, huh. Heard them guards talking 'bout you. Said you

was a cop. Done up for murder. I'm thinking you ain't Kelly no more, boy. Just white meat."

My new friend laughed and shifted his body weight in the bed below. I swung off my bunk, boots first, and caught him flush with a size ten in the side of the head. The connection felt good. His head slammed back against the iron post of the bed frame. That felt even better. I dragged him by the shirt, out of the bunk, and onto the floor. He was heavy and out of shape. He was also most likely a killer, locked up with me in a space eight feet long by five feet wide. Best not to take any chances. Before he could get to his feet, I kicked him again, twice more, solid shots to the back of the head. He was groggy now but still with it. I ripped his shirt over his face so he couldn't bite me. He got one hand around my windpipe and began to squeeze. I wrestled him over to the toilet, broke his grip, and drove his head to the bottom of the metal bowl. He came up for air after about ten seconds, his head slipping free of the shirt. I waited for him to say *enough* but he wasn't saying anything. Just blowing air and trying to grab at me. I was behind him now and that wasn't going to happen. The key was to keep things moving. Keep him off balance. No time to think of a way to get the advantage. I moved him off the toilet and back to the bed. I'd stripped off my pillowcase before he'd even entered the cell. Now I whipped it tight around his neck and began to squeeze from behind. His body was still on the floor, his face and neck soaked and lying on the side of the lower berth. We'd been at it less than thirty seconds and had barely made a sound. I thought I had another fifteen to twenty seconds left in me. Either he'd be dead, I'd be dead, or we'd come to an understanding. I leaned close to my cellie's ear.

"You want to fuck with me? That what you want?"

I twisted the linen tighter around his neck and looked for the results in his face. The mouth was open now. Eyes bulged white and red in their sockets. I could see his chest, full of air that had nowhere to go, and his tongue, playing between a set of yellow teeth and silver fillings. I leaned in again.

"We got a problem, I'll finish this right here. Like you said, I'm done for murder anyhow. Up to you, friend."

I waited. My cellmate gave the slightest nod of his head. I loosened my hold on the pillowcase and he slammed forward into the bed. Taking in great reaches of air, spitting up some blood.

"Fuck the matter with you?" he gasped.

I kicked back up onto my bed. Wary but willing to believe it was finished.

"What's your name?" I said.

"Marcus."

"Well fuck off, Marcus. I ain't nobody's meat. And if I have to kill a motherfucker like you to prove it, that's okay too."

Marcus was leaning forward on his bunk now, rubbing his neck, grabbing some more air and giving me a look of proper disdain.

"If I want you cut, white meat. You get cut."

"You think so?"

"I do. Now stash all the fucking Rambo shit. I don't want to fight you. Just seeing if you was going to be a bitch in here or what."

"Now you know."

"Okay, now I know."

"Great, Marcus. Now leave me the fuck alone."

"You a grouchy ass," Marcus said and spit some more blood onto the cement floor. Then he eased back down in his bunk. I did the same. Marcus, however, couldn't leave it alone.

"You really a cop?"

"Not anymore."

"Who you kill?"

"Shut up, Marcus."

"Was it a bitch? I killed a bitch of mine on the South Side a while back. Shit, ten years ago now. Screwing my brother, you can believe that. Not what I'm in here for though. Fucking cops too dumb for that."

The buzzer rang and a skinny white guard came up. He carried a badge, a nightstick, and a bad complexion. He looked at me, looked at Marcus, and looked at some of Marcus' blood on the floor.

"Fuck's been going on here," he said and poked my cellie with his nightstick. Marcus rolled over and faced the wall. The guard looked up at me.

"What happened here?"

"Slipped and fell," I said.

The guard snorted. "Come on. Detectives want to talk with you."

We walked down a short hallway and into a small holding room. Dan Masters was already there, thumbing through some paperwork.

"Uncuff him."

Masters spoke without looking up. The guard did as he was told and left. I sat down and waited. After a minute or so, Masters restacked his papers and pushed them across the table. I took a look. The top sheet was a release order with my name on it.

"What happened to you?" Masters was looking at five fingers' worth of bruises on my neck.

"Cook County's Welcome Wagon."

The detective shook his head. "That didn't take long. You all right?"

"I'm fine." I picked up the release order. "Tell me about this."

"You're out."

"How do you figure?"

"Appears Evidence lost the murder weapon during processing."

"Convenient."

Masters raised his chin as if I'd asked him to fight. "No murder weapon, no case. In fact, the prosecutor's not even sure there was ever a gun to lose."

"Damn, by this afternoon Johnny Woods will have died from a massive stroke."

The detective didn't find me very funny. "If I were you, I'd shut up and run with it."

Masters looked like he wanted to say more. Instead, he stood up and left. I sat at the table and read through the paperwork. It was all there. A guard took me to the front. Fifteen minutes later, I was processed and back on the street, wondering what in the hell just happened.

CHAPTER 35

I walked out of the Cook County lockup a little after three in the afternoon. A Silver Audi pulled up near the corner of Twenty-sixth and California. Rachel Swenson was behind the wheel. I got in.

"They told me you wanted to post bond," I said. "Thanks."

"That's okay."

"You're a judge. That took some guts."

Rachel twitched her lips once and pushed the car into drive. We moved forward, slowly at first, and then with some purpose.

"You at least going to ask me?" I said.

Rachel flicked on the wipers at the first spattering of rain on her windshield. "Ask you what?"

"If I killed him?"

She moved her eyes back into the weather. "Sounds like he deserved it."

"You think I shot him?" I said.

"As you said, I'm a federal magistrate, Michael. Probably shouldn't be venturing an opinion on that."

"I'm not saying I couldn't have done it."

I felt the car skid on the wet track. Then the judge straightened it out.

"Just that you could have?" she said.

"Just that I could have. That's exactly right."

Rachel merged onto the Stevenson Expressway and accelerated smoothly past seventy miles an hour. The rain was steady now, spiraling down in circles, tap dancing on the roof of Rachel's car and roaring under the tires.

"Janet Woods was released from the hospital early this morning," Rachel said.

"Nothing serious?"

"Depends on who you are and what you consider serious."

She hit the accelerator. The Audi leaped forward, flashing onto the Dan Ryan, then the Kennedy.

"How does your gun disappear from Evidence, Michael?"

"I'm gonna find out right now."

The judge flicked another look my way. "Do that. Because if that gun turns up again, you're looking at murder one."

"I know."

We cruised for a bit, nothing but the storm to keep us company.

"You can get off here," I said.

Rachel slid off the expressway at Fullerton and pulled to the curb near the corner of Halsted and Diversey. We sat and listened to the thump of the rain all around us.

"I need to tell you something," she said, turning halfway to look at me.

"What's that?"

"Sometimes you scare me."

"Sometimes I scare myself."

"I'm serious. You realize someone wanted you to take a very bad fall?"

"Yes."

"And someone else broke a lot of laws to help you avoid the fall?"

"Yes."

"And you don't have any idea why?"

"Like I said, I'm close to some answers."

She plucked at my shoulder with her fingers. "There are limits to what I can do, Michael. To what I will do. You understand that?"

"I understand it. The question is do you?"

"Excuse me?"

"I can read people, Rachel. Pretty damn well, in fact. You're the kind who sticks it out for a friend. No matter what. That's a rare thing. And a wonderful thing. But it can also be dangerous."

Rachel's face cracked into a thin smile. "Don't want another woman on your conscience?"

"That's not it."

"Then what is it?"

I wasn't going to tell her about the mayor. Or the ugly truth about her old boyfriend. But I felt the cold touch of fear for her all the same. It was the worst part of caring about someone. The worst part and, of course, the very best.

"We can't talk about this right now," I said. She nodded, but didn't pretend to understand. I gave her a hug and slipped out of the car. The beautiful judge disappeared into traffic; the future between us simply left to drift.

On Halsted Street, the rain had reduced itself to a drizzle. I looked up and across the road, at the front door of the Hidden Shamrock. All things considered, a sight for sore eyes. I went inside and ordered a pint. Then I sipped and waited. For my answers to start walking through the door.

CHAPTER 36

Ihad taken my pint down a good four inches by the time Dan Masters poked his head into the Shamrock. I was seated at a table by the window and saw him right away, but I waited until he got close before looking up.

"Detective, thanks for meeting me."

Masters chuckled and took a seat. "Fucking Kelly. Guess this might as well happen now. You want to know how it is you got out?"

"I know how I got out, Detective. I want to know why."

"Let's just say I was returning a favor."

"I think you made a mistake."

Masters lifted a finger for the waitress. The detective ordered a Bud and a shot of Jim Beam. Then he got himself comfortable in the chair across from me. I could hear the creak of the gun on his belt and wondered how he'd take it when I told him.

"You're a free man, Kelly. Not everyone likes it. I'll give you that."

Masters tipped up the long neck and let the better half of the bottle drain south.

"When did the thing start with Janet Woods?" I said.

Masters put the bottle down quietly and rubbed the back of his teeth over his lips.

"How did you know about that?"

I didn't know anything about Masters and my client. But I could guess. "Why else would you want to help me by making the murder weapon disappear?"

"You're a friend."

"Cut the bullshit, Dan."

Masters waved a hand my way. "All right. All right. So we started up a little something a few months back. Maybe more than a little something. Anyway, Janet told me you and her had some history too. So you did what you did. For my money, Johnny Woods deserved the bullet. Then I did what I did. Now we leave it. You finish up your drink and go on home."

"I didn't do anything for Janet," I said. "And I didn't kill Johnny Woods."

A seam of flesh twitched under the detective's left eye. "I don't believe it."

"What did you do with the gun?" I said.

"Why?"

"What did you do with it, Dan?"

"Left it with Janet this morning. She was going to dump it for me. For you."

I wasn't so sure I needed the help Janet was offering, but held my peace.

"I need the gun, Dan. And I need to see Janet and the girl."

Masters took a sip of Beam and another slug of beer. "Last I checked, Janet Woods was your client. You need to see her, give her a call."

"I don't think it's going to be that easy, Dan. Does she know I'm out yet?"

A shake of the head.

"Tell her. Then tell her I want to sit down and talk."

"About what?"

"I'll explain it when we all sit down. Just tell her I need to talk."

Masters flexed his shoulders and finished his whiskey. The detective sensed deeper waters in our conversation. Like any cop, he wanted to steer clear. Until he knew exactly how deep.

"Stay on your cell. I'll talk to her tonight and see what's up." Masters got up to go and stopped. Then he sat back down, pulled out an item from inside his overcoat, and put it on the table.

"Almost forgot. One more thing you might be interested in."

The cover was faded, the corners rounded and white with wear and tear. I opened up the *Sheehan's* and saw a red 4 stamped inside.

"Where'd you get this?"

"Taylor. Told me to give it to you if I saw you in jail."

There was an envelope tucked inside the book. My name was written on it. The script was that of a young girl, a lot of rounded letters, and she used circles instead of dots for her *i*'s.

The note inside the envelope, like the girl herself, was anything but young.

Kelly,

I hate and I love. So much to say there and so little time to say it. I hated my stepfather and now he's dead. Thank you for that. I loved the way you care about my mom. And tried to help us. I thought you might want to have this book as a keepsake. Not sure what it means. But it meant an awful lot to Johnny.

Till I see you,
Taylor

I read the note once, then again. Trying to see the spider inside the web. Hoping to find it before it found me. Then I closed up the *Sheehan's* and drummed my fingers across the cover.

"Did Taylor tell you how she got the book?"

"Says her step-dad gave it to her. He must have taken it from the house on Hudson. Probably figured it would be safe with Taylor."

"In case the mayor came calling?"

Masters smiled. "I'm guessing Johnny Woods liked his insurance."

"Didn't work too well for him last night," I said.

"Yeah. Well, I don't know how the book ties in, but if there's hell to be raised, I'm sure you'll do it. Just cut Rodriguez in for the glory if you can."

"Sure."

The detective threw a few dollars on the table and got up a second time.

"Masters . . ."

The cop rocked a bit in his heels and jingled a few coins in his pocket.

"I didn't kill Johnny," I said. "Still not sure who did."

"So tread lightly?"

"Exactly."

"Not a problem, Kelly. There's one thing, however, you need to understand."

"What's that?"

The cop leaned close. Like only a cop can. "Janet loves me. They both do. And that counts for a lot these days."

Before I could say anything more, Dan Masters turned and left. I ordered another pint and opened up the *Sheehan's* Taylor had wanted me to have. It didn't seem any different from the copy I'd looked through at the historical society. That was before I took a closer look at the binding—and found the book within the book.

CHAPTER 37

I headed home and slept in my own bed. I woke up about ten p.m. It was quiet in my apartment. Nothing but the tick of the clock and the muffled sounds of traffic from the street below. I thought about my bunkmate in Cook County, how close I had come to a permanent berth there. Not a good thing to think about, so I stopped. Then I thought about the *Sheehan's* and the document I had prized out of its binding. Both were now sitting in front of me, looking up at me, asking what I planned to do next. I picked up the document and felt its weight. Read through it for the fifth or sixth time, drinking in each word, then rubbing my thumb lightly along the faded print.

After a while, I folded up the document and put it under lock and key. Then I made a pot of coffee and pulled out the prints Fred Jacobs had sent me a night earlier. Laid them on the table beside the *Sheehan's*. I picked up the phone. Rodriguez answered on the first ring.

"You just sit by the phone all night?"

"Heard you were out, Kelly."

"There was a guy I shared a cell with," I said. "First name is Marcus."

"He's in Cook County hospital. Three broken ribs and a busted spleen. Nice work."

"He's a killer. You want the case?"

Rodriguez did, so I gave him the details.

"He told you he killed this woman in 1998?" the detective said.

"Somewhere around there. I got the idea she was an old girl-friend. You should be able to find her in the cold files. When you do, tell Marcus it was courtesy of me."

"You guys really got along, huh?"

"Best of pals. If you can, drop the tip to Fred Jacobs before you go public. I owe him."

"Okay. What else you got for me?"

"Are we still working together?"

"Depends. Did you kill Woods?"

"What do you think?"

"I think no. Course, doesn't help that you were playing around with the dead guy's wife."

"You heard that too, huh?"

"Half of Johnny Woods' block saw you two. Duking it out at six in the morning."

"It's not what you think."

"I told you. I don't believe you killed him. Let's leave it at that."

"I need a favor."

The detective paused. "Is it about Dan Masters?"

"What do you know about Dan?" I said.

"I know enough. What I don't know is why."

Rodriguez knew Masters had pulled the gun that killed Johnny Woods out of Evidence. I wasn't sure how. But I wasn't surprised either.

"The whys might have to wait," I said. "Maybe a day or so."

"Have you talked to Masters?"

"This afternoon. I'm waiting on a call back right now."

Rodriguez hesitated, but not as long as you might think. "What is it you need?" he said.

"Remember the lift you took off my window?"

"The night of the break-in?"

"Yeah. I have a set of prints I need you to run it against."

"The print from your flat was a partial. Not enough points to bring into court."

"This isn't about court, Vince."

Rodriguez chewed on that for a while. "Think I'm going to have to know a little bit more."

So I told him. A little bit more. Then I e-mailed him the set of prints Jacobs had sent me, along with a photo of the person they belonged to. After that I headed back to bed. Dan Masters hadn't called back to set up my meeting with Janet. I hadn't expected him to.

CHAPTER 38

I got in my car on Monday morning and accelerated onto Lake Shore Drive, heading south through traffic. You'd never know it by looking around, but it was against the law in Chicago to use a cell while you were driving. And with good reason. I almost hit an SUV or three as I flipped open my phone and wrestled a business card out of my wallet. It was red with yellow stars.

Hubert Russell's machine picked up, but he cut in before I could leave a message.

"Hello?"

"Hubert."

"I don't know this number."

"It's Michael Kelly. The guy who asked to see the Chicago Fire records."

"Mr. Kelly. Sorry, I don't get a lot of calls I don't recognize. What's up?"

"I got a computer question for you."

"Go ahead."

"It's actually more like a hacking question."

"Even better."

"You told me there wasn't a computer made you couldn't crack."

"That's right."

"How'd you like to prove it?"

There was only a slight pause before Hubert came back over the line.

"I assume this is illegal."

"You assume correctly," I said. "It's also for a good cause."

"Why don't you explain the cause and why it's so good."

So I did. Hubert told me he could help. Even better, he was willing.

"How soon could we do it?" I said.

"I got the software right here. Just need to load it up and we're good to go."

"That easy?"

"Scary as it sounds, yes."

"You around today?"

"Sure, I'm around."

I pulled up in front of the Chicago Historical Society. My watch had just pushed past nine.

"Hang tight, Hubert. I'll call you back."

CHAPTER 39

Teen was standing by the front desk, looking for someone to grin at. She was wearing a dark brown long-sleeve sweater, tan chinos, and brown shoes with large gold buckles.

"The man from the *Tribune*." She offered a sweaty palm and I took it. "How are you, Mr. Kelly? You know, I missed your article."

"Actually, it's not quite ready yet."

"Oh. Anything I can help you with?"

I nodded and moved her gently off the main lobby. "Actually, there is something you can do."

A group of seniors drifted by us and into the gift shop. The volunteer automatically smiled at them and then transferred her giddiness back my way.

"How can I help?"

I took out a photo and put it facedown in front of the volunteer. Along with six other pictures.

"The guy who came in to see the *Sheehan's* a couple of weeks back."

"Yes?"

"When I asked you what he looked like, you told me he was dangerous looking."

Teen lifted her eyes to the ceiling, anxiously looking for the answer to a question I had yet to pose.

"Dangerous looking. Yes, he was."

"Was the man black, Teen?"

She brightened and nodded. "Actually, he was."

Then she frowned. "You don't think I called him dangerous because he was black, do you? That's just not possible. Last year, a black couple moved into the neighborhood, just a block or so from where I live. I see them every week at the Sunset Foods. Lovely people, although I've never actually spoken to them. There are lots of people I don't speak to in the supermarket."

"You see the guy here?"

I flipped over the seven photos. Teen pointed at my guy without missing a beat.

"That's him."

"No doubt?"

"No doubt. See how big he is?"

"Dangerous looking."

"Yes, dangerous looking. Who is he?"

"I'll tell you later. For right now, no questions."

Teen bobbed her head again. Still panting lightly. Still eager.

"The second thing we need to talk about involves your curator," I said.

"Mr. Randolph?"

"Yes."

Teen pressed her lips into a thin line. The first bit of caution crept into our relationship. Not what I needed.

"He's not in this morning," the volunteer said. "He teaches a class at Northwestern."

"I know. Is there somewhere private we can go?"

Teen took me to a small room with beige walls, a table and chairs, a Mr. Coffee, and some vending machines.

"We should be okay in here," she said, and sat down. I followed suit.

"Now what is it, exactly, that you need?"

"Josiah Randolph's diary," I said. "You know about that?"

"Of course. I work on the Omnibus system. Keeps track of all our primary source materials. Would you like to see a demonstration?"

"No."

I gave my response a little punch. Teen jumped in her seat.

"Oh."

"Mr. Randolph showed me Josiah's diary the first time I was here," I said.

"He's awfully proud of his ancestor. Do you know Josiah almost lost his life trying to save Lincoln's Emancipation Proclamation?"

"I'm happy for him. Thing is, I don't think Randolph showed me the whole diary."

Teen shifted in her neatly laundered chinos and ducked my eyes. Exactly what I was hoping for.

"Teen, how long you been working here?"

"Going on sixteen years."

"As a volunteer?"

"Yes."

"Excuse the expression, Teen, but do you like getting treated like the shit off Lawrence Randolph's shoes?"

"Pardon?"

"I saw enough, Teen. You're here to contribute, consult, be part of the team. Not go get coffee for an academic lightweight. The emperor lost his clothes a long time ago. Isn't it time someone let him know?"

I waited. Teen fidgeted. Looked at the door to the break room, a door I had had the good sense to shut before we sat down. Then Teen looked back at me. I could see the girl. First in her class at high school. College, a given. A woman of letters. Except it was 1962. Her parents didn't approve of women going to college. What, really, was the point? So Teen settled down, settled in. Just settled. Married the architect, who, at the time, was just out of school, a friend of the family, and lived down the block. Three kids and some four decades later, it was a good life. A respectable life. But she had more to offer. Much more than a gofer for Lawrence Randolph. Here was her chance. All I had to do was wait.

"What is it you want, Mr. Kelly?"

"I want you to step out, Teen. Help me find the rest of the diary. Find out why primary source materials are being sanitized by your curator. Find out what kind of game Lawrence Randolph is running."

"He's a real prick, you know."

I smiled and moved closer. I thought she'd be willing. I didn't realize how much so.

"I know all about Josiah's diary," Teen said. "Every year, we run internal audits of all our materials. Part of Omnibus. You want to see?"

"No. Tell me about the diary."

She started up again. Then stopped. Gave me a look she probably figured to be crafty.

"Will I get my name in the papers?"

"You want your name in the papers?"

"Of course."

"Consider it done. Now, what about the diary?"

"Okay. Each year I help to run an internal audit. It's done on all the full-time staff, including Mr. Randolph. It's done without their consent and without their knowledge."

Teen's eyes lit up as she dug into the details. "I noticed the discrepancy three years ago. In the society archives, we have more than a hundred thousand primary source documents. More than twenty million pages of material. As I cross-referenced the Omnibus catalogs, I noticed one entry for Josiah Randolph's diary under 'Chicago Fire.' Then I noticed a second entry titled 'Diary Fragments' and filed under 'Miscellaneous.'"

"'Miscellaneous,' huh?"

"Yes, 'Miscellaneous.' I tracked down the woman who had made the entry into Omnibus. Lovely girl. She's a senior now at Northwestern."

"Where did she find her 'Fragments'?"

"Actually, it's a funny story."

"Amuse me."

"As I said, she was just a college kid. Didn't know any better. So she sits down at Mr. Randolph's desk. It was a day like this."

"He was out of the office."

"Yes. She opens up his desk and begins to sort through his personal papers."

"Unheard of."

"Slightly. Anyway, she found two keys in one of the top drawers. The first unlocked the bottom drawer of the curator's desk. The second opened a strongbox she found inside."

"The miscellaneous fragments?"

"She told me they were in the box. She noted their existence, locked up the box, and returned the keys to the curator's top drawer. Then she made a notation about the materials in Omnibus."

"That's it?"

"What else would you expect?"

"What did the fragments say?"

"I have no idea."

"She didn't read them?"

"The purpose of an Omnibus audit is to catalog, not evaluate. She noted the number of pages, got a general sense of what she was looking at, and moved on."

"What about the discrepancy?"

"What about it?"

"Why didn't anyone follow up?"

"Follow up how?"

"Ask Randolph what the fragments were? Why he kept them under lock and key in his desk? How they were different from the rest of the diary he'd made available to the public?"

"This is not an inquisition, Mr. Kelly. Omnibus is designed to catalog."

"I know. Catalog. Not evaluate."

Teen smiled. "That's correct."

"So no one ever followed up with Randolph?"

"I doubt anyone even knows about the Omnibus notations except for myself and the young girl from Northwestern."

"Randolph doesn't know?"

"Certainly not. He'd blow his stack if he knew anyone was poking around his personal papers."

"Let's go," I said, and stood up. Teen got up with me.

"Where are we going?"

"To Randolph's office."

"To do what?"

"Poke around his personal papers."

"You sure that's a good idea?"

"Not really. But it might be."

My volunteer thought about it. Then she led the way out of

the break room and up the front stairs. She nodded and smiled at a half-dozen staff members we passed along the way. Finally she stopped at the closed door to Lawrence Randolph's empty office. Inside was the price of admission. To life beyond the front desk and a daily set of marching orders. To getting past men who nourished their egos on the carcasses of those who were polite enough to serve. To a seat at the table—some sort of table—any sort of table. It was a price the volunteer was apparently willing to pay. Perhaps even eager. Teen gave me a final look, took a deep breath, and pushed the door open. A half hour later, I had what I needed. I sat Teen down, told her who I was and what I suspected. At least, some of it. Then I called Hubert.

CHAPTER 40

S o show me how this works."

Hubert Russell met me at the Starbucks on North and Wells, two blocks removed from the historical society. It was a little past noon. I had a black coffee and my laptop open. Hubert sipped at a vanilla skim latte and was at the wheel.

"Pretty simple," Hubert said. "I've loaded my program onto your hard drive. Now I click on the icon and put it into active mode."

Hubert moved the cursor over a skull and crossbones blinking on my screen.

"Nice icon, Hubert."

The kid smiled. My Mac began to whir, then whine.

"Warming up," Hubert said.

We got a soft beep. My screen went black for a moment and then re-formed with a single bar graph fluctuating on-screen.

"See that graph?"

"I do."

"That represents signal strength. Means there is one person in range of us who is using a WiFi connection."

I looked across the mostly empty coffee shop at Teen. She waved and continued to tap away at her laptop.

"Well, we know who that is."

"That's right," Hubert said. "Now if I click on the graph, watch what happens."

Hubert clicked. Bits of information began to fly across the screen.

"As we speak, your computer is sucking Teen's dry. Copying all her files, programs, passwords, e-mails. Everything."

"And she doesn't even know it," I said.

"Look at her."

I did. Teen waved again and smiled. I motioned for her to come over. She shut down her laptop and the graph disappeared on my screen.

"How much of her hard drive did you get?" I said.

Hubert began to open up files taken off Teen's computer.

"Actually, we got all of it. With this program the poach usually takes less than twenty seconds. See, what happens is there's a flaw in the router that lets you go WiFi. I drop in a decoy and trick the computer into thinking it's talking to itself. When really—"

I held up a hand.

"Enough, Hubert. I believe."

I wanted to pat him on the head but thought better of it. Instead, I checked my watch as Teen drew up a chair.

"What time does he come in?" I said.

"He's in here just about every day around one," Teen said. "Says he likes to get some 'alone time' out of the office."

"Always brings his laptop?"

Teen nodded.

"Okay. Teen, you and I are out of here. Hubert, you sit tight and wait for our boy. You got the picture I gave you?"

Hubert showed it to me.

"Good. When he fires up his laptop and jumps online, you take it all."

"No problem."

The kid from Land Records winked. Teen giggled. Then the volunteer and I walked out of the Starbucks and down Wells Street. I stopped at the Up Down Tobacco Shop and bought a couple of Montecristos. Then we moved over to Topo Gigio's and had a beautiful lunch. Hubert joined us an hour later for tiramisu. As did the entire contents of Lawrence Randolph's laptop.

CHAPTER 41

Rachel Swenson and Vince Rodriguez agreed to meet me at my office. It was a little after eight p.m. Neither was entirely sure why they were there. But they both showed up and that was enough for now.

"What is it that couldn't wait?" Rodriguez said.

"Take a look for yourself."

I threw the *Sheehan's* Masters had given me across the desk. Rodriguez took a look at the book while Rachel read Taylor's note. It had been two days, and no one had heard a thing from Dan Masters or Janet Woods.

"The binding's been sliced open." The detective ran his hand along the book's spine.

"You noticed that."

Rodriguez slanted his face up and across the room. "What did you take out of there?"

I couldn't tell them about that. Not yet, anyway. Still, I needed their help, which made matters difficult.

"Rachel, I need to ask you a favor. Actually, I'm going to need favors from both of you."

Rachel passed Taylor's note across to the detective, along with a look that told me it might be a long hard swim upstream.

"What do you need?" she said.

"You remember the prints I told you about? The ones I was going to compare to the break-in at my flat?"

Rachel nodded. I pulled out a sheet of paper and slipped it across my desk.

"The detective here ran them for me."

Rachel ignored the report. "Just tell me what it says, Michael."

"The partial has only six points of identification. All six matched a print on the set I sent over."

Rodriguez grunted from his hard-backed chair in the corner.

"I told you it doesn't matter," Rachel said. "The match means nothing. You need at least nine points for it to hold up in court."

I lifted a hand.

"Hear me out," I said. "Two weeks ago a man walked into the Chicago Historical Society. Asked a volunteer named Teen for a look at their *Sheehan's* first edition."

"How many people ask to see that book?" Rodriguez said.

"Exactly. Anyway, the volunteer is a nice lady. Do-gooder from the North Shore. Tells me this man was *dangerous looking*. Didn't think much of it at the time. Then I realized how the phrase translates out of white-upper-middle-class American speak."

"And *dangerous looking* means?" Rachel said.

"Black. I went back and double-checked with our volunteer. The guy was black and big."

"Let me guess," Rachel said. "Our suspect on the print happens to be black."

"And he has a history of breaking and entering. Not to mention violent assault."

"I assume you showed his photo to your volunteer friend?" Rodriguez said.

"Along with six others. Took her all of five seconds to pick him out."

I threw a picture across the desk. It was a news photo from Mitchell Kincaid's rally. Behind Kincaid and to his left was his head of security, an angry young man named James Bratton. Big and black—and the man who shot Rachel Swenson with a rubber bullet in the middle of the night.

"I saw Bratton on the news," I said. "At the Kincaid rally last week. Didn't register at first. Then it did. It was ten years ago. I was still a uniform. Arrested him for B and E and assault. He used a crowbar to crank open the first-floor window of an old lady's home on the West Side. Punched her once or twice and took some costume jewelry and cash. Less than a hundred bucks. He pled out and took six months. Records were sealed because he was only seventeen."

Rachel lifted an eyebrow and picked up the photo. "A juvie?"

"I told him already," Rodriguez said. "None of this is admissible. Especially not if his reporter pal lifted juvie prints out of the system."

I kept my eyes on Rachel, who kept her eyes on the photo. Then she looked up and spoke.

"Michael isn't thinking about the criminal end of this. Are you, Michael?"

"Are you?" I said.

"If Mitchell Kincaid's security chief broke into your apartment and shot me, his boss's political career is over before it ever got started. Is that what you think happened?"

I nodded, trying to fit as much regret into the gesture as humanly possible. "I think Bratton was after evidence that would have implicated the mayor's ancestor in a land grab that turned into the Chicago Fire. Johnny Woods was after the same thing. If Bratton got it, I imagine he would have leaked it to the press at the right time."

Rachel shot the picture across my desk with a flick of her fingernail.

"I don't believe it."

"I do," I said.

"You realize what this would do to Kincaid's campaign?"

"It would ruin him."

"Is that the goal here?" Rachel was leaning forward in her seat now, palms rubbing a shine across the wooden armrests.

"No."

"What is it you want, Michael?"

"I want you to approach Kincaid," I said. "Ask him to meet with me."

"Why?"

"Couple of reasons. First, you can do it privately. Discreetly. Second, I don't think Kincaid knew what his staff was up to."

"He didn't."

"For now, let's say I agree. That's why you approach him. Show him what I've got. Ask him to sit down with me."

"What are you going to do?" Rachel said. "Help him write his withdrawal speech?"

Rodriguez jumped in. "And what am I supposed to do? Break-in aside, Bratton might be our guy on the Bryant murder."

"He isn't."

"You don't know that."

I picked up the *Sheehan's* again. Here is where the trust came in. Either it would work, or I'd have to let it go and hope for the best. Where Chicago politics was concerned, that was usually a loser's bet.

"There's more to this than either of you know," I said. "Just give me another day or two. Let this thing play out, and we might be able to save Mitchell Kincaid's career." I glanced over at Rodriguez. "And catch our killer."

Rachel waited for the detective, who lifted his shoulders.

"I can play along, Your Honor. How about you?"

Rachel took another look at the *Sheehan's* and then back at me. "What was in the book, Michael?"

"Set it up with Kincaid," I said. "You'll find out then."

CHAPTER 42

Rachel agreed to make the call and left. I tried to give her a hug but got nothing more than a shoulder and the side of her face. Ah, sweet romance.

"The judge doesn't like being kept in the dark," Rodriguez said.

"Think so?"

The detective chuckled. "You must not keep much of a social life, Kelly. But, I guess that's your problem. Can you pull all this off?"

"There's a chance."

A bottle of Powers Irish surfaced from the depths of a drawer. Rodriguez poured himself a dose and drank it in a single go. Then he stood up and leaned his face across the desk. Rodriguez could be a big man when he wanted to be.

"What was in the book?" he said.

I tasted the edges of my whiskey and leaned back in my chair. I was looking for a bit of leverage. If not in the Powers, at least in the geography of the moment.

"Let me deal with Kincaid. Then we go after the rest of it."

"You sure his security chief's not our killer?"

I nodded.

"This involves the Fifth Floor, doesn't it?"

"How would you feel about that?" I said.

Rodriguez sat back down and turned his chair to look out the window. When he spoke, his voice came from somewhere down the street.

"Not fucking good, Kelly. Not good at all."

"If it goes bad, I'll take the weight."

A smile flickered at the corner of the detective's mouth. "Who the fuck made you the hero?" he said, reaching for the bottle without looking at it.

We both sat quiet. Drank and listened. For something beyond the sound of traffic. All we heard was our respective careers, and perhaps our lives, spiraling down the sewer hole that doubled as the feeding tube for Chicago politics and power.

"Now what about the other thing?" Rodriguez swung around in his chair and pulled close again.

"Johnny Woods' murder?" I said.

"There's that. And there's Dan Masters. He's taken off with Woods' wife, hasn't he?"

"He might be in over his head," I said.

"Masters can take care of himself," Rodriguez said. "Where do you think he is?"

"I don't know, but he'll surface soon enough."

"How can you be so sure?"

"Because the mom and daughter he's with are gonna need some answers."

"Answers you can provide?"

"Maybe, but I might need some help."

"What kind of help?" the detective said.

"The kind that's gonna tell us who pulled the trigger on Woods and why."

I stood up and walked over to Robert Graves' leather-bound

translation of the *Odyssey*. Behind it was a .38 Smith and Wesson snub.

"The gun that killed Johnny." I slid the piece across the desk. Rodriguez didn't touch it.

"You sure?"

"I know my own gun," I said. "This was the piece I found beside Woods' body. The piece that disappeared out of Evidence. I usually keep it behind the *Iliad*. Yesterday I found it three books down. Behind the *Odyssey*. Been fired three times."

"And I assume you have no idea how it got there."

"Actually, I think I know exactly how."

"Should we order some pizza?" Rodriguez said.

"I'm okay with whiskey."

"Yeah. Well, I'm not."

So we ordered pizza. I told Rodriguez how my gun found its way from the Cook County Evidence lockup back into my bookcase. Then I told him what I needed and why. When I finished, the detective left. I put a call in to Big Bob's Saloon and asked for the manager. The turtle races weren't on, so he had a little time. We talked for a while. About Janet Woods and his daytime bartender. After I got off the phone, I sat up, drank some more whiskey, and watched the night grow old. I wondered where Dan Masters was sleeping. And who might be standing over his bed.

CHAPTER 43

I slept hard and late the next day. Walked into my office a little after ten. Mitchell Kincaid was sitting there, his back to the door, reading a magazine. Once Rachel talked to the candidate, I knew he'd meet with me. I just didn't expect it so soon. And I didn't expect him to be alone. Not an attorney in sight.

Kincaid didn't turn when I came in. Just dropped the magazine onto his lap. I walked behind my desk, sat down, and waited.

"Have you seen the latest copy of *Time*?" he said. I shook my head. Kincaid tossed the mag my way.

"They have a list of influential people in this country. Up-and-comers, they call them. My name's right near the top."

"Congratulations."

"Thank you, Mr. Kelly. I guess I always thought it would feel different."

"You expected trumpets?"

"A flourish would be nice."

Kincaid offered an easy smile, one that ran off his face as quickly as it appeared. Then Chicago's would-be savior took a moment. I had seen this moment before. On television. In newspapers. If I opened up the copy of *Time*, I'd probably see it there too. It was the Kincaid profile. Long chin, gray eyes, cheekbones sculpted in shadow and light. An impression of strength, yet delicate enough to convey the intellect that moved underneath. As far as profiles went, Kincaid's wasn't half bad.

The pundits and pollsters might not realize it, but Mayor John J. Wilson did. And it worried him. In a place and time when leadership was in precious short supply, Mitchell Kincaid looked like he was born to the job. And now it wasn't going to happen.

"I noticed the books," Kincaid said. "Cicero, Caesar, Sophocles."

"Something I picked up when I was young."

"I read a bit myself. Don't recall that much, but I do remember *Oedipus Rex*. And a thing called fate."

"Fate, destiny. Free will."

"Exactly. I was sitting here, looking at my picture in *Time* magazine, surrounded by all your books, and thinking about that very thing."

"Sir?"

"This life we lead. The decisions we think we make. Is it all predetermined? All our accomplishments and failures? Locked and loaded when we're born? Or is it up to us?"

"You're asking me if I believe in fate, Mr. Kincaid?"

He tipped his chin my way. "I guess I am. Are we fated to lead the life we do? Or do we really chart our own path?"

"I think we're all given different tools," I said. "Capable of great good and great evil. What we do after that is up to us."

"So you believe in a hybrid?"

"I guess."

"And these tools, they vary from person to person?"

"I think a lot of us spend our lives trying to find out exactly what these tools are and how best to use them."

"People give that a lot of thought?"

I shrugged. "Probably not."

"How about responsibility, Mr. Kelly?"

"How about it?"

"People should hold themselves personally responsible for things that go on in their lives. Good and bad. Regardless of consequence. Agreed?"

"Things they can control? Yes."

"You have introduced the notion of control. A slippery concept."

"Especially in politics, sir."

"Touché, Mr. Kelly. I wish we had met under different circumstances. I think it might have been fun."

"We need to talk, sir."

"I got a phone call last night from someone I respect and admire."

"Let me guess. A judge named Rachel Swenson."

"She speaks highly of you, Mr. Kelly."

I didn't offer a response. Kincaid stood up and found his way to a window.

"My security chief, James J. Bratton. He's a good man. Sometimes confused, but a good man. I've talked with him. I know what he's done. I know that he has, directly or indirectly, tried to gain certain documents he felt might cause great embarrassment to our mayor. He has used whatever means he saw fit to gain those documents, including breaking into your home, the use of force, and physical threats."

Kincaid turned on his heel and walked his eyes across the room.

"I'm here to apologize for that. I was not aware of the existence, or supposed existence, of the Chicago Fire documents until recently. You can believe me or not, as you choose. I'm here to tell you I never endorsed Mr. Bratton's actions. I do, however, accept full responsibility. That is a personal responsibility. With consequences. For myself and my career. As it should be."

Kincaid pulled an envelope from his jacket and slipped it onto my desk.

"This is a copy of a letter I will post after I leave here. To the mayor. With copies to the *Sun-Times* and *Tribune*."

I looked at the envelope but didn't touch it.

"It's my withdrawal from the mayoral race. The reasons I give are personal and undisclosed."

"You don't have to withdraw, sir."

"Yes, I do, Mr. Kelly. Responsibility without consequence is, in fact, no responsibility at all. If I am to be of use to anyone, including myself, in the years to come, I must withdraw. I must reflect. And I must get better. If I am to lead at all."

I picked up the envelope and wondered at its cost.

"What I ask from you, Mr. Kelly, is one thing and one thing only. But it is significant."

"Go ahead."

"I want your silence about this entire matter. Not for my protection. Although I admit, it does help me. But if the story about the fire and this alleged letter was ever given any credence, it would be embarrassing for Mr. Bratton and for the families concerned. Especially, of course, for the mayor."

"And you would have effectively smeared him?"

Kincaid dropped his head a fraction. "Exactly what I'm trying to avoid."

"No one will hear a thing from me, Mr. Kincaid. There is, however, the problem of murder."

Kincaid opened his mouth to speak again. This time I beat him to it.

"I don't believe your aide had anything to do with the death of

Allen Bryant or anyone else. No worries there, sir. But there is someone out there who's willing to kill."

"In order to gain control of these documents? To be honest, I just don't buy it."

"Why not?"

"There would be some political advantage to obtaining the fire documents," Kincaid said. "If they exist. But seriously, murder?"

"This isn't about politics, Mr. Kincaid. And it's not about the Chicago Fire. At least not in the way you're thinking."

"Then what is it about, Mr. Kelly?"

"It's about money, Mr. Kincaid. A boatload of money."

I pulled out a copy of Josiah Randolph's diary from 1871. One more present from my friend Teen.

"This is what your aide was after. Except he didn't know it."

Kincaid took the diary in his hands and opened it. "What is this?"

"Pages from a diary. An account of the Great Chicago Fire, written in 1871 by the curator of the Chicago Historical Society."

Kincaid slipped on a pair of tortoiseshell reading glasses and began to skim. I fixed up a pot of coffee and continued to talk.

"His name was Josiah Randolph. His great-grandnephew runs the society today."

"Did you get this diary from him?"

"Not exactly. Most of the diary was in the public archives. Some of it was a little harder to get a handle on."

"Go ahead," Kincaid said, and kept reading.

"There was no agreement between John J. Wilson and Charles Hume regarding the fire. No evidence I could find that they conspired to start anything."

Kincaid glanced up. "You know that for a fact?"

"I'll tell you what I know and you decide. Josiah Randolph writes in his diary of the moments just before the fire bore down on the historical society. Sit down, Mr. Kincaid. This might take a while."

Kincaid sat. I poured us some coffee.

"The historical society was supposed to be one of the city's 'fireproof' buildings," I said. "On the night of the fire, according to Josiah, most of Chicago's money was lined up outside his basement door, jewels and furs in hand."

"Looking for a place to store their valuables?"

"Exactly. Names like Pullman, Palmer, and Ogden. A real Who's Who. Josiah Randolph took in as much as he could. Then, he heard what sounded like a freight train coming down the block."

"The fire?"

"According to Josiah, heat from the fire began to melt the inside of the society's walls. The flames themselves were still blocks away. That's when Josiah Randolph realized his building wasn't fireproof. In fact, it was anything but."

I found a pack of cigarettes, shook one out, and lit up. Kincaid declined. I shrugged. It went well with the coffee. Then I cracked the window, leaned my heels against the sill, and found the line of my story.

"Josiah figured he had maybe ten minutes to get out of Dodge. After that, the building was going to be gone. So he ran back down to the basement and looked around."

"Trying to figure out what he should save?" Kincaid said.

I nodded. It was good to talk it through out loud. Let me hear how it played, where the holes might be.

"There was one item in particular he tried to take with him."

I flipped open the diary pages and pointed to a section of underlined text. Now that we had gotten down to it, I noticed just a bit of a shake in my hand. That was okay. Fear keeps most men honest. I was probably no exception.

"Josiah talks about it here," I said. "The only handwritten copy of the Emancipation Proclamation. Given to the society by Illinois' favorite son, Abraham Lincoln."

"The New York State Library has Lincoln's handwritten copy." Kincaid spoke as he read. "I've seen it myself."

"That was Lincoln's preliminary copy. The historical society had the final version."

Kincaid nodded and continued to skim the pages of Josiah's diary. Then he stopped and looked up.

"Says here Randolph couldn't save the document."

"The Proclamation was in a wooden frame," I said. "Josiah writes that he couldn't break it and he couldn't get the frame out the basement window."

"So the Proclamation burned," Kincaid said.

"That's what I thought. Then I found a second portion of the diary. The part I told you wasn't available to the public."

I pulled out another sheaf of papers and placed them in front of Kincaid, copies of the diary fragments I had taken from Lawrence Randolph's locked desk.

"After I read these, I had all the originals looked at by a document examiner. There's no doubt. The portion that talks about the Proclamation burning was written with a cheaper, carbon-based ink. The rest of the diary features an ink called iron gall. Same color. Different ink."

"How certain are we?"

"Ink was not mass-produced back then. There were several different qualities and textures. Pretty distinctive. The fragments I am showing you now were written with the original iron-gall ink as well. My expert believes the fragments were clearly part of Josiah Randolph's original diary. I believe they tell us what really happened to the Proclamation. Why don't you take a minute."

I leaned back in my chair and smoked while Kincaid read. After he finished, he put down the diary and took off his glasses. I put out my cigarette and slipped on a pair of latex gloves. Kincaid did the same. Then I laid out on my desk the *Sheehan's* Allen Bryant had been killed for and the parchment I had found within.

"I found it inside this book, Mr. Kincaid. Already verified the cursive. It's Lincoln's Emancipation Proclamation. The final version. Written by the man himself."

Kincaid's fingers ran lightly over the document. He began to read the first few lines, lips moving but no sound forthcoming. Then he looked up. I nodded and he kept reading. When he was done, Mitchell Kincaid sat for a moment. Content, it seemed, simply to be with history. After a while he looked up again. This time, with a smile. Then we talked. About what to do with Lincoln's document. About what to do with Mitchell Kincaid's future. I packed up the Proclamation and gave it to the soon-to-be-ex-candidate. He called for a car to meet him and left, holding his treasure like a newborn. Kincaid's run for mayor might be over. His destiny, however, was just starting to take hold. Now it was time to catch a killer.

CHAPTER 44

The door creaked open. A shaft of light slipped across the floor and tickled the toe of my shoe. I pulled my foot back and waited in the darkness. The door creaked a bit farther. I saw a hand scrabble across the wall, find the light switch, and hit it. The hand's owner was still outside the room talking to someone, backing his way into the office. Then Lawrence Randolph turned and saw me, sitting behind his desk, smiling.

"Hello, Mr. Randolph."

"Kelly, what the hell are you doing in my office?"

"Waiting for you."

Randolph reached for his phone. "I'm calling security."

"There's no need."

Randolph followed my gaze. Behind him, at the door, stood Teen.

"What's she doing here?"

"She'll be right outside. If you feel you're in danger, just give a holler and Teen will come running."

"I'm calling security and having you escorted from the building."

Randolph reached for the phone again. I pulled out the

Sheehan's and laid it on his desk. Then I opened it up and let him see the red number inside.

"That's a number four, Randolph."

The curator's eyes feasted on the *Sheehan's* as he waved Teen away. When we were alone, he held out his hands like one of the statues you'd see in the Queen of All Saints Basilica. Only this statue was real and ready to kill for his God.

"Mr. Kelly. Could I take a look?"

I pushed the book his way. He turned pages, pretended to examine the text. All the while long lengths of finger pried and poked at the book's binding. Feeling for the document he knew was secreted within.

"It's not there, Randolph."

The curator's fingers stopped probing. His eyes reached into mine. "Excuse me?"

"The Proclamation. It's gone." I threw a silver flash drive onto his desk.

"Believe it or not, that drive contains the entire contents of your laptop. We lifted it yesterday afternoon in the Starbucks down the street."

Randolph was sitting now. Eyes moving from the flash drive to the book and back.

"You killed Allen Bryant. You got his name from Johnny Woods and went to his house. You wanted to get your hands on the number four edition before Johnny got there. Didn't work out."

Randolph's eyes hollowed and the corners of his mouth squeezed up into a reluctant smile.

"The e-mails we pulled off your laptop go back more than a year," I said. "You and a skinhead named Clarence Lester. Negotiating the sale of Lincoln's Emancipation Proclamation."

I pulled out a booking photo of Lester. Long, lean face. Chalk-white skin with three teardrops tattooed under one eye. Randolph pulled the shot close with a single finger, took a look, and pushed it back.

"How much were you going to get?" I said.

"You'll never prove it." Randolph nodded at the flash drive. "That's illegal. Wiretapping. Invasion of privacy."

"How much were you going to get?" I said.

"If you hijacked my laptop, then you already know."

"Eight point five million," I said.

The nostrils on Randolph's face seemed to thin and quiver, anxiously scenting cash their owner would never get to spend.

"Close enough," the curator said.

"Where does the Aryan Brotherhood get dollars like that?"

"Think I give a damn, Mr. Kelly? They planned a worldwide webcast. Going to burn the thing online. But that's not the point. Your intercept and any information obtained from it are illegal."

"You keep saying that."

"Yes, I do," he said.

I leaned forward on my elbows, steepled my fingers under my chin, and looked carefully across the desk.

"At first, I thought, why wouldn't you just try to obtain it legitimately? Aboveboard. Sell it at Sotheby's. Probably bring in fifteen, twenty mil."

"Good point," Randolph said.

"Then I realized you couldn't do that. Your great-granduncle was a thief. Never owned the Proclamation in the first place. If you came forward with it, the city, state, and half the world would have jumped in to claim ownership."

I paused and took a look across the room. Josiah Randolph hung on the wall. Same weak chin. Same tight smile. Probably getting a big kick out of the whole thing.

"It had to be someone like the skinheads," I said. "Only way for you to cash in. By the way, you know the Aryan Brotherhood is considered a terrorist organization now?"

I poked again at the silver drive. Randolph flinched as I pushed it his way.

"Lot of latitude today for intercepts like this. Warrantless wiretaps and all that."

I saw the first bit of concern pick at the corners of the curator's arrogance.

"Get the hell out of here," he hissed.

"One thing I don't understand. Why get me involved? Why not just confront Woods about the book? Kill him and take it for yourself?"

"You think murder's that simple?"

"Allen Bryant might think so."

"Mr. Bryant was a nobody. Mr. Woods had entanglements."

"You mean the mayor's office. Let me guess. You thought there was a chance they might actually investigate the death of one of their own?"

"I have no idea what you're talking about, Kelly. Now get out. And take the bitch outside with you."

"I don't think so, Randolph." I placed a final piece of paper on the curator's desk.

"This is your letter of resignation. When you walk out of this office, there will be a team of federal marshals waiting to take you into custody for questioning with respect to Allen Bryant's murder. They'll also take possession of your desktop computer and personal items pursuant to search warrants executed this morning in federal court."

Blood drained south from Randolph's face as I spoke.

"Want a suggestion, Lawrence?"

He nodded.

"Sign this letter. Hand the position over temporarily to your trusted assistant, Teen. Get a good lawyer and hope for the best."

"Why should I do that?"

" 'Cause you're in the system now. I might be able to do you a favor down the road and, believe me, you're going to need every one of them you can get."

Randolph took a look around his soon-to-be-former domain. Soft yellow lights and even softer carpet. A wall of diplomas in golden frames. Pictures of Randolph with the mayor, governor, and any other smiling politician who would grasp his overreaching hand. Books, groaning with pretension and stacked from floor to ceiling. Presiding over it all, Randolph's scheming ancestor, the man who pilfered Lincoln's Proclamation in the first place, a common crook named Josiah. The curator pulled his eyes back to the rather unappetizing present, sniffed once or twice, and did what any sensible man would do.

"I want to cut a deal."

"I can't do that."

"You can help."

"Maybe. Tell me the rest."

Randolph stood up, moved toward the desk, and picked up his oosik.

"That thing help you think?" I said.

Randolph put the oosik down. "Just a toy. I know, you find it strange. You realize my family had the Proclamation in our possession for over a century?"

"Didn't know that."

"Neither did they. Josiah died suddenly from a stroke."

"Couldn't happen to a nicer guy."

"Josiah was brilliant. Created a cover story about the Proclamation for his official diary. Never told anyone he had actually saved it."

"And eventually hid it in his *Sheehan's*."

"In 1974, a pig of an uncle sold the book."

Randolph waved his hands in the air. At the vagaries of time and fate. At the idiocy of others. At the temptations handed down by history. Temptations that were his undoing.

"I found the rest of the diary among Josiah's papers four years ago. The whole story was there. When I realized what Josiah had done, what my family had unwittingly sold—"

"You got greedy."

"The Proclamation belongs to my family. It's my legacy."

"A legacy you wanted to turn around and sell."

"It's mine, Mr. Kelly."

"How did the *Sheehan's* wind up in Woods' hands?"

Randolph wandered over to his wall of books and picked randomly at the volumes there.

"I suspected the number four was in the Chicago area but was never really sure."

"You needed someone to do your legwork. Someone relentless enough to get the job done, but someone you could control."

"Something like that."

"And that's when you decided to bring in the mayor's office and Johnny Woods?"

Randolph turned back my way. "I thought they might bite on the fire story."

"Let them do all the heavy lifting," I said. "Lead you right to the number four."

"That was the idea."

"Didn't quite work out that way," I said.

"Woods lied to me."

"Not a big surprise there."

"No, probably not. He said he'd located the book. Told me Bryant had it at his house on Hudson."

"In actuality, Woods himself had already taken the number four from Bryant," I said.

Randolph nodded. "When we arrived at the house—"

"We?"

"Lester insisted on coming with me that morning. As it turned out, that was probably a mistake."

"Go ahead."

"Bryant was hostile. Told us he had given the book to Woods the previous evening, and why were we so interested, anyway."

I could see the old professor, staring at the skinhead in his living room, a lethal mix of fear and outrage bubbling inside.

"Let me guess," I said. "You didn't believe Bryant."

"I did. Lester wasn't so sure."

"So you killed him."

"Lester wanted to waterboard the professor. Said the CIA did it all the time to get people talking. Are you familiar with the technique?"

"Sure. Stretch him out on a piece of wood and pour water over the guy's face. Victim thinks he's drowning."

"Unless he actually is drowning, which, in the case of Mr. Bryant, was exactly what happened. Terrible accident. For the record, all Lester's doing."

"Spoken like a true rat. They're gonna love you inside, Randolph."

Randolph blinked behind his glasses. "What about our deal?"

"I told you, I'll do what I can. Tell me about the murder. Why all the fuss?"

"Excuse me?"

"The sand in Bryant's mouth. If he was already dead, what was the point?"

The curator puffed himself up as only an academic, even a

wannabe homicidal academic, can do. "I thought we needed to add a bit of complexity to the crime scene."

"Keep the focus on the fire as a possible motive. And maybe turn up the heat a little on Johnny Woods?"

Randolph smiled and walked back to his wall of books. "You've sampled a little history on the Great Fire. You might appreciate this."

The volume was large, dusty, and old. Randolph laid it flat on the desk, open to an onionskin map of 1871 Chicago.

"The fire devoured Chicago in chunks," the curator said. "Block by block. Thousands of people streamed into the streets—streets made of wood and often already aflame. Anyway, where were they to go?"

I turned a page and looked at the illustrations. A dark and boiling river of people, drawn in faded ink, terror on their faces as they ran through a rain of fire and ash. Swarming toward the water. The apparent safety of Lake Michigan.

"According to most accounts," Randolph said, "thousands flocked to the lakefront. Some ran into the water, but found it to be alive with pieces of flaming timber and burning pitch. The air itself, however, was no better. So hot, it peeled the skin off people's bones. To draw a breath was to risk cooking, literally, from the inside out."

Randolph reached over and turned the page for me. To a fresh set of drawings.

"Others coming to the lakefront buried themselves up to their necks in sand. It should have been a prudent move. The earth underneath was wet and cool. There was only one problem."

"The wind."

"Excellent, Mr. Kelly. Columns of superheated air and flames had risen into the sky and tore along the lakefront. Those who survived called them *fire devils*. They turned the beaches into sandstorms—and then into graves. Some, it seems, were buried alive."

I closed the book on faces from long ago. Eyes looking up at a sky filled with death. Mouths half covered in sand. Faces drowning in earth.

"So you fashioned the same fate for Allen Bryant."

"As I said, it was Lester who insisted upon killing the man. I simply provided the proper historical context. May I?"

I stood up. Randolph moved back behind his desk and booted up his computer.

"Now, Mr. Kelly. There is only one more thing I want to show you."

I walked across the room and replaced the volume of history Randolph had given me. Then I sat on a couch along the wall and waited. Rodriguez was already outside with the feds and their warrants. I could give the curator a final minute.

"Your computer play, Mr. Kelly. Clever. As I said, I assume you won't use any of that material officially. Of course, investigators will know exactly where to look in my desktop computer and find it, anyway. Isn't that the notion?"

"That's how it works, Randolph."

The curator finished typing and pushed away from the screen. "Okay, I'm ready to go."

"What did you want to show me?"

"Actually, nothing. Or rather, soon-to-be nothing."

Randolph flipped his screen around so I could get a look. File names were appearing and reappearing in a manic game of hide-and-seek.

"I have a few computer tricks of my own. One is known as a bomb."

I jumped at the computer and hit some buttons. File names kept slipping across the screen.

"What did you do?"

"It can't be stopped, Mr. Kelly."

There was a beep and the file names disappeared altogether. Replaced by a blinking cursor.

"In fact, it's done." Randolph smiled. "All my files and e-mails are erased, on my computer and any computer that received them. Incapable of being reconstructed even with the most sophisticated of programs. A very effective and very lethal bomb."

"I don't believe it."

"You don't have to. Doesn't make it any less real."

Randolph picked up the flash drive I had given him off his desk. "Kind of renders this irrelevant."

He dropped the drive into a wastebasket by his feet and stood up. "Don't feel bad, Mr. Kelly. You're Irish and I'm not. As Charles Hume knew so well, breeding will always tell."

Then Randolph walked out of his office and into the arms of the police. Two hours after that, he walked out of the society with his lawyer. No charges filed and apologies all around. Lawrence Randolph was a killer. And a free man.

CHAPTER 45

I sat in the bowels of the Billy Goat. In the VIP section. Also known as two wooden tables and a collection of chairs. The staff had separated us from the great unwashed by what looked like a green shower curtain. Fred Jacobs sat across from me. It was a little after eleven in the morning and Fred was working on his second Horny Goat. I popped four aspirin and sipped at a cup of coffee that tasted like it had been drained from the Chicago River. I had been up most of the night. First with the feds. Then Rodriguez. Finally, an audience with the judge who had signed the warrants on Lawrence Randolph. Also known as Rachel Swenson.

The FBI and Rodriguez sympathized. Rachel offered various flavors of scorn. Without the information on Randolph's computer, there was virtually nothing to tie him into Allen Bryant's murder. Of course, I still had his entire hard drive at my disposal. Unfortunately, it was poached from Randolph's laptop as he sat inside a Starbucks. Highly effective and just as illegal.

"What about the skinhead Lester?" Jacobs said. The reporter wasn't concerned so much with the niceties of the legal system. He was thinking about his story, heading south fast.

"Rodriguez pulled him in last night."

"Let me guess. Lester never heard of Lawrence Randolph."

"That's about it."

"So they kicked him free?"

I shook my head and ran a hand across three days' worth of stubble. "Feds had a warrant on Lester's apartment. Scored two thousand hits of crank and a dismantled cooker. Rodriguez says he's looking at twenty-five to life. You got the exclusive."

"Not exactly a Pulitzer, Kelly."

I took a look at my watch. "Let's see what the Fifth Floor has to say."

On cue, the green curtain parted and Patrick Wilson walked in. Cook County's chief prosecutor, Gerald O'Leary, was right behind him. The two men took a quick look around. Probably wondering where we hid the microphones and cameras. Then the mayor's cousin spoke.

"Fred, nice to see you again. Mr. Kelly. You both know Gerald O'Leary."

The man who ruined my career offered his hand and I took it. Gerald O'Leary held up well on television. News directors looking to cultivate a source knew better. So they shoveled on the makeup and shot him from high angles, making O'Leary's jowls much less so and taking off ten years in the process. In person, however, the prosecutor didn't fare so well. His face was flushed, his cheeks scored with tiny blue veins. Too much steak, too much butter, too much booze. I wasn't rooting for a massive stroke, but I wouldn't be surprised either.

"How are you, Michael?" O'Leary loved to call me Michael. Like we were old friends. I let him because I didn't have the energy anymore not to.

"Fine, Gerald. Just fine."

We all sat down. Patrick Wilson slipped a hand across the table and touched my arm. "Mr. Kelly, I realize we have some history here."

I looked over at O'Leary. A picture of Mike Royko glared at him from the wall. "I have no problem with Gerald," I said. "Glad to see he's here."

O'Leary swung his large made-for-TV head my way and grinned. "I told you, Patrick. Water under the bridge. Let's move on."

A Billy Goat bartender stuck his nose through the curtain. "Pepsi?" Wilson said.

The nose wrinkled, then spoke. "No Pepsi. Coke."

Patrick Wilson nodded. "Coke it is, then."

The nose disappeared. A minute later, a hand poked through the curtain. At the end of it was a plastic bottle of Coke. Wilson took it and the hand disappeared.

"Okay." The mayor's cousin spoke as he poured his drink into a glass. "Fred has given me some of the details behind your request to meet."

"And the rest you picked up from the Chicago police this morning," I said.

"The chief told us about the warrants served on Lawrence Randolph," O'Leary said. "Unfortunately, they turned up nothing useful concerning Allen Bryant's murder. In fact, they turned up nothing at all. What I don't understand is why this was run through the feds. My office could have handled things."

Patrick Wilson held up a hand. "Gerald. Let's talk about Mr. Kelly's request to meet." He turned my way. "Mr. Kelly. You were going to offer some details."

"Let's start with 1871," I said. "There is no letter. Nothing that implicates the Wilson family in the fire."

The mayor's cousin and consigliere took a sip of his Coke and cleared his throat. O'Leary took his cue and pulled out a Black-Berry.

"You'll have to excuse me for a moment." O'Leary wandered

off, pretending to answer a message he'd never received. Patrick Wilson picked up the thread. But delicately.

"I'm not exactly sure what we're talking about here, Mr. Kelly."

"That's fine," I said. "I have the book Johnny Woods was looking for. I found what was inside. You'll find out about it soon enough. Point is, it has nothing to do with your family."

Wilson printed out a smile and pasted it across his face. "What is it you want from the mayor, Mr. Kelly?"

"Mitchell Kincaid," I said. "He worries the mayor. Politically, that is." I held up a hand. "Don't bother to deny it. He'd worry me too. Kincaid will announce he's withdrawing from the mayoral race this afternoon. Provided we come to an understanding."

The smile dropped off Little Cousin's face. He was used to horse-trading. Usually, however, he was dictating terms.

"There's no understanding here." Wilson glanced toward Fred Jacobs. "I thought I made myself clear on that."

"Fred isn't part of this," I said. "If you can't make a deal, get someone in here who can."

A small vein popped up on Patrick Wilson's temple. I counted twenty beats in about fifteen seconds.

I looked at Jacobs, who stood up and joined O'Leary and his BlackBerry outside.

"What is it you want, Kelly?"

"Three things," I said. "First, you drop the vendetta against a reporter named Rawlings Smith. Jacobs says there's a couple of spots open on the *Tribune* staff. Your office makes the call and puts a word in for him."

Wilson's eyes crinkled a bit at the corners. I don't know what he expected, but my first term seemed to tickle the mayor's man. "What else?"

I took a deep breath before the next one.

"Johnny Woods' murder. You bury it. No charges filed against anyone. Not now. Not ever."

Wilson drew his hands in front of his face and tapped the tips of his fingers together. "As I understand it, there is no murder weapon and not much of a case against you. I don't really see that changing, if that's what you're concerned about. Now what else?"

"I didn't kill Woods. Whether you believe me or not is irrelevant. The condition is that *no one* is ever charged. For any offense in connection with his death."

Wilson leaned back and looked around the room for a little help. A little posturing. Couldn't resist, I guess. Then he came back to the deal. "What else?"

"Lawrence Randolph. I know he's been feeding the mayor information on the fire. He's also a killer. The warrants didn't work. Fine. I want him taken down. And I don't really care how."

Now Wilson laughed out loud and clapped his hands together. "Kelly, you're amusing as hell, you know that. Let this thing go. Set this guy up. How do I know Kincaid will withdraw?"

I pulled out a cell phone. "I'll make the call right now."

Patrick tickled his fingers my way. "Go ahead. Go ahead. You have a deal."

I shook my head. "I need the mayor to sign off. And tell him, if he reneges, the whole thing comes out. Including everything I know about Johnny Woods and the Fifth Floor's obsession with the fire."

Little Cousin slumped back in his chair and ran a hand across his forehead. Then he stood up and buttoned his coat. "Sit tight. This might take a minute."

Wilson left. I was just finishing my coffee when Jacobs slipped back into the room.

"Busting some balls here, Kelly?"

"The Wilson family understands strength. Respects it." I glanced over at the reporter. "You should remember that."

Jacobs ran his hand across his Adam's apple and rolled his eyes toward a menu board tacked to the wall. "*You* should hope they don't make you tomorrow's special."

The green curtain shifted again and a shadow moved on the other side. Patrick Wilson stepped through, a cell phone to his ear, and motioned for us to follow. We ducked outside and into the back of a Lincoln Town Car. O'Leary had already stuffed himself in a corner and was looking out the window. Seven minutes later, we slid to a stop in front of City Hall. Wilson was still on the phone. We walked through the lobby and under a red velvet rope strung in front of an elevator door. It was the mayor's car. The one he took every morning, express, to the fifth floor.

CHAPTER 46

I sat in the same hard wooden chair. Jacobs sat in another. The city lay under the drowse of an afternoon fog. To our left, wisps of gray floated by the windows. To our right, Wilson's desk was draped in polished mahogany and cluttered with all sorts of mayoral things. Behind the desk was a third chair, the padded one, with soft leather and, at the moment, entirely empty.

Jacobs had apparently never been inside the inner sanctum. I was about to tell him where they kept the holy water and candles when the door swung open and the mayor walked in. Jacobs jumped like someone had played "Hail to the Chief." Wilson acknowledged the homage with a nod. Then he walked over to the windows and stared into the soup.

"Good to see you again, Kelly."

The mayor talked without turning. I was still seated and didn't respond. Wilson backed away from the windows and moved behind his desk. Jacobs didn't know whether to stand or sit, so he froze. Wilson moved his eyes over the reporter and then looked at the open door. Jacobs got the hint and left, closing the door on his way out.

"How much does the *Trib* guy know?" Wilson said.

"About what?"

"The fire. And my family."

"He thinks it's an urban legend. Nothing else."

"What do you think?"

"I think there's no letter or document in existence that proves your great-great-grandfather did anything to harm this city."

Wilson folded his hands over his stomach and sank into his flesh.

"John Julius wasn't stupid," the mayor said. "Neither am I."

"I understand that, sir."

"Do you? My great-great-grandfather was a nickel-rubbing, power-greedy bastard. And he always came out on top. It's a trait that runs in the family. Remember that, Mr. Kelly. You could use a friend in this office and by the looks of it—"

The mayor's lips peeled back from his teeth, eyelids lifting for a moment to reveal eyes that were shockingly blue.

"I'm not going anywhere. At least for another term."

"So we have a deal?" I said.

"If Kincaid announces he's not going to run, we have a deal. On one condition."

The mayor held up a hand. I could see the hint of his tongue and he seemed to be slightly out of breath. The whole affair was somehow exciting to him. Rolling dice on the Fifth Floor. Playing God with other people's lives. It was his lifeblood. The lifeblood of Wilson's ancestor and namesake, John Julius. A ruthless need to manipulate, to control, to dominate. Whatever the means and heedless of price. In such a world, there can be only one king. And he answers to no one, save the demon called paranoia.

"And what condition would that be, Mr. Mayor?"

"I need to know what it is you really want."

"I laid it out for Patrick."

Wilson nodded and settled in again. "I understand that. Problem is, Mr. Kelly, it's not enough."

"Excuse me?"

"I know my family's history. Better than anyone. I think you're aware of some things that might cause me problems."

"I told you. I told your cousin. There's no letter."

"Fuck the letter. You still know—or at least think you know—what actually went on in 1871."

"And if I do?"

"Then you have leverage. In my world, that makes you an enemy."

"Funny, some people might think our chat the other night was all about leverage."

Wilson lifted an eyebrow. "You mean the thing with the judge?" I nodded.

"Sean Coyle's an embarrassing story for Rachel Swenson," Wilson said. "But she'd probably survive. Either way, I'm concerned it's not enough to keep you in line."

"All due respect, Mr. Mayor, you might just have to learn to live with that."

Wilson wasn't used to that particular collection of words coming at him. He poured himself a glass of water and took a sip.

"The way we usually do this is with a favor. A personal favor."

"Let me guess," I said. "Something that binds me to you. Gives you back the edge."

The mayor opened up his desk drawer, pulled out a manila folder, and threw it across the desk.

"Another file?" I said. "You guys never run out, do you?"

"Gerald O'Leary ran you off the force. He did it to cover up his own corruption and malfeasance. I told you before, I had nothing to do with it. I can, however, make O'Leary pay."

I looked at the buff-colored folder. Thought about the day they

slipped the cuffs on my wrists. The day I lost my shield, my repu-
tation, my life. It seemed like a long time ago. Until I reached out
and ran my hand across the file's surface. Then it seemed like
yesterday. The mayor laid out his favor.

"Gerald O'Leary has a zipper problem. Wife of thirty-two
years, four kids. Wife's name is Pat. I know her well."

Wilson took another, longer sip of water. The man might be
thirsty, but that didn't prevent him from selling out his colleague
of two decades.

"Anyway, turns out O'Leary is banging this young girl. Monday night maître d' at Gibsons. She's of legal age, but just barely.
Doesn't matter. The pictures will finish him."

"The pictures in here?" I said, and brushed a finger along the
open edge of the folder.

Wilson nodded, as if it were a shame this had to happen at all.

"I see this guy at St. Pat's every Sunday. Really heartbreaking.
Anyway, we get these photos to your pal, Jacobs, O'Leary's career
is done. Marriage done. Everything done."

Wilson turned out his half smile again. There was a bit of food
stuck between his front teeth. Must have been breakfast. I
pushed the folder back into his lap.

"Not interested, Mr. Mayor. In fact, if these snaps see the light
of day, our deal's off."

I stood up. Wilson remained where he was, staring at the chair
I had just vacated. Then he looked up. It was a look that had
served his family for generations. And it wasn't pretty.

"You want to be an enemy?" he said.

"No, Mr. Mayor, I don't. Told you at the beginning. I play
things pretty much as they lie. Straight up."

"Let the chips fall where they may?"

"Call it what you want. You abide by our deal. And you leave
Rachel Swenson alone. Got nothing to fear from me."

The mayor weighed my life, such as it was. Took a while. At least another sip and a half of good mayoral water. Then he shrugged, stretched out all six feet three inches, and came around the desk.

"My guys will call the reporter and set it up on the curator. What's his name?"

"Randolph," I said. "Lawrence Randolph."

"Yeah, Randolph. Okay, we got it."

"What's it gonna be?" I said.

Wilson shrugged. "They'll come up with something." Then His Honor leaned in for a final word. "Just remember one thing, Kelly. It's my city you live in. Every inch of it."

The mayor placed a hand on my shoulder and gave it a squeeze. "Now go get yourself something to eat. We just opened up a new place at Millennium Park. Great burgers."

Wilson's hand slipped off my shoulder and down my arm. Then he turned and walked to his windows. I opened the door and took a final look. The mayor had his back to me, looking out over his city, edges of buildings peeking through a torn curtain of gray. In an hour or so, the afternoon fog would be swallowed whole by an early dusk. Night would steal in and lights would come on: in the Sears Tower, the Hancock, and across two miles of steel and concrete in between. The darker it got, it seemed, the better the view. At least from the fifth floor.

CHAPTER 47

The hall outside the mayor's office was empty. I was halfway toward the elevator when Willie Dawson stuck his head from around a convenient corner.

"Kelly," the mayor's aide whispered.

I shuffled over, trying to look furtive albeit not understanding why. Willie hustled me into a small office. It contained a wooden table with a cardboard box on top of it.

"He didn't flame-broil your ass, like I suggested."

"Thanks, Willie."

"Should have flame-broiled your ass. Like a goddamn BK Whopper. Yessiree. 'Gonna regret it,' I told him."

"What do you want, Willie?"

"Want? From you? Nothing. You're nothing but trouble."

Willie gestured down to the box on the table between us. For the first time I registered holes, poked into the box's cover.

"Mayor wants you to have this."

Willie took off the top. Inside was a pink baby's blanket. Nestled inside the blanket was a puppy, brown and white with long ears and gold markings.

"What's this?"

"The mayor's springer had her litter. Mayor says you need one. Told me to make sure you got a female."

I looked down. The pup opened one eye, then the other. I tried to look away, but it wasn't easy. The pup yawned and rolled over on her back. Apparently, it was time for a belly rub.

"Pick her up, Kelly."

I did. The pup licked the side of my face, burrowed her head into my chest, and promptly fell asleep. I looked over at Willie, who was fighting it but smiling all the same.

"You have that effect on all women?"

"Funny guy, Willie. I can't take care of a puppy."

"Mayor didn't ask if you wanted his gift. If you understand what I mean?"

I looked down again at the pup, dug in and already offering up a light snore. I shrugged. What the hell.

"What do I feed her?"

"Instructions are in the box."

"What's her name?"

"You the daddy, Kelly. You decide. Now if I were you, I'd disappear. Sooner the better."

Two minutes later I was out the door, mayoral pup still in my arms, trying to hail a cab. It wasn't easy, but I made it home. Cabbie talked at me the entire ride. About crate training, housebreaking, and something called doggie day care. I nodded and wondered what the hell language he might be speaking. My new friend didn't seem nearly so concerned. In fact, she didn't crack an eyelid the whole way home.

CHAPTER 48

The cabbie dropped me in front of my flat. I carried Her Highness upstairs and put her down just inside the front door. The as-yet-to-be-named pup took a look around and another look back at me. Then she made her way into the bedroom. I followed. She was sitting on the floor and staring up at my bed. I shook my head no. The pup had other ideas. She got a running start, bounced off the side of my box spring, and landed, snout first, on the floor. I laughed. The pup yelped. She might have considered it a bark, but, trust me, she was kidding herself. I leaned against the door frame and watched as she took another go at the promised land, otherwise known as a soft mattress. The pup came up short again, hitting the ground, butt first this time, with a thud. She got up a bit slower, walked over, and sat down in front of me.

"What do you want me to do?"

She cocked her head, wagged her tail, stretched her paws out in front of her, and wiggled her butt in the air. I'd discover later this was a signal. The pup wanted to play. At the time, I thought she was probably going to go to the bathroom. Instead, she yelped again. Once, twice. Then a whole series of them. Finally, I did what any new parent would do. I caved, picked up the pup, and set her down on the bed. She ran around in circles for half a minute or so, then found a spot on my pillow. Thirty seconds later, she was asleep again. I turned off the light and closed the door. What the fuck.

I was back in the front room of my apartment, thinking about the cold beer in my fridge, when I heard a light tap on the door. I forgot about the beer, picked up my gun, and thumbed off the safety. I had been home less than five minutes and figured my visitor to be no coincidence. Whoever it was had been waiting, watching, as I came in. The only encouraging sign, they were knocking at my door. Not knocking it down. I was half hoping for a certain female federal judge named Swenson to be on the other side. What I got was nothing close.

"Kelly, can I come in?"

Dan Masters was wearing a Lucky Strike T-shirt and smelling like fast food and cheap hotels. One hand held a cigarette cupped against his palm. The other rattled a set of keys to a rental car. The detective wasn't wearing a badge and I didn't see a gun.

"When was the last time you slept, Masters?"

"Don't worry about me. Can we come in?"

Masters stepped back and I looked down the hallway. Janet sat on the stairs and looked at the wall less than two feet away. Taylor stood nearby, staring at nothing out the window. I leaned back in the doorjamb.

"My two friends," I said, and turned back into my apartment. Masters followed, closing the door behind him.

"You want a drink?" I said.

"No, thanks."

I opened up a drawer and pulled out copies of three insurance policies Vince Rodriguez had dug out for me.

"A hundred and a half in coverage on Johnny Woods," I said, and threw them on the table. "Most of it taken out in the last three months."

Masters turned his head sideways to look at the policies. Like he was looking at one of those modern paintings no one could ever understand or even know which way to hang. Then he straightened up and looked at me.

"You got a glass of water?"

I walked out to the kitchen. The detective got his drink while I waited. I was thinking about the two women in my hallway. I suspected Masters was as well. I don't think either of us was happy about any of it.

"I knew about the insurance," Masters said. "At least some of it. Two days ago, Janet tried to cash one of them in."

I nodded and got that beer from the fridge. "Let me guess. There was a hold on payment."

The ghost of a grin played at the corners of Masters' eyes. "They told her the Chicago PD had been making inquiries. Then they told her if she had any questions, she should follow up here."

"I bet she was pissed."

Masters finished his water and filled up again. "Slightly. I figured it was you and Rodriguez. Wanting to flush her back to Chicago."

"Looks like it worked," I said, and walked back into my living room. "Maybe we should bring the ladies in and hash things out."

"One more second." Masters took a seat on the couch. I leaned against the wall. He took a final hit on his cigarette and rubbed it into an ashtray.

"I need this settled," he said. "Tonight."

"They killed him, Dan. Used my gun to do it. Then they sent

me over there. Probably tipped the police to the house right after I left them. I'm telling you and I'd know better than anyone. I didn't shoot Johnny Woods. I don't know anyone else who could've."

"And they would have expected you to lie down and take the rap?"

"Hell, no. But who's going to believe me? Neighbors saw me trading fists with Woods outside his house. I'm talking from a jail cell. And it's my gun. If you hadn't come along and deep-sixed the evidence, they'd have been free and clear."

Masters nodded. The skin looked thin around his eyes, and there was a sudden quiver making a living just below his lip. "Janet's not what you think, Kelly."

I thought of her. At a wonderful place called twenty years old. Enjoying her youth, her looks, her life. Waiting for the rest of it to happen. And here it was.

"You don't know what I think about Janet Woods," I said. "Let's keep it at that."

"Fair enough. What happens after we talk?"

"What do you want to happen?"

Masters shrugged. "Leave town again. Probably best for them. Either way, I need to go."

"Downtown knows you grabbed the gun?"

"They know it, but can't prove it. Still, it would be tough. I can drop a word before I leave that you had nothing to do with it. Or the murder."

"Don't bother. I'm good with the mayor. We all are." Then I told him about the deal I had cut.

"So Johnny Woods is forgotten?"

"Forgotten," I said.

"Why'd you do that?"

I thought about the night Dan Masters came home from the

job early and found his wife. The night his life ended. Then I thought about Janet Woods' face and her daughter's future.

"Seems to me like no one's getting a free ride," I said.

The detective rubbed a hand across his lower lip. "You think I'm crazy to run with them. Maybe I am. One thing, though, I know for sure. If I try to go it alone, it's a short walk to the gun."

I couldn't say he was right. But I wasn't ready to take the weight if I was wrong.

"It's your play, Dan. But if I were you, I'd sleep with one eye open."

"You think Janet would come after me? For what?"

"Not Janet."

I turned over one of the insurance policies. Highlighted in yellow was the name of the policy's beneficiary: Taylor Woods.

"If I were you, it's the kid I'd worry about."

CHAPTER 49

Masters led them into my apartment. Janet looked a little shook; Taylor, a little bored. He sat them down at a table overlooking the street.

It had been a week, but Janet's face was still dark and puffy. It looked like it hurt to smile. She tried, anyway. Reached out and patted my hand. Taylor Woods sat in profile, near my front window, listening to an iPod and watching traffic that didn't exist move on the street below.

"Surprised to see me?" I said.

"I'm sorry, Michael." The minute the words were out of Janet's mouth, I half wanted to believe her. Exactly the reason I almost spent a lifetime inside an Illinois jail cell. Needed to remember that.

"Don't be sorry. You did what you did. We are where we are. Let's deal with it."

My client rested her eyes on mine and nodded. This part, at least, she could talk about. The rest would have to wait.

"Dan just told us about the arrangement you made with the mayor."

"You mean about the murder you're going to walk away from."

"Johnny was a bastard, Michael. You know that."

"I offered you help."

"You offered me nothing. Can't you see I needed to do this? Do it this way?"

"So you could look yourself in the mirror?"

"Something like that."

"I wonder," I said, and took a slow sip of beer. Janet pulled out some cigarettes and lit up. It was nice. Just like old times. Until I pulled out the insurance policies and pushed them across the table.

"I wonder," I said, "how much of it you did to get rid of Johnny and how much you did for the money."

Janet leaned on her cigarette and blew smoke across the room. Toward her daughter, who was still doing a wonderful job ignoring us all.

"The insurance was her idea." Janet dragged the words out in long ugly syllables. Dragged them out and let them sit. On the middle of the table, where they festered and then began to stink.

"Taylor was always about the money. The money, the money. If we were going to kill him, why not get rich as well."

"I wouldn't call a hundred fifty K rich," I said.

"You got that right," Janet said, and laughed. A hard and flinty thing. Taylor turned to the sound of it, her smile a knowing echo of her mother's greed.

"Asshole still beat her silly." That was Masters, stepping in again where he didn't belong. "She showed me the X-rays. You saw it yourself, Kelly."

I remembered her face, remembered the bruises. "Probably not as much as you think, Dan."

Vince Rodriguez had done more than put a string on Janet Woods' insurance cash. I'd asked him to run a check on the - bartender at Big Bob's. His name was Chris Granger. I threw a criminal jacket on the table. Janet picked it up and took a look inside.

"Your bartender pal," I said. "How many of your bruises carry his name?"

She didn't offer a response. Didn't need to. Masters opened up the jacket and ran his eyes down Granger's rap sheet.

"Armed robbery, petty theft, extortion. Three arrests for assault." The cop looked up. "What are you saying?"

"Some of the beatings were probably real," I said. "Maybe most of them. I'm guessing Woods was hitting her pretty regular. It just wasn't enough."

Masters dropped Granger's jacket back onto the table. The ex-con's mug shot peeked out from the file. "And you're saying she hired Granger?"

I shrugged. "She was in the bar three times in the week and a half before Woods was shot. I saw her there once myself. According to his boss, Granger was bragging about getting some extra cash. About doing something kinky to a hot-looking customer. Something he'd do for nothing is what he told his buddies. I figure he gave her the last beating. At the very least. The one that got me over to the Woodses' house."

"She was almost dead, Kelly."

"If it was going to work, she had to play it tough. To convince me. Convince the police. Convince whomever."

Janet crossed one leg over the other and ran a hand across her cheek. "It's called owning the bruises, Michael."

I nodded. "Exactly. And you knew that going in. Let me ask you a question. Was any of it real?"

"He hit me, Michael. Johnny did that."

"Used to be *he beat me.* Now it's just *hit.*"

Janet dropped her eyes to the floor and studied the cracks in her life. We had shared a romance once that was wonderfully young. Years later, the echo of a consequence that was impossibly sad. Now there was nothing left. Nothing more my client could use to draw me in. And she knew it.

"Who pulled the trigger?" I said.

Janet didn't look up. Taylor tapped her foot. I kept talking.

"I assume the original plan was strictly self-defense. You hire me. Get me familiar with the pattern of abuse. Whether the bruises were from Johnny or someone you hired—didn't really matter. You shoot Johnny. I testify about what I saw and you walk away clean. Am I missing something?"

I waited. Still no answer.

"Then Taylor sees the gun in my office. The two of you figure out a better way. Why take the chance on self-defense when you can frame someone like me? With my own gun, no less?"

I glanced over at Masters. He was looking at the girl. I moved my eyes back to my client.

"The night at your house was part of it," I said.

Janet finally looked up and shrugged. "We wanted you to stay the night."

"Neighbors like to look out the windows," I said. "You figured they'd see me leaving. Ties me in as your lover."

"We didn't plan on Johnny being outside. Funny thing is, he never said a word about it."

"Whose idea was it, Janet?"

She angled her face to one side and blew more smoke into the mess that lay between us.

"Whose idea was what, Michael?"

"Letting me take the weight for Johnny's murder. Leaving my gun at the scene. Putting it back in my office after the detective here screwed everything up by grabbing it out of Evidence. I assume the police would have been tipped to it eventually."

I felt Masters flinch a bit at that. He hadn't known about the gun resurfacing on my bookshelf. I didn't think so. I continued talking to Janet, all the while drawing a bead on the brains behind the frame.

"I'm guessing it was your little girl over there," I said. "She even sent me Johnny's book, thinking I was still in jail. If a guard got hold of her note, it would have tied me in even deeper. Or am I still not giving you enough credit?"

Janet dropped her cigarette into an empty beer bottle and studied my ceiling. Masters leaned his forearms on his knees and watched his shoes. Taylor stared out the window and listened to her tunes. We all sat that way for a while: myself, my two clients, and a beat-to-hell-and-back detective. Each trying hard to look at anything except another human being in the room. Finally, Masters made a move to go. The other two got up with him. The detective pulled me aside at the door.

"Don't bother looking for us, Kelly."

"Why would I bother?"

"It's just your way."

I looked over at the kid, scrolling through her iPod, oblivious to the grown-up world around her.

"The girl pulled the trigger, didn't she?"

Masters hesitated. Maybe he didn't know. Maybe he didn't want to know. But I knew. And I knew I wouldn't make the case. Even if I could. Not at fourteen years old. Not even if she was a killer.

"Never mind," I said. "It's no one's problem anymore."

And then all three of them left. I watched from my front window, through the latticework of branches that crowded my flat. Dan Masters stopped at the corner and touched Janet on the sleeve. The two talked for a moment. Then Masters held out an arm. She sank into his shoulder. He dropped his head against hers. The two of them walked like that to a Toyota Corolla that sat in front of a hydrant and was decorated with a ticket. Taylor followed five paces behind, sneakers scuffling, headphones on, thumbs working furiously at the marvelous entertainment technology offered to America's youth. Masters got behind the wheel. Janet sat beside him. The girl stopped under a streetlight and took a look up toward my window. I think she might have smiled. I know she waved. Then she climbed into the backseat of the car. The soon-to-be-former Chicago detective turned the engine over and the Corolla disappeared down the street. Another nuclear family, just living the American dream.

I STEPPED BACK from the window, saw an envelope on the table, and recognized Taylor's handwriting in the loops and circles of my name. There was no note inside, just a couple of photos. Cheap, grainy shots I'd seen in a million and a half Vice jackets. Only this time I knew the girl being violated. Knew the face. Knew the pain. Two generations' worth.

I took the photos into the kitchen and watched them burn in the sink. Janet Woods had been right when she said it was only a matter of time until Johnny Woods went after Taylor. Janet just didn't know how right she was, or how little time she actually had. But her daughter knew. Better than anyone, Taylor knew.

CHAPTER 50

It was cold and windy along the lakefront. The water was dishwater gray, and a thick curl of white froth ran along the surface. I zipped up my coat and walked south toward North Avenue Beach.

Two months hence, summer would be in the offing. Early morning joggers and yoga in the sand, the city standing tall on one side, nothing but blue water on the other. The quiet cry of a seagull overhead and the small talk of Gold Coast locals, walking their dogs along the footpaths and getting their coffee before the day heated up.

Around ten a.m. the lifeguard shack would open and the beach would start to happen. Music floating out over the water, eclectic strands mixing and mingling into a harmonious whole. The lazy smell of suntan oil, treadmills grinding out miles at the outdoor gym, beer and brats cooking at the beach house. People lying out on their blankets, reading paperbacks, talking, sizzling under the sun, and, of course, flirting.

In the early afternoon, North Avenue would sprout thin white poles and netting as far as the eye could see. Young professionals would descend from their high-rises and climb out of the Loop, looking for some beach volleyball. Running, jumping, sweating, more bare skin, more suntan oil, more beer, and, of course, more flirting.

As the sun dipped behind the city's skyline, North Avenue Beach would grow quiet again. A man and a woman might play a final solitary game of volleyball. The runners would return, as would the dogs, their owners in tow. Night would creep up and over the lake, draining it of color and leaving a vast black emptiness at the edge of the city. Nothing visible, nothing tangible, except the sound of tomorrow, knocking gently against the breakwater.

Those were the thoughts that kept me warm as I walked along the beach. A pigeon loitered nearby, caring not a whit for my musings and keeping an eye on the doughnut I'd gotten to go along with my coffee. I took a bite and threw it at the black-eyed beast, who pecked it into pieces and made off with as much as he could carry. I took the lid off the coffee and breathed in the heat, thinking it might warm me up. All it did was make my coffee cold.

A solitary figure waited near the North Avenue bridge. Vince Rodriguez was wearing a blue cashmere topcoat, black leather gloves, and rose-tinted sunglasses. He was reading a *Sun-Times* and spoke without looking up.

"See the paper today?"

I hadn't. Vince turned over the front page. It was a picture of the mayor and Mitchell Kincaid, framed against a statue of Abraham Lincoln, heads together, undoubtedly thinking something deep. It was a nice shot. A shot JFK and Bobby would be proud of. The headline under the photo read:

KINCAID AND WILSON: OUR LINK TO LINCOLN.

I scanned the article. It detailed Mitchell Kincaid's vision: a Lincoln Annex to the Chicago Historical Society. A state-of-the-art home for everything and anything that was Abraham Lincoln. Its centerpiece, of course, would be the newly discovered Emancipation Proclamation. Kincaid called it his destiny and wanted to fund the annex privately. Mayor Wilson wouldn't hear of it; his city would foot the bill. It would cost forty million dollars, but who was counting? Certainly not Chicago's taxpayers. I dropped my eyes to the bottom of the article, saw a quote from the annex's assistant curator, and smiled. Longtime volunteer Teen McCann was looking forward to the challenge and the living history that was Lincoln.

"How long will it take to build?" I said.

"They say two years, minimum. In the interim, Kincaid is going to take the Proclamation around the country. Museums, churches, schools. Educate the people about the history behind the document as well as its message."

"Going to make quite a name for himself," I said.

Rodriguez nodded. "Local Dems already have him plugged into a run for Senate."

"Who's stepping down?"

The detective smiled and tugged his gloves tight. "Way I hear it, a seat's suddenly going to open up next year."

"Wilson making that happen?"

"Of course. Kincaid's his guy now. Three months ago, they wanted to cut his heart out. Now, the mayor's gonna push him."

"All the way to the U.S. Senate."

Rodriguez shrugged. "The way Wilson sees it, he helps this guy go national and Kincaid forgets all about running for mayor. Forever. Wilson becomes a kingmaker and Chicago gets a big friend in D.C."

"Everyone's happy," I said.

"Something like that."

It was a smart play: clean, efficient, bloodless. Mayor Wilson all over. I took a sip of cold coffee. We reached Fullerton Avenue and walked through the underpass toward Rodriguez's car.

"What did you think of Fred Jacobs' story?" I said.

It had been little less than a month since my meeting with the mayor. Two weeks later, Chicago's Vice unit picked up Lawrence Randolph on a West Side stroll. The curator had a fourteen-year-old boy in his car. The *Trib* ran Jacobs' story on page one the following day.

"He got it mostly right," Rodriguez said.

"An anonymous tip, huh?"

Rodriguez kept walking.

"Let me guess," I said. "To make it even sweeter, Vice swept all the older kids off the stroll. Left only the babies out there."

Rodriguez stopped. "Now why would they do that?"

"That way when Randolph showed, they'd be sure it was sex with a minor," I said. "Felony offense. I figure he'll do ten years, minimum. Hard time."

Behind his sunglasses Rodriguez laughed a cop's laugh, a chill that echoed without ever making a sound. "Way I hear it, he's going to be locked up with his buddies from the Aryan Nation. But that's the Fifth Floor. They tend to play for keeps."

The detective gave a soft whistle and hit a button on his key chain. His car beeped and the doors unlocked. I opened up the passenger side. There was a coat in the front seat with an edge of purple underneath it. Rodriguez covered up the flowers and moved the coat into the back. Then he slipped off his glasses and turned the engine over. I got in and we waited for the car to warm. Rodriguez ticked on the radio and found an all-news station. Then the detective pulled out a postcard. It had cactus trees and sand on it.

"Got this yesterday."

Dan Masters had managed three sentences. One was about the weather. The second was about a house he had bought. The third was a thank-you. Rodriguez had shepherded Masters' paperwork through the department. Made sure he got full credit for time served. And benefits. It wasn't enough to live happily ever after. But it was a start.

"Sounds like he's doing okay," I said.

"He doesn't mention Janet or the girl."

"Probably a good thing."

"How about the P.S.?" Rodriguez said.

I had read it once but took a second look.

P.S. Say hi to Kelly. Tell him I'm sleeping fine.

"I think the P.S. is a good thing too," I said.

Rodriguez slipped the postcard back inside his pocket. "You wish we'd taken them in?"

I caught a flash. Bright eyes, auburn hair, and the cold smile of mother and daughter. "I'm not really sure what I wish."

Rodriguez turned down the radio and pulled his coat close around his body. "For what it's worth, I'd have played it the same way."

"Thanks, Detective."

Rodriguez nodded. I hadn't told anyone about the photos Taylor had left in my flat. Didn't see the point. Johnny Woods was dead. Now we'd all live with the rest of it.

"You heading over today?" I said.

Rodriguez reached back for his coat. And the purple flowers underneath. It was May first, Nicole Andrews' thirty-fifth birthday.

"Yeah. Thought I might drop these off."

They were orchids, lightly scented, lovely to look at, and impossibly fragile. Rodriguez cupped the blossoms with the side of one hand and then laid them in his lap.

"You want to come?" he said, but didn't mean it.

I shook my head. "Think I'll head over later."

The detective nodded and stared at a spot of nothing in the

rearview mirror. He might cry when he got to Nicole's grave. He might just feel the hole inside. Either way, after a while, he'd leave. The orchids would stay. In this weather, they'd be lucky to make it through the night.

"Give you a lift back to your place?"

I opened the car door. "That's okay, Vince. I'm gonna walk for a bit."

I got out of the car and watched Rodriguez drive off. Then I turned into the wind, for the long, cold walk home.

CHAPTER 51

It was a small ritual between friends. At least, it seemed small. Until one of the friends got herself murdered. Then everything changed.

It was the day after Nicole's birthday. Ten years ago. The day the ritual was born. We had gone out for drinks with some people the night before. Then it was over. Nicole was officially twenty-five. Another year stretched out ahead of her. That's when we decided to go out again. To celebrate again, the day after Nicole's birthday. Just the two of us. I remember my friend smiling and tugging lightly at my sleeve.

"It'll be great, Michael. Just me and you. Nothing fancy. Just lunch. A little way to decompress. Ease out of the birthday thing."

"Kind of like coffee after a big meal," I said.

"Really good coffee," Nicole replied.

"Okay. Really great coffee."

And so we did. Picked out a Chinese restaurant on Clark Street, a hole in the wall that never seemed to have a customer. Nicole thought it was perfect for a post-birthday birthday party. We ate lunch, split a bottle of wine, and toasted the year. It was quiet. It was nice. And the ritual was born. Every year, twice a year. First Nicole's birthday, then mine. Same table. Same waiter. Lunch and a bottle of wine.

IT WAS 12:03. The day after my friend's thirty-fifth. I walked down to the restaurant. Our waiter was there. The place was empty, like it always was. I asked for a bottle of wine. Then I made it a half. I ordered a plate of noodles and steamed vegetables. The food came in about twelve minutes. I ate it in less than three. The noodles tasted like nothing. The conversation was even less. Then I paid the bill and opened up the fortune cookie. It read, *Better times are around the corner.* I nodded to the waiter, left the restaurant, and took a look at my watch. It was 12:24.

Ten minutes later I was inside Graceland Cemetery. I spent a couple of minutes at my brother's grave. Then I walked the fifty yards or so to Nicole's. Rodriguez's purple bouquet was front and center. There were a couple of other offerings around the head-stone. Everything looked a little tattered, a little worn. I stood there for a while. Then I pressed a knee into the grass. Like I'd done before. I told my friend she'd just turned thirty-five, in case she didn't know. I told her about our lunch and wished her a happy birthday. Then I told her about the case. About Lawrence Randolph. About a mother, her daughter, and the demons that walked with them.

"Michael?"

The voice came creeping up and over my shoulder. I stood and turned toward it. Rachel Swenson was wearing a short black coat. Her hair was swept up away from her face and pinned back under a maroon stocking cap. Her cheeks were red and she looked like she'd been crying.

"Hey," I said.

"Hey. I didn't mean to bother you."

"You didn't."

We began to walk.

"I just came by for her birthday," I said.

"I know. Nicole told me."

I glanced over, but Rachel was looking straight ahead.

"Told you what?" I said.

"She told me about you guys. How you'd go out to lunch on the day after."

"She told you that, huh?"

"Yes, Michael, she did. She told me it was one of the treasured things in her life."

I nodded and kept my head down. Rachel slipped an arm around my waist. I pulled her close and we kept walking.

"Everything turn out okay with Kincaid?" I said.

"Everything turned out just fine."

"Thanks for trusting me," I said.

She stopped and kissed me on the cheek. A soft breeze pushed us out of the graveyard and down Clark Street. I closed my eyes and let the sun warm my face. Chicago's winter had finally broken. For the first time in a long time, it seemed like spring was going to happen.

"You like puppies?" I said, and opened my eyes.

Rachel smiled and nodded. I stopped again and considered this beautiful woman who could say so much, sometimes by saying nothing at all. I lifted her chin and kissed her on the lips. We held each other for a moment and let the world fall away. Then we walked as far as the Gingerman Tavern. We stopped there and ordered a couple of beers. They were cold and tasted good. We held hands, under the table, and talked about the future. Finally, after a while, it was time to go home.

EPILOGUE

I don't know why I needed to know. But I did. Call it the Oedipus that exists in all of us.

It was early on a Thursday morning, a little more than two months after Janet Woods had left town with her daughter. Rachel Swenson was asleep beside me, breath barely audible. I slipped out of bed, into my living room, and picked up the phone. An hour later, I had the piece of paper I needed in my hands. Taylor Woods' birth certificate. According to the county's Bureau of Vital Records, she was actually baptized Taylor Collins, Janet's maiden name, on January 25, 1992. That meant Taylor was sixteen years old. Not fourteen as she and her mother claimed. It also meant Janet might never have terminated the pregnancy she told me about when I agreed to take her on as a client. And that Taylor Woods might very well be my daughter.

I heard Rachel stirring in the bedroom, folded up the birth certificate, and pushed it into the deepest part of a bottom drawer. I wanted to know. Now I did. Like Oedipus, however, I had no idea where that knowledge might lead. Or whether I was ready for the journey.

There are a few unassailable items of fact surrounding the Great Chicago Fire of 1871. First, it started in or around Catherine O'Leary's barn on the night of October eighth. Second, it burned for more than twenty-four hours and destroyed more than seventeen thousand buildings. Finally, while there is no smoking gun (excuse the pun) pointing us to the definitive cause of the fire, most historians agree it was almost certainly accidental in nature. This final point underscores the obvious: this is a work of fiction. While I have tried to be faithful, wherever possible, to Chicago's geography, buildings, and institutions, the characters and events depicted herein are entirely fictional. Names, characters, places, and incidents, past and present, either are the product of my own imagination or are used fictitiously. Any resemblance to actual persons, living or dead, events or locales is entirely coincidental.

If you are interested in the history of the Great Fire, there is a wealth of information available. I would highly recommend the following titles: *The Great Chicago Fire*, Robert Cromie; *The Great Chicago Fire and the Myth of Mrs. O'Leary's Cow*, Richard F. Bales; *The Great Chicago Fire, in Eyewitness Accounts and 70 Contemporary Photographs and Illustrations*, David Lowe; and *Smoldering City: Chicagoans and the Great Fire, 1871–1874*, Karen Sawislak.

In addition, a trip to The Chicago History Museum, formerly known as The Chicago Historical Society, is a must. The museum has an extensive collection of primary and secondary source materials, as well as a marvelous staff available to help you navigate it all.

ACKNOWLEDGMENTS

This is my second novel. I would first like to thank the folks who bought and, hopefully, enjoyed *The Chicago Way*. I hope you've enjoyed *The Fifth Floor*.

I would also like to thank my agent, David Gernert; a marvelous Chicago writer and friend, Garnett Kilberg-Cohen; my editor at Knopf, Jordan Pavlin; and all the folks at Knopf and Vintage/Black Lizard who have provided such amazing support for my first two novels. I would especially like to thank Laura Baratto, Erinn Hartman, Jim Kimball, Leslie Levine, Jennifer Marshall, Maria Massey, Russell Perreault, and Zachary Wagman.

A special thanks to all the bookstore owners, librarians, reading clubs, Web sites, and others who help to promote writers and get their work into the hands of the reading public. With all the wonderful titles and authors in the marketplace, it is tough for any new writer to "break through." Without this special network of people, it would be virtually impossible.

Thanks to my friends and family for all their love and support. Special thanks to the following people: my mom and dad, my brother and sisters, Sister Eileen Harvey, Frank Harvey, Mike and Lily Lyons, Dickie and Alice Lyons, Katie Reardon, Martha and Richard Shonter, and Rick Shonter.

Finally, thank you, Mary Frances. I cannot imagine doing any of it without you.